A Penguin Special
Protest and Survive

Robert Chavas
27 may 1981
Bruxelles.

a Christian response:
"protest + survive"

Protest and Survive

Edited by E. P. Thompson and
Dan Smith

Penguin Books

Penguin Books Ltd, Harmondsworth,
Middlesex, England
Penguin Books, 625 Madison Avenue,
New York, New York 10022, U.S.A.
Penguin Books Australia Ltd, Ringwood,
Victoria, Australia
Penguin Books Canada Ltd, 2801 John Street,
Markham, Ontario, Canada L3R 1B4
Penguin Books (N.Z.) Ltd, 182–190 Wairau Road,
Auckland 10, New Zealand

Filmset, printed and bound in Great Britain by
Hazell Watson & Viney Ltd, Aylesbury, Bucks
Set in VIP Baskerville

Contents

PART ONE

1   E. P. Thompson
    Protest and Survive 9

2   Henry T. Nash
    The Bureaucratization of Homicide 62

PART TWO: Europe: Theatre of War 75

3   Alva Myrdal
    The Superpowers' Game over Europe 77

4   Dan Smith
    The European Nuclear Theatre 110

PART THREE: The Armourers: Bureaucracies and
    Economics 127

5   David Holloway
    War, Militarism and the Soviet State 129

6   Emma Rothschild
    The American Arms Boom 170

7   Dan Smith and Ron Smith
    British Military Expenditure in the 1980s 186

8   Mary Kaldor
     **Disarmament: The Armament Process in
         Reverse** 203

PART FOUR: Europe: Theatre of Peace 221

9   **Appeal for European Nuclear
         Disarmament** 223

10   Ken Coates
     For a Nuclear-free Europe 227

11   Bruce Kent
     Notes from the Concrete Grass Roots 246

Further Reading *compiled by Harry Dean* 257

Acknowledgements and Notes on Contributors 264

PART ONE

CHAPTER ONE

E. P. Thompson
Protest and Survive

The following letter appeared in *The Times* on 30 January 1980, from an eminent member of Oxford University:

Reviving Civil Defence

From Professor Michael Howard, FBA
Sir,

The decision to provide bases in this country for United States cruise missiles; the future of our own 'independent' strategic deterrent; the extent of our provisions for civil defence: all these have surely to be considered together as part of a single defence posture. No evidence emerged in the course of last Thursday's debate (January 24) that this is being done by the present Government.

The presence of cruise missiles on British soil makes it highly possible that this country would be the target for a series of pre-emptive strikes by Soviet missiles. These would not necessarily be on the massive scale foreseen by Lord Noel-Baker in your columns of January 25. It is more likely that the Russians would hold such massive strikes in reserve, to deter us from using our sea-based missiles as a 'second strike force' after the first Soviet warheads had hit targets in this country.

This initially limited Soviet strike would have the further objective, beyond eliminating weapons in this country targeted on their own homeland, of creating conditions here of such political turbulence that the use of our own nuclear weapons, followed as this could be by yet heavier attacks upon us, would become quite literally 'incredible'.

Civil defence on a scale sufficient to give protection to a

substantial number of the population in the event of such a 'limited' nuclear strike is thus an indispensable element of deterrence. Such measures should not be covert and concealed. On the contrary, they should be given the widest possible publicity; not only so that the people of this country know that they will be afforded the greatest possible degree of protection in the worst eventuality, but so that the credibility of our entire defence posture should not be destroyed through absence of evidence of our capacity to endure the disagreeable consequences likely to flow from it.

In the absence of a serious civil defence policy, the Government's decision to modernise or replace our 'independent deterrent' will be no more than an expensive bluff likely to deceive no one beyond these shores, and not very many people within them.

Yours faithfully,

M.E. Howard,

Chichele Professor of the History of War,

All Soul's College, Oxford.

I have cited this letter in full in order to ensure that, in the discussion which follows, the views of the author are not misrepresented, and also because it is a concise and cogent statement of a view held by influential persons in our country. According to this view we should place ourselves at once in a state of readiness for nuclear war, by extensive measures of civil defence, and these measures (it is argued) may actually make war less likely, by adding to the 'credibility' of our 'posture of deterrence'. Those who advocate this policy are not 'warmongers' (or they suppose that they are not such), although they form an influential part of that lobby which advocates every kind of preparation for war. I find their views to be not only odd and perverse, but also exceedingly dangerous, but I do not suppose that the fearful terminus to which they are directing our history is one which they intend.

Let me state clearly, then, that I accept that Professor Howard himself is innocent of any warlike intention. But his letter contains most serious assertions, and I will proceed to examine these. One part of these is composed of speculations as to future events; the other concerns the postures and pretences appropriate in the theatre of nuclear diplomacy. I will attend now to the first.

According to his scenario, the enemy – which enemy is plainly stated to be the Russians for as many years ahead as speculation can go – will make a pre-emptive strike against Britain with nuclear missiles. This is not anticipated to occur before 1983, since the decision that 160 or more United States cruise missiles should be based on British soil was taken by NATO (without consultation with the British parliament) on 12 December 1979, at Brussels; and it will take about three years before their manufacture is complete and they have been transported and sited in this country.

Professor Howard considers that the presence of these missiles on our soil will make it 'highly possible' that this country will be the target, not for one, but for *a series of pre-emptive strikes*, at some time in 1983 or thereafter. So far from 'deterring' the Russians, he supposes that the presence of these missiles here may provoke and draw down upon us these strikes. We may agree that his reasoning here is sound.

I am less happy with the next step in his reasoning. He does not suggest that there will be any counter-strikes by British-based missiles against the Russians. On the contrary, he supposes that the Russian strikes, although 'limited', would succeed in 'eliminating' all of these 160 cruise missiles. And that the Russians will hold more 'massive strikes' in reserve to 'deter us from using our sea-based missiles' against them. In the absence of adequate measures of civil defence, these first 'limited' strikes would create conditions of 'political turbulence' in this country, preventing 'us' (but I am not now sure who 'us' can be, unless the typesetter has inadvertently dropped the capitals into the lower case) from massive nuclear retaliation. If, however, a sufficient proportion of the surviving population were prevented from acts of 'political turbulence' by measures of civil defence, then a proper military strategy could be pursued by NATO, and massive second-stage nuclear exchanges could freely commence.

It will be seen that the purpose of civil defence is political and provisional. It is to ensure the necessary degree of stability in that short interval between the first and the second (retaliatory) nuclear strike. Professor Howard does not take his speculations any further. He does not tell us whether the 'massive strikes' of the second stage would seal the entrances to the air-raid shelters and block up their air-ducts.

We may suppose, at least, that these second strikes will be effective in bringing 'political turbulence' to a prompt end, and thereby in removing the necessity for further civil defence. At this stage the professor passes over to the consideration of the correct degree of mendacity to be exercised in our current defence 'posture', and we will consider that element in his argument later on.

Now, as to the scenario, we will commence by noting that Professor Howard, in a letter to *The Times* whose intent is to advocate much greater expenditure and publicity on civil defence, does not, in any single clause, indicate any detail of what such defence might consist in, nor how effective it might be. His terms are all general. He wishes there to be 'measures', which afford 'the greatest possible degree of protection', and 'evidence' of 'our capacity to endure the disagreeable consequences likely to flow from' our present military and diplomatic strategies. But he does not indicate what measures might be possible, nor does he even explain what could be 'disagreeable' about the expected event.

Professor Howard is perhaps himself a little uneasy on this count. For he reassures us that these pre-emptive strikes by Russian missiles 'would not necessarily be on the massive scale foreseen by Lord Noel-Baker in your columns of January 25'. He wishes us to suppose that this 'series of strikes', which 'eliminate' the 160 cruise missiles scattered on our soil, are to be, as these things go, a mild and local affair.

I have therefore consulted the letter from Philip Noel-Baker in *The Times* of 25 January. Lord Noel-Baker is the recipient of the Nobel Peace Prize for his work for international conciliation over very many years. We may take it that he keeps himself well informed. In his letter he notes that 'many voices are being raised in the United States, Britain and elsewhere to argue that nuclear wars could be fought without total disaster; some even suggest that nuclear war could be won'. He then goes on to detail the findings of Mr Val Peterson, who was appointed United States Civil Defense Administrator twenty-five years ago, and who organized many exercises, national, regional and local, at the height of a previous Cold War.

Mr Peterson drew the following conclusions from his successive exercises. In 1954 the national exercise was estimated to have had a yield of twenty-two millions of casualties, of whom seven millions would have been dead. In 1956 fifty-six millions, or one third of the population of the United States, were presumed as casualties. In 1957:

If the whole 170 million Americans has Air Raid Shelters, at least 50 per cent of them would die in a surprise enemy attack. In the last analysis, there is no such thing as a nation being prepared for a thermonuclear war.

From evidence of this order Lord Noel-Baker concludes:

Any use of nuclear weapons will escalate into a general war . . . There is *no* defence against such weapons; and . . . nuclear warfare will destroy civilisation, and perhaps exterminate mankind. To hope for salvation from Civil Defence is a dangerous self-deluding pipe dream.

Professor Howard has at least taken care to cover himself against this argument. The series of strikes envisaged in his scenario 'would not necessarily be on the massive scale' which Lord Noel-Baker foresees. What he foresees is possible (we should note), and perhaps even probable, but not 'necessarily' so. That is a large relief. But, then, on what scale are we to suppose that a more 'limited' attack might be? If we are to be futurist authorities on war, or even historians of war, then we should be exact as to weaponry and as to its effects.

There is a good deal of talk around today, from 'defence correspondents', military strategists and the like, which leads us to suppose that the military, on both sides of the world, are capable of delivering very small nuclear packs, with the greatest accuracy and with no lethal consequences outside the target area. Professor Howard's speculations are evidently supported by some such assumptions: the Russians are to 'eliminate' 160 cruise missiles, but only local damage will be done.

Now there are two points here which require examination. The first concerns the known power and probable effects of these weapons. The second concerns the strategic assumptions of those 'experts' who suppose that any nuclear war could be limited in this way. We will now turn to the first.

There appeared in *The Times*, nine days before Professor Howard's letter, a major article ('The Deterrent Illusion', 21 January) by Lord Zuckerman. The author was the government's chief scientific adviser from 1964 to 1971, and, in addition to drawing upon his own extensive experience, he also draws, in this article, upon that of eminent United States scientists and advisers.

Lord Zuckerman's testimony (which should be read in full) is wholly dismissive of the notion of a 'limited' nuclear strike, confined to military targets only:

It is still inevitable that were military installations rather than cities to become the objectives of nuclear attack, millions, even tens of millions, of civilians would be killed, whatever the proportion of missile sites, airfields, armament plants, ports, and so on that would be destroyed.

And he explains that strategists, in calculating the estimated effects of missile strikes, employ the acronym CEP (Circular Error Probable) for the radius of a circle within which 50 per cent of strikes would fall.

Thus we have to deal with two factors: the 50 per cent of missiles which fall *within* the CEP, and the 50 per cent which fall *without* and which 'would not necessarily be distributed according to standard laws of probability'. Lord Zuckerman does not tell us the presumed CEP for a 'limited' strike aimed at a single missile base, and this is perhaps an official secret. But in the debate that was eventually held in the Commons (*Hansard*, 24 January) *after* NATO's decision to base cruise missiles here, statements were made which enable an impression to be offered.

I must first explain that the strategy of nuclear warfare has now become a highly specialized field of study, which has developed its own arcane vocabulary, together with a long list of acronyms: CEP, MIRV (multiple independently targeted re-entry vehicle), ICBM (inter-continental ballistic missile), ECCM (electronic counter-counter measures), MEASL (Marconi-Elliott Avionics Systems), and, as the plum of them all, MAD (mutual assured destruction).

In this vocabulary nuclear weapons are sub-divided into several categories: *strategic* – the inter-continental missiles of immense range and inconceivable destructive power, which may be submarine-launched or sited in silos and on tracks behind the Urals or in the Nevada desert; *theatre* (long, middle or short-range), which may be bombs or missiles, carried on aircraft or permanently sited, or moved around at sea or on land on mobile launch platforms; and *tactical*. Sometimes NATO strategists refer to 'theatre' weapons as 'tactical' ones, and sometimes they are referring to smaller battlefield nuclear devices – land-mines, artillery shells, etc., which could be mixed in with 'conventional weapons'.

These several degrees of weaponry form 'a chain of deterrence'. Mr Pym, the Defence Secretary, spoke in the House of Commons on 24 January of 'an interlocking system of comprehensive deterrence . . . a clear chain of terrible risk', with the pistol and the grenade at one end and the MX missile at the other.

It is generally agreed that 'the West' has some advantage in *strategic* weapons, although this fact has been concealed from the Western public in recent months in order to direct attention to long and medium-range *theatre* weapons, where it it said that the Soviet Union has recently attained an advantage by replacing the SS 4 and SS 5 missiles with the very deadly SS 20, and by introducing the Backfire bomber. It is to meet this 'threat' to parity in the middle link of the chain that cruise missiles are to be introduced by NATO in Western Europe.

On 3 December 1979 Mr David Fairhall, the *Guardian*'s defence correspondent and a very zealous apologist for NATO, published a map (see p. 17) which illustrates how NATO apologists perceive the European 'balance'. It will be seen from this map that the Soviet threat is very serious, since it is marked in heavy dotted lines and thick arrow-heads, whereas NATO's response is delicately etched. It will also be seen that NATO's existing, pre-modern weaponry (the Pershing I, the F 1-11 and the Vulcan) is pitiful, and will not even be able to destroy Rome or Naples, nor any part of Greece. So that if it were not for the submarine-launched ballistic missiles (Polaris, Poseidon and Trident), NATO would be reduced in a nuclear war to stinging itself, like a scorpion, to death.

Either NATO or the map is pretty silly, or both. The point, however, is that present strategic thinking supposes a 'limited' nuclear war, with 'theatre' weapons. Europe is such a 'theatre', and this limited war will be localized to a small area from the Urals to the Western coast of Ireland. In this scenario, 'strategic' weapons (ICBMs and the like) will be held back for a 'second strike', so that neither Siberia nor the North American continent will be under any immediate threat. Professor Howard has adopted this scenario, in supposing the Russians will employ their own

THE EUROPEAN NUCLEAR BALANCE

Trident

Polaris/Poseidon

Baku

Miles 1000

Murmansk

Cruise missile

Leningrad

Moscow

Kiev

Pershing II

Vulcan

F111

Pershing /

Paris

Berlin

London

SS4

SS20

SS5

Backfire

Badger/Blinder

With grateful acknowledgements to the Guardian

17

'theatre' weapons (SS 20 or Backfire bombers) in a pre-emptive strike upon our cruise missile ('theatre') bases.

Let us now examine this scenario more exactly. Sir Frederick Bennett (Torbay) affirmed in the Commons debate on 24 January that the warheads of these Russian theatre missiles 'have at least the destructive capacity of the bombs dropped on Nagasaki and Hiroshima', although Mr Churchill (Stretford) had different information. 'By today's standards Hiroshima's bomb was a puny and miserable weapon' and (he said) each SS 20 missile carried a pack equivalent to 100 Hiroshima bombs.

It will be seen that two well-informed Conservative spokesmen differed in their information by a factor of one hundred. This is a trivial disagreement (since both are agreed that these missiles are capable of very great destruction). But it serves to illustrate the fact that, when we come to hard information, the air is very much fouled up today.

The reasons for this are easy to identify, but they illuminate a part of the problem, so we will digress to explain them. First, it is axiomatic that each military bloc has an interest in misleading the other, and this is done both by concealing information and by deliberately spreading disinformation.

In general, each bloc is at pains to deny and conceal its own areas of greatest military strength, and to advertise a pretence to strength in areas where it is weak. The intelligence agencies which report on each other's resources are themselves an interest-group, with high ideological motivation, and on occasion they deliberately manufacture alarmist reports.

Lord Zuckerman gives evidence as to the steady flow of 'phoney intelligence' and 'far-fetched' predictions as to Soviet military power which have influenced United States planning over the past twenty years. There is no reason to suppose that this fouling-up of information takes place only in Western capitals.

The name of the game, on both sides, is mendacity.

Indeed, /deterrence/ might itself be defined as the biggest and most expensive Lie in history; and it was, in effect, defined in this way by our Defence Secretary, Mr Pym, in the debate on 24 January: 'Deterrence is primarily about what the other side thinks, not what we may think'.

The debate on that day was the first to be held in parliament on the subject of nuclear weapons for fifteen years, and it lasted for about five and a half hours. It was distinguished throughout by the paucity of hard information, although it should be said that Mr Pym imparted some new information, and more than had come at any time from the previous administration.

Mr Pym announced the near-completion of the 'Chevaline' programme to 'modernize' the warhead of our Polaris missiles – a programme costing £1,000 millions, which had been carried out in the deepest secrecy, and without the knowledge of the full Cabinet, and in defiance of official Labour policy, on the authority of Mr Callaghan and two or three of his particular friends.

Thus the House was given this information *after* the decision had been taken, the money had been spent, and the work had been done. I do not know how £1,000 millions was tucked away in a crease in the estimates and hidden from view (just as the many millions expended on internal security services, telephone-tapping, etc., are hidden from view), but it suggests that the level of official mendacity is today very high indeed.

In any case, let us be fair, Mr Pym did give the House this information, and we may suppose that he did so in order to embarrass Mr Callaghan, Mr Fred Mulley, Mr Healey and Dr David Owen (the co-partners in this expensive deception), and to reduce them to silence or assent on other matters of nuclear weapon 'modernization' in the ensuing debate.

In this he succeeded very well. (We may suppose that he held other, 'second-strike', secret material back as a further deterrent.) But apart from this malicious little political detonation, the yield of new information in the debate was low.

The second reason why the air is fouled-up is that the military and security elites in both blocs, and their political servitors, cannot pursue their expensive and dangerous policies without continually terrifying the populations of their own countries with sensational accounts of the war preparations of the other bloc.

To be sure, the plain facts are terrifying enough without any embroidery. But it is necessary to persuade the native populations that the other side is stealing a lead in order to justify even greater preparations and expenditure at home.

This is as necessary in the Soviet Union as it is in the West, despite the absence of any open public debate over there on the issues. For the Soviet military budget is very heavy, and this entails the continual postponement and disappointment of people's expectations as to improving services and goods. In particular, a quite disproportionate concentration of the nation's most advanced scientific and technological skills takes place in the military sector – as it does, increasingly, even in this country. The threat from the West, whether it exists or not (and in Soviet perception it certainly does), has become a necessary legitimation for the power of the ruling elites, an excuse for their many economic and social failures, and an argument to isolate and silence critics within their own borders.

In the West we have 'open debate', although it is contained by all-party 'consensus' and is not permitted to intrude in any sharp way into our major media. I have discussed elsewhere the ways in which this is carefully controlled by the preparation and selective release of 'official information'.

An interesting example of this manipulation came out towards the end of the Commons debate. In responding, Mr Barney Hayhoe, the Under-Secretary for Defence, sought to allay fears expressed by the patriotic Mr Peter Shore (Labour's shadow Foreign Secretary) that the NATO programme of missile 'modernization' might not be *large* enough to keep up with Soviet missile programmes. Mr Hayhoe replied:

The United States is planning to introduce cruise missiles, carried on B 52 bombers, for the strategic role. It is planning an armoury of 2,000 or 3,000 missiles . . . forming only one part of a huge strategic triad alongside ICBMs and submarine-launched ballistic missiles, and all due to enter service in two or three years' time.

This programme is to be *in addition* to the existing United States 'strategic' resources (which are generally agreed to be already in excess of Russia's, and which have always been so).

Now I am not an expert in these matters, and I do not usually follow the specialist press. But in the previous three months, and especially in the weeks preceding the NATO decision of 12 December, I had followed the general press with care. I have on my desk still a thick file of clippings from the defence correspondents of the more serious daily, weekly and Sunday papers. Yet this was the first mention I met with of these rather substantial United States plans, which are to be added to NATO's little provision.

The entire 'debate' in Britain prior to the NATO decision was not a debate at all, but an exercise in official information. It was conducted in the press and television on the basis of letting the people believe that there was a massive build-up of Soviet SS 20s and Backfire bombers, all aimed at NATO; but with the United States, the dominant power in NATO, removed from the equation. NATO's programme of nuclear weapons 'modernization' could then be presented as a tardy and inadequate response to the Soviet threat. Nothing at all was mentioned, in the general press, as to this little addition to the Western sum ('2,000 or 3,000 missiles') as part of 'a huge strategic triad'.

Since that decision – and as some members of the British public have begun to ask awkward questions – official information has given way, in some quarters, to downright official lying. I am not complaining at the fact that Mr Pym, when on 17 June he announced on television the sites chosen by the US Air Force for their missiles, pleaded, with a catch in his throat, that these were intended only for the 'defence' of our peace and our liberty. This is exactly what Mr Brown, Mr Ustinov or any other Minister of Defence (as Ministers of War are now laughably called the world over) tells his own people. That is only to be expected.

I am objecting more to the kind of statement given, with increasing frequency, in parliament and in the press, of the following order:

One new Russian SS missile, with all Europe in its sights, is installed every five days; there are already 160 of these monsters in place ... The Russian nuclear force threatening Europe's cities will build up to something like 2,000–3,000 warheads by the mid 1980s. Against it is a NATO plan, still on paper, to deploy Pershing II and cruise missiles – but only some 500 of them.

That is from the leading editorial of the *Sunday Times* for 6 July 1980. I am sorry to single out this newspaper, since it is only repeating what is said on all sides. But a paper which pretends to objectivity and authority ought to be judged by stricter standards than those which pretend only to propaganda.

What is directly false in this passage is that 160 of 'these monsters' (the SS 20) are faced only by 'a NATO plan, still on paper' to introduce Pershing IIs and cruise missiles. What they face are substantial long-range nuclear weapons assigned to the NATO 'theatre': these include F 1-11 and Vulcan bombers, with a range of some 3,000 nautical miles; the British 'independent' Polaris, which is assigned to NATO command, as well as (in Soviet perception) the French 'independent' weapons also; and the United States Poseidon, forty of which are also assigned to NATO command. These United States Poseidons each carry some ten independently targeted warheads, making 400 in all.

This is before we take into any account further United States 'strategic' resources, which can be attached to any particular theatre at will.

The SS 20 is based on land and the Poseidon is based at sea, and, until lately, it had been supposed, in the war-games rooms, that they traded off against each other. What has happened is not the introduction of some wholly new dimension of threat (the SS 20 came into production in 1976, the Backfire bomber in 1974), but a redefinition of the rules of the game. Our Western experts have suddenly decided to hold their hands over Poseidon, Polaris, etc., and to pretend that they do not exist. This is done as a public information exercise, aimed not at the Russians but at us, to frighten up into believing that we are naked and defended by only a plan 'still on paper' against Russian 'monsters'.

This is a contemptible exercise, since the true facts could easily be ascertained by any editorial writer. And, in fact, any competent Russian editorialist can make a very much better case against cruise missiles than our 'experts' can make against the SS 20. For the plain fact is that the critical accounting must be done, not between the Warsaw Pact and NATO (with the USSR and USA both removed from the equation), but between the two giant superpowers. And in this accounting, the cruise missile can hit targets in western Russian, whereas the SS 20 can get nowhere near to the USA. Hence in Russian perception these lethal and accurate weapons, all under American control, are being given forward bases on the European continent where they can strike at Russian installations or cities, thus creeping beneath the 'strategic' thresholds imposed by SALT II.

Moreover, they can strike at Russia both fast and far. The Pershing II, from its West German bases, could descend on Russian targets in only four minutes. Mr Pym, on that same telly fireside chat (17 June), assured the British people, with tears in his eyes, that cruise missiles did not 'escalate' nuclear armaments – no, not at all. For each cruise missile, one F 1-11 or older warhead would be withdrawn. What he neglected to mention was that the cruise can stretch into Russian territory some 500 miles deeper than the existing 'theatre' bombers, if we allow these to return to their home bases. Where Vulcan bombers can hit Leningrad, the cruise and Pershing II can (like Polaris or Poseidon) hit Moscow.

If I was a Russian, that would seem to me like escalation. It would make me feel uneasy, just as, if the Russians had weapons which could it Hull and Norwich, but then introduced missiles with a stretch to reach London, Bristol and Birmingham, I would feel uneasy here.

I am not suggesting that Russian missiles are not multiplying, nor that they are not menacing to us. They are both. The mobile SS 20, with its triple warhead, is a foul, unnecessary, and threatening weapon, and I hope that those who contest the introduction of cruise missiles into this country will also let the Russian embassy know their views of those weapons. I have been illustrating two different points. First, the logic of 'deterrence', in which both sides play a never-ending game of leapfrog, justifying their actions at each stage by blaming the other, whereas in fact a good deal of the thrust to 'modernize' weapons is planned quite independently (ten or twenty years ahead of the event) by the armourers of each side.[1] Second, I have sought to emphasize that the whole basis of our information is corrupt, and that every official statement, on both sides, is either an official lie or a statement with direct propagandist intent which conceals as much as it reveals.

As to the actual facts of the 'nuclear balance', objective research by such bodies as the Stockholm International Peace Research Institute gives rise to conclusions more complex than anything that we have been offered in our press or on our screens. Thus, in one count of strategic weapons, by individual bombers and missiles, the Soviet Union appears to be a little ahead of the United States; whereas by a different count of actual warheads (that is, MIRVs, or independently targeted re-entry vehicles) the United States appears as having many more weapons (9,000 to 5,000) than Russia. This is, of course, before 'modernization'. The available information has been examined with care by Dan Smith in *The Defence of the Realm in the 1980s*, and his fourth chapter, 'Of Numbers and Nukes', is essential reading. The particular case of cruise missiles and SS 20s has been given a definitive examination by Milton Leitenberg in a paper (*NATO and WTO Long Range Theatre Nuclear Forces*) available from the Armament and Disarmament Information Unit at the University of Sussex. Those who wish to be informed on these problems – and very much better informed than most Members of Parliament – should obtain these, read them, and then pass the information on, since it is becoming very clear that neither the press nor the television will do this honestly for us.

We are now in a position to conclude this digression, and to return to the arguments of Lord Zuckerman and of Professor Howard.

Lord Zuckerman has shown that we must take into account two variables when considering the effect of the 'series of pre-emptive strikes' which Professor Howard envisages as being drawn upon us by cruise missile bases: the 50 per cent of missiles falling within the CEP, and the remainder falling without.

We have seen that the SS 20 is the 'theatre' missile which we must expect to strike Britain, and that the lowest estimate of its destructive capacity is 'at least' that of the bomb dropped on Hiroshima. This bomb (Mr Churchill reminded the House on 24 January) caused the death of 100,000 persons within hours, and of a further 100,000 who have died subsequently, in the main from radiologically-related diseases.

The SS 20 is reputed to be an accurate missile, although not as accurate as the cruise, and the CEP might be down to a few hundred yards. But the meditated strategy of both sides is to send, not one accurate missile at each target, but missiles in clutches of thirty or forty. The late arrivals will be buffeted about a good deal by the immense detonations of the first-comers, so that the C E P for a clutch is likely to be enlarged to several miles.

An American officer has now, at long last, told the waiting Mr Pym where these missiles are to be based, and they will be, not at Upper Heyford and Lakenheath – as had been supposed – but at Greenham Common, near Newbury, and Molesworth, near Huntingdon. In my view the reason for this unexpected choice is that both of the latter bases had long been disused, and, by making them operative once more, the United States Air Force is able to *add* two major bases to their existing clutch in this country. As Mr William Rodgers remarked in the debate on the defence estimates (28 April), in the only sensible statement to come from him on these matters in the past year: 'Ask the Services how much money they would like and they will always say "More".' The US Air Force told Mr Pym: 'More!', and they will therefore be able to keep Upper Heyford and Lakenheath in full operation as well, and ready for whatever 'modernized' aircraft succeed to the F 1-11s.

If strikes were made against these newly-designated bases, then Newbury is likely to fall within the C E P, but Reading and Huntingdon may fall without. Within the C E P we must suppose some fifteen or twenty detonations at least on the scale of Hiroshima, which will then discharge immense quantities of radioactive effluvia over the surrounding countryside.

This is to suppose that the Soviet strike is homing on to clearly-defined and immobile targets. But this is not the case. We are now told that the missiles will be carried in packs of four on mobile launching vehicles, and in times of 'emergency' will be dispersed from their bases into the surrounding districts.

There has been a great deal of double-talk about all these questions. On the one hand, we have been told that these are defensive weapons, which could never be used for a first strike. But if we are to suppose the Russians to be a hideous

26

enemy, already armed with 'monsters', then packing all these missiles at Greenham Common and at Molesworth is to present to them perfect targets for two immense 'Pearl Harbors'. And, equally, the sudden deployment of missile-launchers from these bases (which would be monitored by satellite observation) would be the signal to an enemy that 'emergency' had come.

In any case, there is not much point in arguing about where these missiles are sited, since this decision has been taken, not only above our heads, but above Mr Pym's head also. In a BBC TV phone-in programme in February he said:

From the point of view of siting the cruise missiles I don't think it makes a great deal of difference. It is really a security and defence and strategic consideration, and of course one must take public opinion into account as far as one possibly can.

(*Cambridge Evening News*, 6 February 1980)

This was a politician's way of saying that the US military would take the decision, and that public opinion would go unconsulted and disregarded. Three weeks before this Mr Pym gave a somewhat more honest reply to questions from the Member for Swindon (Mr David Stoddart), whose watchful constituents had already informed him of the (then) Official Secret that Greenham Common was being cased by the US Air Force. 'I urge the Secretary of State', said Mr Stoddart, 'to keep these updated nuclear weapons well away from Swindon.' Mr Pym responded thus:

The siting of these weapons in no way affects the vulnerability or otherwise of a particular place. It is a mistake for anyone to think that the siting of a weapon in a particular place . . . makes it more or less vulnerable. We are all vulnerable in the horrifying event of a holocaust.

(*Hansard*, 15 January 1980)

I do not know whether the citizens of Swindon find this

reassuring or not. Mr Pym was saying that the Americans intend to spread and scatter these weapons before launching them, so that the enemy will have to spread and scatter his strike over a very much larger area in order to have any hopes of 'eliminating' them. This area will be considerable. A person with the name of Lord Strathcona and Mount Royal (if that can really be the name of a person) announced in the House of Lords on 17 June that the launchers would be scattered from the bases to a distance of 50 miles or more before firing; and Mr Pym was reported in the *Guardian* on 18 June to have mentioned 100 miles. I do not intend to do all of the readers' work for them, so may I recommend them to get out a map of Britain, and draw circles of a diameter of 50, and then of 100, miles around Greenham Common and Molesworth, and find out for themselves what major centres of population – in addition to London, Bristol, Leicester, Norwich and Birmingham – these circles take in.

Thus if the Russians really wanted to find the cruise missile-launchers out, then there would have to be CEPs dotted all across southern, central and eastern England. There is nothing very special being prepared by NATO for Reading or Huntingdon: Luton, Sheerness and Southampton will be just as 'vulnerable', and there is no way of describing a series of nuclear strikes against cruise missiles except as a 'holocaust'.

This is before we take account of Lord Zuckerman's other variable – the 50 per cent of strikes which would fall outside the Circular Error Probable. These will be missiles whose navigational or homing devices are inaccurate or which, perhaps, are brought down on their path. It would be over-optimistic to suppose that every one of these would fall on Salisbury Plain or on that barren patch of the Pennines around Blackstone Edge. I have taken a ruler to a map of Europe, and I cannot see any way in which an SS 20 dispatched from Russia could home in on Newbury without passing directly over central London.

If by misadventure a strike outside the CEP fell on a

major city the damage would be considerable. Lord Louis Mountbatten told an audience in Strasbourg in May 1979 that 'one or two nuclear strikes on this great city . . . with what today would be regarded as relatively low yield weapons would utterly destroy all that we see around us and immediately kill half of its population'. And Lord Zuckerman adds that 'a single one-megaton bomb' – and the warhead of the SS 20 is said to be $1\frac{1}{2}$ megatons – 'could erase the heart of any great city – say, Birmingham – and kill instantly a third of its citizens'.

There is no room in this island to 'scatter' missiles without bringing multitudes into mortal danger, and there is no room to 'search' without inflicting a holocaust. As Lord Zuckerman has said:

> There are no vast deserts in Europe, no endless open plains, on which to turn war-games in which nuclear weapons are used into reality. The distances between villages are no greater than the radius of effect of low-yield weapons of a few kilotons; between towns and cities, say a megaton.

We are now at last prepared to cast a more realistic eye upon Professor Howard's scenario.

According to this, the 'initially limited Soviet strike' might, in the absence of civil defence precautions, create conditions of 'political turbulence' which would prevent 'us' from using our own nuclear weapons in retaliation. This would be regrettable, since it would inhibit the escalation from 'tactical' or 'theatre' to 'second-strike', sea-based nuclear war. But he envisages civil defence measures 'on a scale sufficient to give protection to a substantial number of the population', enabling this number to endure the 'disagreeable consequences' which would ensue.

The object of civil defence, then, is not so much to save lives as to reduce the potential for 'political turbulence' of those surviving the first strike, in order to enable 'us' to pass over to a second and more fearsome stage of nuclear warfare.

It is Professor Howard's merit that he states this sequence honestly, as a realist, and even allows that the consequences will be disagreeable.

We are still entitled, however, to inquire more strictly as to what measures would be *on a scale sufficient*, what proportion of the population might constitute *a substantial number*, and what may be indicated by the word *disagreeable*.

It is not as if nuclear weapons are a completely unknown quantity, which have only been tested in deserts and on uninhabited islands. They have been tested upon persons also, in 1945, at Hiroshima and Nagasaki, and to some effect. These effects have been studied with care; and the beneficiaries of this sudden donation of advanced technology were so much struck by the disagreeable consequences that they have continued to monitor its effects to the present day.

One remarkable consequence of those two detonations is that the survivors in those two cities, and the descendants of the sufferers, were transformed into advocates, not of revenge, but of international understanding and peace. To this day work for peace is regarded as a civic duty, and the mayors of Nagasaki and Hiroshima regard this work as the principal obligation of their office.

For example, in 1977 an International Symposium on the Damage and After-Effects of the bombing of these two cities was inaugurated, and a number of reports of this work are now in translation. I have read condensations of these, as well as other materials from Nagasaki.

It had been my intention to condense this material still further, and to remind readers of the effects of the first atomic bombings. I have now decided to pass this matter by, for two reasons. The first is that I have found the task beyond my powers as a writer. After reading these materials, whenever I approached my typewriter I was overcome by such a sense of nausea that I was forced to turn to some other task.

The second reason is that, at some point very deep in their consciousness, readers *already know* what the consequences of these weapons are. This knowledge is transmitted to children even in their infancy, so that as they run around with their space-weapons and death-rays they are re-enacting what happened thirty years before they were born.

There is, however, one area of convenient forgetfulness in this inherited memory. The moment of nuclear detonation is remembered vaguely, as a sudden instant of light, blast and fire, in which instantly tens of thousands of lives were quenched. It is thought of as a stupendous but instantaneous moment of annihilation, without pain or emotional suffering.

But this is not accurate. It is now estimated that 140,000 were killed 'directly' by the bomb on Hiroshima, and 70,000 by that on Nagasaki, with an allowance for error of 10,000 either way in each case. But the bombs were dropped on 6 and 9 August, and the accounts for *immediate* casualties were closed on 31 December 1945. This reflects the fact that a very great number of these deaths – especially those from burns and radioactivity – took place slowly, in the days and weeks after the event.

Michiko Ogino, ten years old, was left in charge of his younger sisters when his mother went out to the fields to pick eggplants. The bomb brought the house down on them all, leaving his two-year-old sister with her legs pinned under a crossbeam:

> Mamma was bombed at noon
> When getting eggplants in the field,
> Short, red and crisp her hair stood,
> Tender and red her skin was all over.

So Mrs Ogino, although the clothes were burned from her body and she had received a fatal dose of radiation, could still run back from the fields to succour her children. One after another passing sailors and neighbours heaved at the beam to release the trapped two-year-old, failed, and, bowing with Japanese courtesy, went on their way to help others.

Mother was looking down at my little sister. Tiny eyes looked up from below. Mother looked around, studying the way the beams were piled up. Then she got into an opening under the beam, and putting her right shoulder under a portion of it, she strained with all her might. We heard a cracking sound and the beams were lifted a little. My little sister's legs were freed.

> Peeled off was the skin over her shoulder
> That once lifted the beam off my sister.
> Constant blood was spurting
> From the sore flesh appearing . . .

Mrs Ogino died that night. Fujio Tsujimoto who was five years old, was in the playground of Yamazato Primary School, Nagasaki, just before the bomb dropped. Hearing the sound of a plane he grabbed his grandmother's hand and they were the first into the deepest part of the air-raid shelter. The entrance to the shelter, as well as the playground, was covered with the dying. 'My brother and sisters didn't get to the shelter in time, so they were burnt and crying. Half an hour later, my mother appeared. She was covered with blood. She had been making lunch at home when the bomb was dropped.'

My younger sisters died the next day. My mother – she also died the next day. And then my older brother died . . .

The survivors made a pile of wood on the playground and began to cremate the corpses. My brother was burned. Mother also was burned and quickly turned to white bones which dropped down among the live coals. I cried as I looked on the scene. Grandmother was also watching, praying with a rosary . . .

I am now in the fourth grade at Yamazato Primary School. That playground of terrible memories is now completely cleared and many friends play there happily. I play with my friends there too, but sometimes I suddenly remember that awful day. When I do, I squat down on the spot where we cremated our mother and touch the earth with my fingers. When I dig deep in the ground with a piece of bamboo, several pieces of charcoal appear. Looking at the spot for a while, I can dimly see my mother's image in the earth. So when I see someone else walking on that place, it makes me very angry.

I will not quote any more of the testimony of the children of Nagasaki (*Living Beneath The Atomic Cloud*). What it makes clear is that the 'instant' of detonation was protracted over days and weeks, and was full, not only of physical misery, but of unutterable yearning and suffering. A great river runs through Hiroshima, and each year the descendants set afloat on it lighted lanterns inscribed with the names of the family dead, and for several miles the full breadth of this river is one mass of flame.

After this we still have to consider the future tens of thousands who have died subsequently from the after-effects of that day – chiefly leukaemia, various cancers, and diseases of the blood and digestive organs. The sufferers are known as *hibakashu*, a word which ought to be international. Some *hibakashu* suffer from the direct consequences of wounds and burns, others from premature senility, others from blindness, deafness and dumbness, others are incapable of working because of nervous disorders, and many are seriously mentally deranged. Only two comforts can be derived from the expert *Nagasaki Report*: *hibakashu* have been distinguished by their mutual aid, sometimes in communities of fellow-sufferers: and the genetic effects of the bomb (which are still being studied) do not as yet appear to have been as bad as was at first apprehended.

We may now push this distressing matter back into our subconscious, and reconsider the possible effect of 'a series of pre-emptive strikes', with scores of weapons very much more powerful than those bombs, upon this island.

It is true that the inhabitants of Hiroshima and Nagasaki were very little prepared for this advanced technology, and, indeed, in Nagasaki the 'All Clear' had sounded shortly before the detonation, so that the populace had trooped out of their conventional shelters and the women were working in the fields and the children playing in the playgrounds when the bomb went off.

Our own authorities might be able to manage the affair better. With greater warning, stronger houses, and with some more effective measures of civil defence, some lives might be saved, and perhaps even 'a substantial number'. Indeed, two Conservative MPs have calculated that effective measures might reduce deaths in a nuclear war in this country from about thirty-five millions to just twenty millions, and I will allow that fifteen millions in savings is a substantial number indeed.

Nevertheless, two comments must be made on this. The first is that the death or mortal injury of even the small figure of twenty millions might still give rise to the conditions of 'turbulence' which Professor Howard is anxious to forestall. The incidence of disaster would not be evenly spread across the country, with hale and hearty survivors in all parts standing ready, with high morale, to endure the hazards of the 'second strike'.

Air Marshal Sir Leslie Mavor, Principal of the Home Defence College, addressing a civil defence seminar in 1977 said that 'the main target areas would be so badly knocked about as to be beyond effective self-help. They would have to be more or less discounted until adjoining areas recovered sufficiently to come to their aid.' Those parts of the country 'holding no nuclear targets' might come through 'more or less undamaged by blast or fire'.

Their difficulties would be caused by fall-out radiation, a large influx of refugees, survival without external supplies of food, energy, raw materials . . .

(*The Times*, 16 January 1980)

This seems a realistic assessment. There would be some total disaster areas, from the margins of which the wounded and dying would flee as refugees; other intermediate areas would have energy supplies destroyed, all transport dislocated, and persons, food and water contaminated by fall-out; yet others would be relatively immune. But even in these immune areas there would be some persons in a state of hysterical terror, who would be ready (if they knew how) to intervene to prevent the second stage of Professor Howard's scenario.

The second comment is that we do not yet have any realistic notion of what might be *a scale sufficient* to effect *substantial* savings, nor what measures might be taken. We may certainly agree with the professor that no such measures are either planned or contemplated. The defence correspondent of *The Times*, Mr Peter Evans, in an illuminating survey in January, discovered that measures have been taken to ensure the survival of the high personnel of the State. This has long been evident. There will be bunkers deep under the Chilterns for senior politicians, civil servants and military, and deep hidey-holes for regional centres of military government. That is very comforting.

The population of this country, however, will not be invited to these bunkers, and it is an Official Secret to say where they are. The population will be sent off, with a do-it-yourself booklet (*Protect and Survive*), to wait in their own homes. They will be advised to go down to the ground floor or the cellar, and make a cubby-hole there with old doors and planks, cover it with sandbags, books and heavy furniture, and then creep into these holes with food and water for fourteen days, a portable radio, a portable latrine, and, of course, a tin-opener.

I have for long wondered why sociologists and demographers keep writing about 'the nuclear family', but now it is all at length set down and explained.

Now this might save some lives, but it will also make for an unhappy end to others. For the principal effects of nuclear weapons are very intense heat, blast and radioactive emissions. Within a certain distance of the centre of the detonation all houses, cars, clothes, the hair on dogs, cats and persons, and so on, will spontaneously ignite, while at the same time the blast will bring the houses tumbling down about the cubby-holes. We must envisage many thousands of nuclear families listening to Mr Robin Day's consensual homilies on their portable radios as they are baked, crushed or suffocated to death.

Those outside this radius might be afforded a little temporary protection. But when they eventually emerge (after some fourteen days) they will find the food and water contaminated, the roads blocked, the hospitals destroyed, the livestock dead or dying. The vice-chairman of Civil Aid, who is a realist, advises thus: 'If you saw a frog running about, you would have to wash it down to get rid of active dust, cook it and eat it' (*The Times*, 14 February 1980). And, according to Professor Howard's scenario, people will still be living in expectation of 'yet heavier attacks'.

If we are to learn from the experience of the people of Nagasaki and Hiroshima, then I think it is, after all, unlikely that many survivors will be devoting their energies to 'political turbulence', since, unless they know the entrances to the governmental deep bunkers, they will have nothing to turbul against. Most will be wandering here and there in a desperate attempt to find lost children, parents, neighbours, friends. A few of the most collected will succour the dying and dig among the ruins for the injured.

The measures outlined in *Protect and Survive* do not seem to me to be on *a scale sufficient* to reduce the consequences of a nuclear strike to the compass of a small word like 'disagreeable'. It is possible to imagine measures on a greater scale. The evacuation of whole cities, as is planned in the USA and perhaps in the Soviet Union, is inoperable here because this island is too small. But one might imagine the excavation of vast subterranean systems beneath our towns, complete with stored food and water, generating systems, air-purifying systems, etc.

This might save *a substantial number* of lives, although one is uncertain what it would save them for, since above ground no workplaces, uncontaminated crops or stock would be left.

The logic of this development, then, will be to remove these activities underground also, with subterranean cattle-stalls, granaries, bakeries, and munitions works.

It is certainly possible that, if civilization survives and continues on its present trajectory until the mid-twenty-first century, then the 'advanced' societies will have become troglodyte in some such fashion. But it would not be advisable to suppose that our descendants will have then at length attained to 'security', in the simultaneous realization of the ultimate in 'deterrence' with the ultimate in 'defence'. For the military will by then have taken further steps in technology. Earth penetrators already exist, which can drive death underground. All this will be perfected, 'modernized', and refined. There will be immense thermonuclear charges capable of concussing a whole underground city. And, in any case, by the time that humanity becomes troglodyte, it will then have been already defeated. 'Civilization' will then be an archaic term, which children can no longer construe.

We will now turn to the second assumption which underpins Professor Howard's arguments. This concerns 'tactical' or 'theatre' nuclear war.

The professor supposes a 'theatre' war confined to Europe, which does not escalate to confrontation between the two superpowers. We will not chide him too much on this supposition, since it is now commonplace in the strategic thinking of both blocs. Indeed, it is commonplace not only as idea but also as fact, since immense sums are spent on both sides to match each other's weapons at 'tactical' and 'theatre' levels.

We have seen that poor Mr Pym (who has now at last been told by an American officer what to do) is quite as simple on this matter as Professor Howard. Both suppose a 'chain of deterrence', according to which war may not only start at any level but it may be confined to that level, since at any point there is a further fearsome threshold of 'deterrence' ahead.

This is not the same as the proposal that *local* or *regional* wars with nuclear weapons may take place. That is a reasonable proposal. If the proliferation of these weapons continues, it is possible that we will see such wars: as between Israel and Arab states, or South Africa and an alliance of African states. Whether such wars lead on to confrontation between the superpowers will depend, not upon the logic of weaponry, but on further diplomatic and political considerations.

This proposition is different. It is that nuclear wars between the two great opposed powers and their allies could be confined to this or that level. This is a silly notion at first sight; and, after tedious and complex arguments have been gone through, it emerges as equally silly at the end. For while it might very well be in the *interests* of either the USA or the USSR to confine a war to Europe, or to the Persian Gulf, and to prevent it from passing into an ultimate confrontation, we are not dealing here with rational behaviour.

Once 'theatre' nuclear war commences, immense passions, indeed hysterias, will be aroused. After even the first strikes of such a war, communications and command posts will be so much snarled up that any notion of rational planning will give way to panic. Ideology will at once take over from self-interest. Above all, it will be manifest that the only one of the two great powers likely to come out of the contest as 'victor' must be the one which hurls its ballistic weapons first, furthest and fastest – and preferably before the weapons of the other have had time to lift off.

This was the commonsense message which Lord Louis Mountbatten, shortly before he was murdered, conveyed to a meeting in Strasbourg. He referred to the introduction of 'tactical' or 'theatre' weapons:

The belief was that were hostilities ever to break out in Western Europe, such weapons could be used in field warfare without triggering an all-out nuclear exchange leading to the final holocaust.

I have never found this idea credible. I have never been able to accept the reasons for the belief that any class of nuclear weapons can be categorized in terms of their tactical or strategic purposes . . .

In the event of a nuclear war there will be no chances, there will be no survivors – all will be obliterated. I am not asserting this without having deeply thought about the matter. When I was Chief of the British Defence Staff I made my views known . . . I repeat in all sincerity as a military man I can see no use for any nuclear weapons which would not end in escalation, with consequences that no one can conceive.

The same firm judgement was expressed by Lord Zuckerman in *The Times* on 21 January 1980: 'Nor was I ever able to see any military reality in what is now referred to as theatre or tactical warfare':

The men in the nuclear laboratories of both sides have succeeded in creating a world with an irrational foundation, on which a new set of political realities has in turn had to be built. They have become the alchemists of our times, working in secret ways which cannot be divulged, casting spells which embrace us all.

Professor Howard takes his stand on these irrational foundations, and practises alchemy in his own right. The spells which he casts on the public mind are presented as 'civil defence'. He calls for measures (unnamed) which must be 'given the widest possible publicity', in order to ensure 'the credibility of our entire defence posture', a posture which might otherwise be seen to be 'no more than an expensive bluff'.

The professor supposes that he is a tough realist, who is drawing conclusions which others, including politicians, are too timorous to draw in public. If we spend thousands of millions of pounds upon nuclear weapons, then we either intend to use them or we do not. If we intend to use them, then we must intend to receive them also. Or we must seem to intend so.

But, as he knows, there are no practicable civil defence measures which could have more than a marginal effect. He is therefore telling us that 'we' must replace one expensive bluff by a bluff even more expensive; or he is telling us that 'we' have decided that we are ready to accept the obliteration of the material resources and inheritance of this island, and of some half of its inhabitants, in order to further the strategies of NATO.

These are two distinct propositions, and it is time that they were broken into two parts. For a long time the second proposition has been hidden within the mendacious vocabulary of 'deterrence'; and behind these veils of 'posture', 'credibility' and 'bluff' it has waxed fat and now has come of age.

The first proposition is that nuclear weapons are capable of inflicting such 'unacceptable damage' on both parties to an exchange that mutual fear ensures peace. The second is that each party is actually preparing for nuclear war, and is ceaselessly searching for some ultimate weapon or tactical/strategic point of advantage which would assure its victory. We have lived uneasily with the first proposition for many years. We are now looking directly into the second proposition's eyes.

Deterrence has plausibility. It has 'worked' for thirty years, if not in Vietnam, Czechoslovakia, the Middle East, Africa, Cambodia, the Dominican Republic, Afghanistan, then in the central fracture between the superpowers which runs across Europe. It may have inhibited, in Europe, major 'conventional' war.

But it has not worked as a stationary state. The weapons for adequate 'deterrence' already existed thirty years ago, and, as the Pope reminded us in his New Year's Message for 1980, only 200 of the 50,000 nuclear weapons now estimated to be in existence would be enough to destroy the world's major cities. Yet we have moved upwards to 50,000, and each year new sophistications and 'modernizations' are introduced.

The current chatter about 'theatre' or 'tactical' nuclear war is not a sophisticated variant of the old vocabulary of 'deterrence'; it is directly at variance with that vocabulary. For it is founded on the notion that either of the superpowers might engage, to its own advantage, in a 'limited' nuclear war which could be kept below the threshold at which retribution would be visited on its own soil.[2]

Thus it is thought by persons in the Pentagon that a 'theatre' nuclear war might be confined to Europe, in which, to be sure, America's NATO allies would be obliterated, but in which immense damage would also be inflicted upon Russia west of the Urals, while the soil of the United States remained immune. (In such a scenario it is even supposed that President Carter and Mr Brezhnev would be on the 'hot line' to each other while Europe scorched, threatening ultimate inter-continental ballistic retribution, but at last making 'peace'.) This has been seen as the way to a great victory for 'the West', and if world-wide nuclear war seems to be ultimately inevitable, then the sooner that can be aborted by having a little theatre war the better.

The trouble with all this, from the Pentagon's point of view, is that it requires rewriting the war games-plan, and in this rewriting Soviet strategists have been unaccountably uncooperative. Mr Lawrence Freedman, who is Head of Policy Studies at the Royal Institute of International Affairs, and who is evidently a very great expert, noted in *The Times* (26 March 1980):

Recent moves in NATO have encouraged plans for selective, discrete strikes rather than all-out exchanges ... Unfortunately, the Soviet Union has shown little interest in Western ideas on limited nuclear war.

'Missiles in Western Europe would give the American President an intermediate option', stopping short of 'putting

American cities at risk', writes another expert, Mr Treverton of the Institute for Strategic Studies (*Observer*, 19 November 1979). And the President's national security adviser (and architect of the Iranian helicopter fiasco), Zbigniew Brzezinski, has recently discussed the current reviews of 'our nuclear targeting plans' in the course of an interview in *The New York Sunday Times* (30 March 1980):

All of these reviews are designed ... to avoid a situation in which the President would be put under irresistible pressure to preempt, to avoid leaving the United States only the options of yielding or engaging in a spasmodic and apocalyptic nuclear exchange.

Question: Are you saying that you want the United States to be able to fight a 'limited' nuclear war?

Brzezinski: I am saying that the United States, in order to maintain effective deterrence has to have choices which give us a wider range of options than either a spasmodic nuclear exchange or a limited conventional war ...

That is a politician's way of saying 'yes'. European war is to be one 'choice' or 'option' for United States strategists, although what might appear to be 'limited' on that side of the Atlantic might appear to be spasmodic and apocalyptic on this. The cruise missiles which are being set up in Western Europe are the hardware designed for exactly such a 'limited' war, and the nations which harbour them are viewed, in this strategy, as launching platforms which are expendable in the interests of 'Western' defence. While Russia might not *wish* to rewrite the games-plan, since some of its most populous and highly industrialized regions are *within* the 'theatre' whereas all of the USA is not, nevertheless (it is supposed) her hand might be forced if faced with the alternatives of such a war or of outright ICBM obliteration.

If all this sounds crazy, then I can only agree that crazy is exactly what it is. But, then, as a frequent visitor to the United States I must report that there is a dangerous tendency to craziness in the American view of the world. Protected geographically by two huge oceans, on a continent that has never been invaded or even subjected to aerial attack, the people suffer from a diminished reality-sense in which wars are always something which happen 'over there'. These illusions are fed with massive media propaganda, and are excited by electoral humbug, until crowds can shout (of the Iranians) 'Nuke them!' without any notion of what the words mean. It is against all this that the generous and responsible American peace movement has to work.

Mr Pym has told the House of Commons that the cruise missiles to be sited at Greenham Common and Molesworth are to be 'owned and operated by the United States'. Their use must be sanctioned by the President of the United States on the request of the Supreme Allied Commander, NATO, who is always an American general. He has also made some evasive parliamentary provisos about 'consultation', but it is clear enough that in any 'emergency' (or on the plea of an emergency) such consultation will be null. In every crisis, someone else's finger will be upon 'our' trigger.

Cruise missiles are *committing*: strategically and also politically. They place us, with finality, within the games-plan of the Pentagon. It was for this reason that Senator Nino Pasti, formerly an Italian member of the NATO Military Committee and Deputy Supreme Commander for NATO Nuclear Affairs, has declared: 'I have no doubt that the tactical nuclear weapons deployed in Europe represent the worst danger for the peoples of the continent':

In plain words, the tactical nuclear weapon would be employed in the view of NATO to limit the war to Europe. Europe is to be transformed into a 'nuclear Maginot line' for the defence of the United States.

(*Sanity*, July/August 1979)

Meanwhile the United States is urgently seeking for similar platforms in the Middle East for another small 'theatre' war which might penetrate deep into the Caucasus.

43

And an even uglier scenario is beginning to show itself in China, where greed for a vast arms market is tempting Western salesmen while United States strategists hope to nudge Russia and China into war with each other – a war which would dispel another Western phobia, the demographic explosion of the East. The idea here is to extract the West, at the last moment, from this war – much the same scenario as that which went disastrously wrong in 1939.

These little 'theatre' wars (not one of which would obediently stay put in its theatre) are now all on the drawing-boards, and in the Pentagon more than in the Kremlin, for the simple reason that every 'theatre' is adjacent to the Soviet Union, and any 'tactical' nuclear strike would penetrate deep into Russian territory.

The plans for the European 'theatre' war are not only ready – the 'modernized' missiles designed for exactly such a war have been ordered, and will be delivered to this island in 1983. And at this moment, the advocates of civil defence make a corresponding *political* intervention. Let us see why this is so.

These advocates wish to hurry the British people across a threshold of mental expectation, so that they may be prepared, not for 'deterrence', but for actual nuclear war.

The expectations supporting the theory of deterrence are, in the final analysis, that deterrence will *work*. Deterrence is effective, because the alternative is not only 'unacceptable' or 'disagreeable': it is 'unthinkable'.

Deterrence is a posture, but it is the posture of MAD (mutual assured destruction), not of menace. It does not say 'If we go to nuclear war we intend to win': it says 'Do not go to war, or provoke war, because neither of us can win'. In consequence it does not bother to meddle with anything so futile as 'civil defence'. If war commences, everything is already lost.

Those who have supported the policy of deterrence have done so in the confidence that this policy would prevent

44

nuclear war from taking place. They have not contemplated the alternative, and have been able to avoid facing certain questions raised by that alternative. Of these, let us notice three.

First, is nuclear war preferable to being overcome by the enemy? Is the death of fifteen or twenty millions and the utter destruction of the country preferable to an occupation which might offer the possibility, after some years, of resurgence and recuperation?

Second, are we ourselves prepared to endorse the use of such weapons against the innocent, the children and the aged, of an 'enemy'?

Third, how does it happen that Britain should find herself committed to policies which endanger the very survival of the nation, as a result of decisions taken by a secret committee of NATO, and then endorsed at Brussels without public discussion or parliamentary sanction, leaving the 'owning and operation' of these weapons in the hands of the military personnel of a foreign power, a power whose strategists have contingency plans for unleashing these missiles in a 'theatre' war which would not extend as far as their own homeland?

The first two questions raise moral, and not strategic, issues. My own answer to them is 'no'. They are, in any case, not new questions. The third question is, in some sense, new, and it is also extraordinary, in the sense that even proposing the question illuminates the degree to which the loss of our national sovereignty has become absolute, and democratic process has been deformed in ways scarcely conceivable twenty years ago.

But arguments such as those of Professor Howard are designed to hurry us past these questions without noticing them. They are designed to carry us across a threshold from the *unthinkable* (the theory of deterrence, founded upon the assumption that this must *work*) to the *thinkable* (the theory that nuclear war may happen, and may be imminent, and,

45

with cunning tactics and proper preparations, might end in 'victory').

More than this, the arguments are of an order which permit the mind to progress from the unthinkable to the thinkable *without thinking* – without confronting the arguments, their consequences or probable conclusions, and, indeed, without knowing that any threshold has been crossed.

At each side of this threshold we are offered a policy with an identical label: 'deterrence'. And both policies stink with the same mendacious rhetoric – 'posture', 'credibility', 'bluff'. But mutual fear and self-interest predominate on one side, and active menace and the ceaseless pursuit of 'tactical' or 'theatre' advantage predominate on the other. Which other side we have crossed over to, and now daily inhabit.

Professor Howard himself has perhaps thought the problem through. His letter appeared to me, when I first read it, as a direct political intervention.[3] His language – his anxiety as to possible 'political turbulence', his advocacy of measures which are not 'covert or concealed' – appeared to reveal an intention to act in political ways upon the mind of the people, in order to enforce a 'posture', not of defence but of menace; and in this it corresponded, on a political level, with the menacing strategic decisions of NATO last December at Brussels.

The essence of the political problem was clearly stated, at the height of the old Cold War, by John Foster Dulles:

In order to make the country bear the burden, we have to create an emotional atmosphere akin to a war-time psychology. We must create the idea of a threat from without.

But that was when the problem was only in its infancy. For the country – that is, *this* country – must now not only be made to bear a burden of heavy expense, loss of civil liberties, etc., but also the expectation, as a definite and imminent possibility, of actual nuclear devastation.

Hence it becomes necessary to create not only 'the idea of a threat from without' but also of a threat *from within*: 'political turbulence'. And it is necessary to inflame these new expectations by raising voluntary defence corps, auxiliary services, digging even deeper bunkers for the personnel of the State, distributing leaflets, holding lectures in halls and churches, laying down two weeks' supplies of emergency rations, promoting in the private sector the manufacture of Whitelaw Shelters and radiation-proof 'Imperm' blinds and patent Anti-Fall-Out pastilles and 'Breetheesy' masks, and getting the Women's Institutes to work out recipes for broiling radioactive frogs. And it is also necessary to supplement all this by beating up an internal civil-war or class-war psychosis, by unmasking traitors, by theatening journalists under the Official Secrets Acts, by tampering with juries and tapping telephones, and generally by closing up people's minds and mouths.

Now I do not know how far all this will work. There are tactical problems, which those who live outside All Souls are able to see. Whitehall's reluctance to issue every householder with a copy of *Protect and Survive* is eloquent testimony to this. For there is a minority of the British people who are reluctant to be harried across this threshold. These people have voices, and if they are denied access to the major media, there are still little journals and democratic organizations where they are able to speak. If the mass of the British public were to be suddenly alerted to the situation which they are actually now in – by 'alarmist' leaflets and by broadcasts telling them that they have indeed every reason for alarm – then the whole operation might backfire, and give rise to a vast consensus, not for nuclear war, but for peace.

I suspect that, for these reasons, Professor Howard is regarded, by public-relations-conscious persons in the Establishment, as a great patriot of NATO and an admirable fellow, but as an inexperienced politician. The people of this country have been made dull and stupid by a diet of Official Information. But they are not all *that* stupid, and there is still a risk – a small risk, but not one worth taking – that they might remember who they are, and become 'turbulent' before the war even got started.

I suspect that the strategy of high persons in the Cabinet Office, the security services, and the Ministry of Defence, is rather different from that of Professor Howard. There is preliminary work yet to do, in softening up the public mind, in intimidating dissidents, in controlling information more tightly, and in strengthening internal policing and security. Meanwhile planning will go forward, and at the next international crisis (real or factitious) there will be a co-ordinated, univocal, obliterating 'civil defence' bombardment, with All-Party broadcasts, leafleting and the levying of volunteers, and with extreme precautions to prevent any dissenting voices from having more than the most marginal presence.

So that I think that Professor Howard is a little ahead of his times. But the *arguments* which Mr Howard has proposed, are, exactly, the arguments most deeply relevant to the present moment. That is why I have spent all this time in examining them.

I have sought, in these pages, to open these arguments up, to show what is inside them, which premises and what conclusions. I have not been trying to frighten readers, but to show the consequences to which these arguments lead.

Nor have I been trying to show that Professor Howard is a scandalous and immoral sort of person. I do not suppose myself to be a more moral sort of person than he. He cannot have put forward his ghastly scenario with any feelings of eager anticipation.

And, finally, although I am myself by conviction a socialist, I have not been grounding my arguments on premises of that kind. I do not suppose that all blame lies

48

with the ideological malice and predatory drives of the capitalist 'West', although some part of it does.

Socialists once supposed, in my youth, that socialist states might commit every kind of blunder, but the notion that they could go to war with each other, for ideological or national ends, was unthinkable. We now know better. States which call themselves 'socialist' can go to war with each other, and do. And they can use means and arguments as bad as those of the old imperialist powers.

I have based my arguments on the *logic* of the Cold War, or of the 'deterrent' situation itself. We may favour this or that explanation for the origin of this situation. But once this situation has arisen, there is a common logic at work in both blocs. Military technology and military strategy come to impose their own agenda upon political developments. As Lord Zuckerman has written: 'The decisions which we make today in the fields of science and technology determine the tactics, then the strategy, and finally the politics of tomorrow'.

This is an inter-operative and reciprocal logic, which threatens all, impartially. If you press me for my own view, then I would hazard that the Russian state is now the most dangerous in relation to its own people and to the people of its client states. The rulers of Russia are police-minded and security-minded people, imprisoned within their own ideology, accustomed to meet argument with repression and tanks. But the basic postures of the Soviet Union seem to me, still, to be those of siege and aggressive defence; and even the brutal and botching intervention in Afghanistan appears to have followed upon sensitivity as to United States and Chinese strategies.

The United States seems to me to be more dangerous and provocative in its general military and diplomatic strategies, which press around the Soviet Union with menacing bases. It is in Washington, rather than in Moscow, that scenarios are dreamed up for 'theatre' wars; and it is in America that the 'alchemists' of superkill, the clever technologists of 'advantage' and ultimate weapons, press forward 'the politics of tomorrow'.

But we need not ground our own actions on a 'preference' for one of the other blocs. This is unrealistic and could be divisive. What is relevant is the logic of process common to both, reinforcing the ugliest features of each others' societies, and locking both together in each other's nuclear arms in the same degenerative drift.

It is in this sense that NATO's 'modernization' programme, and the Soviet intervention in Afghanistan, taken together, may perhaps be seen as a textbook case of the reciprocal logic of the Cold War. NATO's plans were certainly perceived by Soviet leaders as menacing, and vigorous efforts were made by Mr Brezhnev and others to prevent them. This perception of menace hardened, on 12 December 1979, when NATO endorsed the full programme at Brussels – and when, in the meantime, the United States Senate, under pressure from the arms lobby, failed to ratify SALT II. In response, the hard arguments and the hard men had their way amongst the Soviet leadership, and, two weeks later, the Soviet intervention in Afghanistan took place. NATO 'modernization' was not a decisive factor, in the view of the Russian historian, Roy Medvedev (to whom I addressed some questions last June), since the intervention in Afghanistan had been meditated and prepared over a much longer period. But it signalled to those Soviet leaders who favoured 'the military option' that, in relation to Europe, they now had 'nothing to lose'.

Throughout this essay I have been attempting to disclose this reciprocal logic of process, which is driven forward by the armourers of both superpowers. And what I have been contending for, against Professor Howard, is this. First, I have shown that the premises which underlie his letter are *irrational*.

Second, I have been concerned throughout with the use of *language*.

What makes the extinction of civilized life upon this island probable is not a greater propensity for evil than in previous history, but a more formidable destructive technology, a deformed political process (East and West), and also a deformed culture.

The deformation of culture commences within language itself. It makes possible a disjunction between the rationality and moral sensibility of individual men and women and the effective political and military process. A certain kind of 'realist' and 'technical' vocabulary effects a closure which seals out the imagination, and prevents the reason from following the most manifest sequence of cause and consequence. It habituates the mind to nuclear holocaust by reducing everything to a flat level of normality. By habituating us to certain expectations, it not only encourages resignation – it also beckons on the event.

'Human kind cannot bear very much reality'. As much of reality as most of us can bear is what is most proximate to us – our self-interests and our immediate affections. What threatens our interests – what causes us even mental unease – is seen as outside ourselves, as the Other. We can kill thousands because we have first learned to call them 'the enemy'. Wars commence in our culture first of all, and we kill each other in euphemisms and abstractions long before the first missiles have been launched.

It has never been true that nuclear war is 'unthinkable'. It has been thought and the thought has been put into effect. This was done in 1945, in the name of allies fighting for the Four Freedoms (although what those Freedoms were I cannot now recall), and it was done upon two populous cities. It was done by professing Christians, when the Western Allies had already defeated the Germans, and when victory against the Japanese was certain, in the longer or shorter run. The longer run would have cost some thousands more of Western lives, whereas the short run (the bomb) would cost the lives only of enemy Asians. This was perfectly thinkable. It was thought. And action followed on.

What is 'unthinkable' is that nuclear war could happen

to *us*. So long as we can suppose that this war will be inflicted only on *them*, the thought comes easily. And if we can also suppose that this war will save 'our' lives, or serve our self-interest, or even save us (if we live in California) from the tedium of queuing every other day for gasoline, then the act can easily follow on. We *think* others to death as we define them as the Other: the enemy: Asians: Marxists: non-people. The deformed human mind is the ultimate doomsday weapon – it is out of the human mind that the missiles and the neutron warheads come.

For this reason it is necessary to enter a remonstrance against those who use this kind of language and adopt these mental postures. They are preparing our minds as launching platforms for exterminating thoughts. The fact that Soviet ideologists are doing much the same (thinking us to death as 'imperialists' and 'capitalists') is no defence. This is not work proper to scholars.

Academic persons have little influence upon political and military decisions, and less than they suppose. They do, however, operate within our culture, with ideas and language, and, as we have seen, the deformation of culture is the precedent condition for nuclear war.

It is therefore proper to ask such persons to resist the contamination of our culture with those terms which precede the ultimate act. The death of fifteen millions of fellow-citizens ought not to be described as 'disagreeable consequences'. A war confined to Europe ought not to be given the euphemisms of 'limited' or 'theatre'. The development of more deadly weapons, combined with menacing diplomatic postures and major new political and strategic decisions (the siting of missiles on our own territory under the control of alien personnel), ought not to be concealed within the anodyne technological term of 'modernization'. The threat to erase the major cities of Russia and East Europe ought not to trip easily off the tongue as 'unacceptable damage'.

I am thinking of that great number of persons who very

much dislike what is going on in the actual world, but who dislike the vulgarity of exposing themselves to the business of 'politics' even more. They erect both sets of dislikes around their desks or laboratories like a screen, and get on with their work and their careers. I am not asking these, or all of them, to march around the place or to spend hours in weary little meetings. I am asking them to examine the deformities of our culture and then, in public places, to demur.

I will recommend some forms of action, although every person must be governed in this by his or her own conscience and aptitudes. But, first, I should, in fairness to Professor Howard, offer a scenario of my own.

I have come to the view that a general nuclear war is not only possible but probable, and that is probability is increasing. We may indeed be approaching a point of no-return when the existing tendency or disposition towards this outcome becomes irreversible.

I ground this view upon two considerations, which we may define (to borrow the terms of our opponents) as 'tactical' and 'strategic'.

By tactical I mean that the political and military conditions for such war exist now in several parts of the world; the proliferation of nuclear weapons will continue, and will be hastened by the export of nuclear energy technology to new markets; and the rivalry of the superpowers is directly inflaming these conditions.

Such conditions now exist in the Middle East and around the Persian Gulf, will shortly exist in Africa, while in South-East Asia Russia and China have already engaged in wars by proxy with each other, in Cambodia and Vietnam.

Such wars might stop just short of general nuclear war between the superpowers. And in their aftermath the great powers might be frightened into better behaviour for a few years. But so long as this behaviour rested on nothing more than mutual fear, then military technology would continue to be refined, more hideous weapons would be invented, and the opposing giants would enlarge their control over client states. The strategic pressures towards confrontation will continue to grow.

These *strategic* considerations are the gravest of the two. They rest upon a historical view of power and of the social process, rather than upon the instant analysis of the commentator on events.

In this view it is a superficial judgement, and a dangerous error, to suppose that deterrence 'has worked'. Very possibly it may have worked, at this or that moment, in preventing recourse to war. But in its very mode of working, and in its 'postures', it has brought on a series of consequences within its host societies.

'Deterrence' is not a stationary state, it is a degenerative state. Deterrence has repressed the export of violence towards the opposing bloc, but in doing so the repressed power of the State has turned back upon its own author. The repressed violence has backed up, and has worked its way back into the economy, the polity, the ideology and the culture of the opposing powers. This is the deep structure of the Cold War.

The logic of this deep structure of mutual fear was clearly identified by William Blake in his 'Song of Experience', *The Human Abstract*:

> And mutual fear brings peace;
> Till the selfish loves increase.
> Then Cruelty knits a snare,
> And spreads his baits with care . . .
>
> Soon spreads the dismal shade
> Of Mystery over his head;
> And the Catterpiller and Fly
> Feed on the Mystery.
>
> And it bears the fruit of Deceit,
> Ruddy and sweet to eat;

> And the Raven his nest has made
> In its thickest shade.

In this logic, the peace of 'mutual fear' enforces opposing self-interests, affords room for 'Cruelty' to work, endangers 'Mystery' and its parasites, brings to fruit the 'postures' of Deceit, and the death-foreboding Raven hides within the Mystery.

Within the logic of 'deterrence', millions are now employed in the armed services, security organs and military economy of the opposing blocs, and corresponding interests exert immense influence within the counsels of the great powers. Mystery envelops the operation of the technological 'alchemists'. 'Deterrence' has become normal, and minds have been habituated to the vocabulary of mutual extermination. And within this normality, hideous cultural abnormalities have been nurtured and are growing to full girth.

The menace of nuclear war reaches far back into the economies of both parties, dictating priorities, and awarding power. Here, in failing economies, will be found the most secure and vigorous sectors, tapping the most advanced technological skills of both opposed societies and diverting these away from peaceful and productive employment or from efforts to close the great gap between the world's north and south. Here also will be found the driving rationale for expansionist programmes in unsafe nuclear energy, programmes which cohabit comfortably with military nuclear technology whereas the urgent research into safe energy supplies from sun, wind or wave are neglected because they have no military pay-off. Here, in this burgeoning sector, will be found the new expansionist drive for 'markets' for arms, as 'capitalist' and 'socialist' powers compete to feed into the Middle East, Africa and Asia more sophisticated means of kill.

The menace of this stagnant state of violence backs up also into the polity of both halves of the world. Permanent threat and periodic crisis press the men of the military-industrial interests, by differing routes in each society, towards the top. Crisis legitimates the enlargement of the security functions of the state, the intimidation of internal dissent, and the imposition of secrecy and the control of information. As the 'natural' lines of social and political development are repressed, and affirmative perspectives are closed, so internal politics collapses into squabbling interest-groups, all of which interests are subordinated to the overarching interests of the state of perpetual threat.

All this may be readily observed. It may be observed even in failing Britain, across whose territory are now scattered the bases, airfields, camps, research stations, submarine depots, communications-interception stations, radar screens, security and intelligence HQ, munitions works – secure and expanding employment in an economic climate of radical insecurity.

What we cannot observe so well – for we ourselves are the object which must be observed – is the manner in which three decades of 'deterrence', of mutual fear, mystery, and state-endorsed stagnant hostility, have backed up into our culture and our ideology. Imagination has been numbed, language and values have been fouled, by the postures and expectations of the 'deterrent' state. But this is matter for a close and scrupulous inquiry.

These, then, are among the strategic considerations which lead me to the view that the probability of great power nuclear warfare is strong and increasing. I do not argue from this local episode or that: what happened yesterday in Afghanistan and what is happening now in Pakistan or North Yemen. I argue from a general and sustained historical process, an accumulative logic, of a kind made familiar to me in the study of history. The episodes lead in this direction or that, but the general logic of process is always towards nuclear war.

The local crises are survived, and it seems as if the decisive moment – either of war or of peace-making and reconciliation – has been postponed and pushed forward into the future. But what has been pushed forward is always worse. Both parties change for the worse. The weapons are more terrible, the means for their delivery more clever. The notion that a war might be fought to 'advantage', that it might be 'won', gains ground. There is even a tremour of excitement in our culture as though, subconsciously, human kind has lived with the notion for so long that expectations without actions have become boring. The human mind, even when it resists, assents more easily to its own defeat. All moves on its degenerative course, as if the outcome of civilization was as determined as if the outcome of this sentence: in a full stop.

I am reluctant to accept that this determinism is absolute. But if my arguments are correct, then we cannot put off the matter any longer. We must throw whatever resources still exist in human culture across the path of this degenerative logic. We must protest if we are to survive. Protest is the only realistic form of civil defence.

We must generate an alternative logic, an opposition at every level of society. This opposition must be international and it must win the support of multitudes. It must bring its influence to bear upon the rulers of the world. It must act, in very different conditions, within each national state; and, on occasion, it must directly confront its own national state apparatus.

The Campaign for European Nuclear Disarmament, which is already gaining active support in many parts of Western Europe, as well as a more cautious attention in some parts of Eastern Europe, has as an objective the creation of an expanding zone freed from nuclear weapons and bases.[4] It aims to expel these weapons from the soil and waters of both East and West Europe, and to press the missiles, in the first place, back to the Urals and to the Atlantic ocean.

The tactics of this campaign will be both national and international.

In the national context, each national peace movement will proceed directly to contest the nuclear weapons deployed by its own state, or by NATO or Warsaw Treaty obligations upon its own soil. Its actions will not be qualified by any notion of diplomatic bargaining. Its opposition to the use of nuclear weapons by its own state will be absolute. Its demands upon its own state for disarmament will be unilateral.

In the international, and especially in the European, context, each national movement will exchange information and delegations, will support and challenge each other. The movement will encourage a European consciousness, in common combat for survival, fostering informal communication at every level, and disregarding national considerations of interest or 'security'.

It is evident that this logic will develop unevenly. The national movements will not grow at the same pace, not be able to express themselves in identical ways. Each success of a unilateral kind – by Holland in refusing NATO cruise missiles or by Romania or Poland in distancing themselves from Soviet strategies – will be met with an outcry that it serves the advantage of one or other bloc.

This outcry must be disregarded. It cannot be expected that initiatives on one side will be met with instant reciprocation from the other. Very certainly, the strategists of both blocs will seek to turn the movement to their own advantage. The logic of peace-making will be as uneven, and as fraught with emergencies and contingencies, as the logic which leads on to war.

In particular, the movement in West and East Europe will find very different expression. In the West we envisage popular movements engaged in a direct contest with the policies of their own national states. At first, Soviet ideologues may look benignly upon this, looking forward to a weakening of NATO preparations which are matched by no actions larger than 'peace-loving' rhetoric from the East.

But we are confident that our strategy can turn this

rhetoric into acts. In Eastern Europe there are profound pressures for peace, for greater democracy and international exchange, and for relief from the heavy burden of siege economies. For a time these pressures may be contained by the repressive measures of national and Soviet security services. Only a few courageous dissidents will, in the first place, be able to take an open part in our common work.

Yet to the degree that the peace movement in the West can be seen to be effective, it will afford support and protection to our allies in Eastern Europe and the Soviet Union. It will provide those conditions of relaxation of tension which will weaken the rationale and legitimacy of repressive state measures, and will allow the pressures for democracy and detente to assert themselves in more active and open ways. Moreover, as an instrinsic part of the European campaign, the demand for an opening of the societies of the East to information, free communication and expression, and exchange of delegations to take part in the common work, will be pressed on every occasion. And it will not only be 'pressed' as rhetoric. We are going to find devices which will symbolize that pressure and dramatize that debate.

Against the strategy which envisages Europe as a 'theatre' of 'limited' nuclear warfare, we propose to make in Europe a theatre of peace. This will not, even if we succeed, remove the danger of confrontation in non-European theatres. It offers, at the least, a small hope of European survival. It could offer more. For if the logic of nuclear strategy reaches back into the organization and ideologies of the superpowers themselves, so the logic of peace-making might reach back also, enforcing alternative strategies, alternative ideologies. European nuclear disarmament would favour the conditions for international detente.

As to Britain there is no need to doubt what must be done to protest and survive.

We must detach ourselves from the nuclear strategies of

NATO and dispense with the expensive and futile imperial toy of an 'independent' deterrent (Polaris). We must close down those airfields and bases which already serve aircraft and submarines on nuclear missions. And we must contest every stage of the attempt to import United States cruise missiles on to our soil.

When I first sat down to write this essay, in February 1980, it seemed to the handful of us in Britain, France, West Germany and Eastern Europe who were then discussing such a campaign that we were only whistling in the dark. On every side of us the armourers were having their way. Only in Holland and Belgium did it seem that a popular movement of conscience could still bring any influence to bear upon political decisions.

Now we know differently. The movement has taken off, and it is, already, too large and too various for any group or interest to manipulate it for sectional ends. In Britain this is true most of all. In every part of the country groups have been forming themselves, under many auspices and names – CND, World Disarmament, END, local councils of peace, and local campaigns against cruise missiles. It is a confused and confusing scene, developing too fast for any central organization. One thing only is clear. No one is going to nobble this movement: these groups are for themselves. We hope in this book to provide a service to these hundreds of groups – and also to all readers who not only wish to act, but who know that clear argument and sound information are actions in their own right.

Notes

1. See the essays by Dan Smith, Mary Kaldor, David Holloway and Emma Rothschild below.
2. For the history of the concept of 'theatre' warfare, see Alva Myrdal's essay below.
3. Since I wrote an earlier version of this, in the form of

a pamphlet, Professor Howard has told me, with courtesy, that I have misrepresented his views on some points. He is not an advocate of cruise missiles (which he does not think will 'do much good'), but intended in his letter to draw necessary conclusions from the decision to bring them here. No doubt he will defend his own views more fully in due course, and also explain further his objections to cruise missiles.

4. For the European Appeal, see below.

CHAPTER TWO

Henry T. Nash
The Bureaucratization of Homicide*

Men in blue, green, and khaki tunics and others in three-button
business suits sit in pastel offices and plan complex operations in
which thousands of distant human beings will die.

(Richard J. Barnet)

During the 1950s and 1960s, the hot years of the Cold War,
I held several jobs with the Department of Defense (DOD).
I remember most vividly my job with the Air Targets
Division of the Air Force where I worked as an intelligence
analyst. Here I helped select targets in the Soviet Union at
which, in the event of a war, Air Force officers would fire
nuclear warheads.

As an analyst in the Political and Economics Section of
the Air Targets Division my responsibility was to 'nominate'
as targets buildings identified as Communist Party headquarters located in various Soviet cities. In order for a
nominated target to win its way into the Bombing Encyclo-
pedia (the official Secret Air Force catalogue of strategic
targets in each communist country), a Significant Summary
Statement was prepared which briefly (roughly 50 words or
less) described each target and its strategic importance.
While I worked at selecting and justifying political targets,
fellow-analysts in other offices were busy identifying different types of strategic targets – petroleum depots, airfields,
or industrial centres. Each of us made nominations for the
integrated Air Force strategic target list and we each hoped

* Editors' note: this essay was first published in The Bulletin of Atomic
Scientists in April 1980.

that our targets would be chosen for a DOD strategic plan of nuclear attack designed to bring about a rapid, unconditional surrender of Soviet forces. Like myself, my colleagues were graduates of liberal arts colleges and many were taking evening graduate courses in fields such as international relations or economic theory. Most of us had vague hopes of a college teaching job some day but, meanwhile, taking courses meant improving our professional credentials and this made it easier to live with the more mundane aspects of our nine-to-five life.

Today, as a professor in a small liberal arts college, I am frequently visited by haunting memories of my work with Air Targets. I'm surprised how clear these memories are; the details of my work, the faces and names of my colleagues and the atmosphere of the place where I worked – a grey, creaking two-storey temporary barracks-like building, anchored to Constitution Avenue by the weight of a large, heavy windowless cinderblock room in which classified documents were read and filed. But the haunting memories are tied less to people and place than to a nagging and disturbing question – what was it about work with Air Targets that made me insensitive to its homicidal implications? I and my colleagues, with whom I shared a large office, drank coffee and ate lunch, never experienced guilt or self-criticism. Our office behaviour was no different from that of men and women who might work for a bank or insurance company. What enabled us calmly to plan to incinerate vast numbers of unknown human beings without any sense of moral revulsion? At least no signs of moral revulsion surfaced when we were having an extra martini or two at lunch to celebrate the inclusion of some of our government control centres in a Joint Chiefs list of prime Soviet targets.

The Cold War made selecting targets for attack in the Soviet Union seem respectable. Within the Defense Department one was struck by the atmosphere of a war to be waged

63

and won. Crisis conditions made targeting seem imperative, which, in turn, made it morally acceptable.

Another factor was that the complex vastness of the Defense Department prevented any intelligence analyst from determining how his work might be used by higher-ranking officials. The relationship between cause and effect was obscured. Because of the size of the Defense bureaucracy, managerial efficiency called for the compartmentalization of work and, within our intelligence operation, one basis for compartmentalization was the 'need to know'. This meant that analysts were permitted to know something only if it were needed to complete an assigned task. Without a need to know, access was prohibited. Thus, in the case of the Air Targets Division, I had access to targeting information pertaining to Soviet government control centres but I did not have access to data concerning other categories of targets, such as Soviet petroleum depots or air bases. Working on tasks of limited yet clearly defined scope appealed to analysts who might otherwise have felt at sea in the vastness of the bureaucracy. Need to know, initially designed to help reduce intelligence leaks, restricted each analyst's appreciation of the larger context of which his job was a small part. Obscuring the 'big picture' helped promote peace of mind.

While some administrative arrangements prevented analysts from grasping how all the parts fit together, others helped analysts achieve a sense of professional security and personal gratification. For example, analysts usually worked as members of a committee, team or task force. Although this group–think process often blunted the expression of individual insights and diluted strong conclusions, it offered something of value to individual team players. A well-received team product provided reinforcement through shared, mutual congratulations while, in the case of a negative or critical reaction, the individual player could absolve himself from personal responsibility by blaming less insightful team members or by joining fellow-teammates in blaming the unappreciative system. The team made it possible to savour the gratification of praise and muted the unappealing impact of criticism.

It was not only the protective structure of the team that shielded the individual analyst from serious challenges or the ignominy of being proven wrong; the broad theoretical or conjectural context within which research was carried on offered security as well. The fact that most study requirements were cast in terms of long-range predictions ('The Stability and Cohesion of the Soviet Government Control System: 1985–90', for example, or 'Sources of Soviet Petroleum in the Year 2000') provided protection. It was difficult if not impossible for any potential critic to prove that a colleague was incorrect, or put him on the spot, if the study consisted of speculative generalizations about probable future developments concerning a broad, complex subject. Analysts were cognizant of this invulnerability and liked it.

Another facet of DOD research was the practice of developing reports in terms of the so-called 'worst case' situation. With regard to assessments of Soviet military capabilities, for example, analysts strained to depict the most extreme and threatening dimensions of the Soviet Union's ability to develop the full resources of its military potential. The worst case approach to 'research' was encouraged by the Department of Defense since, to the extent that Soviet military potentialities were described in their most horrendous dimensions, the Department strengthened its chances to motivate Congress to provide increased defence funds. Furthermore, the worst case approach imposed no constraints on the analyst's imaginative freedom to estimate future levels of enemy weaponry. Again, under these circumstances an analyst's conclusions were less susceptible to effective challenge. Further immunity from criticism was assured by the fact that each analyst's conclusions, or those of his team, would be immediately classified and access to the finished product restricted to those who held proper clearances and the need to know.

65

Ascertaining enemy capabilities in terms of the worst case disposed analysts to perceive relations among nations as being hostile, combative and consequently threatening. This encouraged the view that America's interests were best protected through superiority in arms. Thus, what was initially only an approach to intelligence research (the worst case) came to colour the analyst's world-view, an outlook that was buttressed by compatible attitudes in the Defense environment. The worst case inevitably disposed Defense analysts to concentrate on assessing enemy capabilities, primarily military, without ascertaining what enemy intentions might be. Worst case thinking implied that enemy intentions were known (maximum aggressiveness) and that a concentrated effort to list enemy capabilities was required. Worst case rendered legitimate the ideological conviction that stressed the critical importance of 'standing up to the Russians'. This could be best done through the acquisition of more weapons since, of course, the only thing the Russians respected was force.

What all of this fostered in the workaday concerns of Defense analysts was a persistent preoccupation with the state of military technology – the numbers game. Assembling, or at least being familiar with, lists, tables, and catalogues of the estimated number and characteristics of enemy weapons was an essential part of being a respected intelligence analyst. As the arms race continued and the United States and the Soviet Union acquired more and more weapons, there were more and more items to count and describe. The strong technological and quantitative orientation of these tasks held the attention of analysts and the relationship of weapons to human life was an incidental consideration. During a NATO war game I remember the surprise expressed by an Air Force colonel when he was informed of the number of casualties that resulted from his striking an 'enemy' urban centre with a one-megaton weapon. It took the simulated reality of a war game to bring home the human dimensions of this act. The colonel quickly regained his composure, reassuring himself that this was, after all, only a game.

In retrospect, in the anxious atmosphere of the Cold War, and in the setting of the Department of Defense where arms were considered the means of survival, thinking about the social characteristics of an enemy society constituted an unrewarding, almost irresponsible pursuit. How useful was it to grasp the intricate dynamics of another society if you were the most powerful nation in the world and had already decided to seek security through military intimidation? The significance of military power in determining the behaviour of government officials was illustrated by remarks made by Pham Van Dong, Premier of North Vietnam, and Henry Kissinger, then President Nixon's national security affairs adviser. These remarks enabled Richard Barnet to contrast the capacities of the leaders of North Vietnam and America to comprehend each other's political motivations.

I was struck by how well the Vietnamese politician understood Nixon's character and situation as well as the pressures that operated on him. The Premier had the ability to put himself in Nixon's place. Kissinger, on the other hand, while evidencing respect and even a little admiration for his adversary's skill, seemed to have no genuine understanding of what motivated him. In Hanoi, Nixon was a human being, not liked, but seriously considered. In the White House, Pham Van Dong was a chessboard figure. Those with power easily convince themselves that they do not need to understand their adversaries. Those without power know they cannot afford not to understand.[1]

A circular three-step form of logic offered comfort to Defense bureaucrats. Superior military power disposed defence planners not to take the trouble to comprehend their victims. Not knowing whom one was planning to kill made the sombre prospect of using weapons much less onerous. Therefore, it was possible to think of arms superiority as the best means of achieving national security.

Also contributing to the atmosphere of intelligence work

was the stress given to security clearances. Every analyst was required to have a security clearance and with a clearance was granted access to documents bearing security classifications up through Top Secret. Clearance usually required a six- to twelve-month probe of an applicant's past – where he had lived and worked, whom he knew, and organizations he had joined. I can recall how we criticized the clearance process, pointing out how subjective the process was because of the weight given to impressions of neighbours and casual acquaintances. Despite the many critical comments about clearances, I also had the impression that being cleared had its rewards. These were personal and had to do with being confronted by a screening process, passing the test, and then enjoying final acceptance. Being cleared represented a flattering experience sharpened by the quality of selectivity, not unlike the feeling accompanying acceptance by a fraternity or country club. You knew you were chosen. Being included confirmed that you had been found worthy by those unseen and unnamed officials somewhere in the upper reaches of the bureaucracy who managed America's security needs. It was a perverse gratification in a way – to feel rewarded simply for things one refrained from doing in the past – but most analysts quietly savoured the fact that someone had considered them fit to share vital national secrets in the cause of security.

Among those finally cleared for work at Defense, there were some upon whom was bestowed a higher, more selective, *special* clearance. Special clearance meant that one was granted access to unique intelligence acquired by means of highly secret techniques, such as electronic sensors used to intercept another nation's official communications or specially trained deep-cover agents in high places. When I was 'chosen' for a special clearance, my immediate feeling was one of achievement and pleasure. I also remember the earlier feeling when I was not cleared for special intelligence and how important it seemed to me to be one of the three or four who were cleared among the twenty or so analysts in the Political and Economics Section. With subdued envy I would watch those chosen few leave our office several times a day to check the 'take' in the 'back room', the guarded, windowless cinderblock cubicle filled with combination safes. These special people would periodically read over my work to see if some fact or point of emphasis should be altered on the basis of what they were privileged to see and I was not. Intelligence community decorum made it inappropriate to question any changes made by this select few. One simply exhibited a silent respect for superior knowledge.

Thinking back on DOD security practices, I realize that levels of clearance represent just another dimension of information fragmentation. When I was denied access to special information I felt that I was not as fully informed as others and, because of this, I was not as fully a part of, or as responsible for, the ongoing work. If nuclear weapons were being assigned to a section of Kiev or Kharkov, I imagined that someone else was more responsible than I.

Along with Civil Service grade and job experience, Special intelligence clearances also helped establish a hierarchy within the office. Hierarchical relationships, wherever they exist, create a distraction of their own by causing one to think about where one stands in relation to others. Within the intelligence community, not everyone had the special clearance and, largely because of this fact, one came to want it. If this sign of more complete acceptance was not extended, one wondered why. Yet there was no way to determine why, nor was there any way to correct the situation. Doubts and hopes were generated which distracted attention from the substance of one's work. A preoccupation with the structure, process, and mechanics of day-to-day existence was encouraged by the atmosphere of the Department of Defense and one quickly became absorbed by these concerns. What was done with the end product of work assumed a secondary importance.

If, on the other hand, a moment arose when one's thoughts happened to fasten on the human consequences of developing and using arms, there was consolation to be found in the Defense environment. The unsavoury aspects of such ruminations were blunted by the reminder that America's victims deserved their fate and that it was the victims who were responsible for bringing a nuclear holocaust down on their own heads. Describing the Soviet leadership as evil, corrupt, immoral, sadistic, power-mad and inhuman – plus being communists – provided at least a partial justification for their elimination. Vilifying the enemy, describing him in demeaning terms, is a longstanding government practice intended to legitimize the killing of others. In World War II, the enemies were Nazi pigs and yellow-bellied Japs. During the Cold War referring to communists as Red Fascists helped to link them with legitimate victims of World War II. Later, in the Vietnam War, the North Vietnamese were seen as aggressive communists and were therefore evil. Killing them was further facilitated by depicting them as 'slants' and 'gooks'. Since gooks were only half human, their eradication was 'no big deal'. Besides, if the Vietnamese were seen as caring less than Americans about this temporal life, if they didn't mind dying all that much, killing them became a less traumatic experience.

Finally, the language of the Defense world deserves attention. As America emerged in the 1950s as a world power committed to the use of military capabilities for national security, a variety of new words became part of the language of the foreign affairs bureaucracy. Beyond its usual function of facilitating communication, language in Defense, and in the intelligence community in general, helped to obscure the reality of what the work was all about – to distract attention from the homicidal reality and give a brighter hue to the ominous. Presumably certain words and expressions 'took hold' because civil servants felt comfortable with them. Certain words helped link Defense work with familiar and positive experiences of each individual's past and thereby reinforce the innocuous quality of ongoing projects. Some examples of Defense language can help clarify these observations.

Changing the name of the War Department to the Defense Department, Strike Command to Readiness Command, and the Air Force's use of the maxim 'peace is our profession' are examples of this. Impressions of the benign were strengthened by the careful construction of acronyms, such as PAL (Permissive Action Link), an electronically controlled DOD system of interconnected locks used to prevent the unauthorized launching of an inter-continental ballistic missile.

The vocabulary of Defense, to the extent that phrases such as 'power vacuum' and 'power equilibrium' could be used, had the ring of respected and predictable laws of the physical sciences that had nothing to do with such things as war and annihilation. Weapons were called military 'hardware', thereby evoking impressions of something familiar, useful, and available in a neighbourhood store. I recall the time in the late 1950s when the term 'baby H-bomb' was commonly used in referring to low yield, small tactical nuclear weapons suitable for use in limited wars. This image of the lovable 'baby' bomb helped to make a typical question in war planning such as 'should we deliver ten or fifteen baby nukes on the Irkutsk Party headquarters?' seem like an innocent inquiry. Adding further to the impression that weapons were part of warm household relations was a 1968 Air Force *Fact Sheet* statement that described the Minuteman III missile as '. . . the newest member of the ICBM family'. The practice of referring to nuclear weapons by terms conventionally used to suggest everyday human experiences was evident with America's first use of atomic bombs in Japan – the Hiroshima bomb was named 'Little Boy' and it was the weight of 'Fat Man' that fell on Nagasaki.

As America's involvement in the Vietnam War grew deeper, the Defense vocabulary expanded and displayed an even greater imaginative and anaesthetizing flair. Bombing raids became 'surgical strikes' and the forced movement and impounding of Vietnamese citizens were part of America's 'pacification program' – terms suggesting images of the hospital operating room or a Quaker meeting. The enemy was not killed, but, instead, was 'taken out', 'wasted' or 'blown away' as a consequence of 'executive action' or a 'protective reaction' foray. A military ground offensive was termed 'aggressive defense' and spraying an area with machine-gun fire was nothing more than 'reconnaissance by fire'. James C. Thompson, sensitive to the contribution of bureaucratic jargon to the development of professional callousness, wrote:

In Washington the semantics of the military muted the reality of war for the civilian policy-makers. In quiet, air-conditioned, thick-carpeted rooms, such terms as 'systematic pressure', 'armed reconnaissance,' 'targets of opportunity' and even 'body count' seemed to breed a sort of games-theory detachment. Most memorable to me was a moment in the late 1964 target planning when the question under discussion was how heavy our bombing should be, and how extensive our strafing . . . An Assistant Secretary of State resolved the point in the following words: 'It seems to me that our orchestration should be mainly violins, but with periodic touches of brass.'[2]

Americans are no longer fighting in Vietnam but the use of language for political purposes continues. Recent examples are the efforts by Defense planners to make the controversial neutron bomb, a small nuclear warhead (or nuclear 'device') that produces twice the radiation of ordinary nuclear bombs, seem both appealing and palatable by referring to it as a 'radiation enhancement weapon'. Since the neutron bomb is designed to kill people while sparing buildings, some prefer to suggest a certain kitchen-cosiness by calling it the 'cookie cutter'.

I have been back to Washington a number of times to talk with old friends. Each time I visit the Pentagon or wait in the visitors' lobby at CIA headquarters in Langley, Virginia (where the grounds are called 'the campus'), I catch myself staring at the men and women who pass by. I overhear snatches of conversations and am struck by the amount of laughter. It's all very much as I remember it – people whose speech and behaviour suggest their sociability, but also their strong conviction that they are doing what needs to be done and it is therefore right. Nothing in the air seems sinister or hints of guilt. There is still the working atmosphere of a bank or insurance company.

In her book *Eichmann in Jerusalem*, Hannah Arendt analyses why few Nazis or Germans were able to express a sense of guilt for the monstrous crimes they committed in the final solution to the Jewish question. Arendt's explanation was that the Nazi bureaucracy provided mechanisms for establishing distance between the individual and the reality of genocide. It was important for those who did the actual killing to know that they were not responsible for the planning. And those who planned never had to kill. The Nazi state was administered by ordinary men and women performing routine acts no one of which seemed, in itself, unacceptably sinister. This aspect of the holocaust is suggested by Arendt's statement that her study of Adolf Eichmann is a 'report on the *banality* of evil'.

What I look for when I return to Washington and talk to former colleagues is the reassurance that things have changed. It does seem that the tensions of the Cold War have lessened. Public statements coming from the highest levels of government indicate that this is the case. The American-Soviet dialogue is less shrill. But within the heart of the bureaucracy, among the career civil servants of ten or twenty years, there is a holding back from the risks of detente and I wonder if things have really changed. I fear that my memories of the Air Targets Division are more relevant than I wish to believe.

My memories of my experiences in the intelligence community would become less relevant if analysts today were able to stand back from their day-to-day activities and begin to examine the implications of their work with more objectivity. Thought can sensitize men and women to the implications of their actions and this could impose new inhibitions on the behaviour of the foreign affairs bureaucracy. One wonders:

... could the activity of thinking as such, the habit of examining whatever happens to come to pass or to attract attention, regardless of results and specific content, could this activity be among the conditions that make men abstain from evil-doing or even actually 'condition' them against it?[3]

There are, as I have indicated, forces within the system that work against such self-examination but the tentative move toward a policy of detente offers a setting within which this could begin to happen. Referring once again to Arendt, to the extent that critical self-examination does not occur, the individuals comprising the bureaucracy are abandoning a human undertaking which she considers to be of the highest value, the activity of thinking. Many of the tragedies of the past are attributable less to the evil or stupidity of man than to his thoughtlessness.

Notes

1. Richard J. Barnet, *Roots of War* (Penguin Books, Harmondsworth and Baltimore, 1973), p. 60.
2. James C. Thompson, Jr, 'How Could Vietnam Happen? An Autopsy', in Stephen L. Spiegel (ed.), *At Issue* (St Martin's Press, New York, 1977), p. 384.
3. Quoted by Richard J. Bernstein in a review of Hannah Arendt's *The Life of the Mind*, Book Review, *The New York Times*, 28 May 1978, p. 1.

PART TWO

Europe:
Theatre of War

CHAPTER THREE

Alva Myrdal
The Superpowers' Game over Europe*

Since World War II, world history to a large extent has
been determined by the tidal waves of relations between the
two superpowers, the United States and the Soviet Union,
and the repercussions of these for all other nations. Running
from an uneasy war-time alliance through an almost
immediately following sharply hostile cold war, the history
of the superpowers' postwar antagonism has been inter-
rupted occasionally by the seeking of accommodation in the
act of balancing each other.

For a long time, as the cold war escalated, the hostility
between the two superpowers and their allies was, on the
Western side, motivated by a need for defence of the 'free
world' against the 'communist conspiracy for world revolution'. On the Eastern side, the motive was to stand up
against 'monopoly capitalism', 'neocolonialism', and
'imperialism'. The arms race was pursued by both sides
under the assumption of an imminent risk of a military
showdown between the two systems, or, at least, of a
constant danger of encroachment from the other ideological
camp.

A central element in the development of the relations
between the superpowers has been the arms race going

* *Editors' note:* this is an abridged version of Chapter II of Alva Myrdal,
The Game of Disarmament (Pantheon, New York, 1976; Manchester University Press, 1977). Although Dr Myrdal's study was completed in 1976, and
preceded NATO's decision to 'modernize' its 'theatre' weapons (cruise
missiles and Pershing IIs), this essay sets the scene for that decision, and
analyses the strategic arguments underpinning the notion of nuclear
warfare in the 'European theatre'.

against the strivings for disarmament. The detente of recent years led to a more polite choice of vocabulary as well as some, though limited, approaches to freer economic, scientific, and cultural relations and, generally, widened communications. The Helsinki Conference held in the summer of 1975 represented a kind of codification of the ideas of detente, but without any firm commitments regarding implementation. Detente, however, did not lead to a reversal or even a cessation of the arms race. The main new element was rather the institutionalization of the continuous character of the arms race. The two superpowers now stand more armed than ever with gigantic arsenals which continue to be increased.

The history of postwar disarmament endeavours can only be told as one of repeated lost opportunities, in which the crucial and determining factor has been sparring by the superpowers. From the beginning, both have excelled in high rhetoric about the goal of disarmament, often employing acrimonious polemics against each other's positions. But beneath the surface they have increasingly acted as if there were between them a conspiracy not to permit a halt, still less a reversal, of the arms race.

Other nations have been tied up in alliances. Although the Soviet bloc had already been established and solidified, Europe was more firmly structured by the formation of NATO in 1949 and WTO in 1955. In other parts of the world, various regional or bilateral accords usually created less tightly regulated arrangements. Within these alliances, despite all pronouncements of mutuality and partnership, the power has remained firmly in the hands of the two superpowers.

Spurred on by the superpowers' arms race, most other countries have militarized unprecedentedly, not least the underdeveloped countries. The superpowers have actively contributed to this militarization by military aid and by the politicization of development aid.

They have not acted in concert to prevent or stop wars in

various parts of the world, as the Charter of the United Nations prescribes that the great powers should do. In these wars, as in the Middle East, they have often taken sides, even when they have not got themselves involved in active warfare, as the United States did in Indochina. Still, they have until now been careful not to let their contributions to and involvement in these wars lead to an open military confrontation between themselves.

Talking disarmament while relentlessly building up their own armaments to dazzling levels; prodding and aiding allied countries to do the same, though on a necessarily more modest scale; making the world more dangerous; compelling even nonaligned countries to keep their defences high – this is how peoples and governments of the lesser powers have experienced superpower politics after the war.

While these repercussions are played out all over the world, the two superpowers in their competitive antagonism are fixated on each other. Their posture is, I believe, well illustrated by the old Viking tale of the fighters who are required to carry on their knife-duel hitched together by a belt around their waists.

The primary motivating force for the superpowers has been that each must be second to none. Such a goal can, of course, never be permanently fulfilled. That this is their absurd ambition can be concluded from their constant measuring and comparing of military might. Sometimes this ambition is revealed unblushingly:

> No power on earth is stronger than the United States of America today. None will be stronger than the United States of America in the future. This is the only national defense posture which can ever be acceptable to the United States.[1]

Whenever the will of the United States Congress falters regarding military expenditures, the Pentagon propaganda machine releases news about an approaching bomber gap or missile gap or megatonnage gap or some other alleged advance in the Soviet armoury. The Soviet government is not dependent on a scrutinizing congress and the internal debate there is muted. But it can be safely assumed that those responsible for the Soviet budget are egged on by their military establishments which deliver correct or incorrect information about threatening changes in American capabilities. Thus are both powers pursuing an arms race within the arms race.

The simple idea that the main motivation of the arms race between the superpowers is for each to match the other in destructive capacity is continuously revealed in official statements on both sides. Initially the Soviet Union started from a position of inferiority, but it has gradually advanced towards equality in the gross kill-effect of nuclear weapons deployed or in production. In regard to technology, the United States has always been and is for all foreseeable time far ahead. But in practical terms, especially from the beginning of the SALT negotiations in 1969, the two superpowers have acknowledged that what they possibly can agree upon is the establishment of essential parity – which each of them then attempts to surpass in order to reach superiority.

Fear of what the opposite side may be aiming for then acts on both as a force to drive the arms race onward. The military planners exploit this situation, the politicians do not oppose them, and the citizens therefore allow the two defence systems to spiral steadily upwards in an action-reaction pattern. As long as the arms race is permitted to go on, more than momentary stability can never be secured.

Apart from identifying the most dynamic elements in the arms race, we should also ask: how much is enough? Is there any rationale for continuing the quest to match the other side at ever higher levels – and for trying to surpass it? Such are the questions left unformulated by the superpowers themselves in bilateral negotiations and official statements to the public in their own countries.

Independent experts have often approached these problems and effectively pointed out how vast is the overkill capacity of both superpowers. The immediate aim of such observations has been to demonstrate the need to reach an agreement between them to scale down their nuclear ambitions. Seldom, however, is the question raised whether one of the superpowers could unilaterally and safely cease the competition and even decrease its nuclear arsenal without risking its deterrent effect.

Independent analysts all agree upon one thing: the overkill capacity of each of the superpowers is far beyond 'enough', even if the ambition should be to kill all of mankind. Often this argument is made in the form of estimating their ability to kill each human inhabitant so many times over. The theme can be played with many variations. Jules Moch, who for a long time was the leading French spokesman in favour of disarmament in the United Nations and on its various committees, made a striking calculation in his book *Destin de la paix* (1969). Taking into consideration how many tons of explosives are needed to kill the average number of people on each area of a square kilometre, he figured out that stocks of nuclear weapons already then available were sufficient to annihilate the total world population 690 times over.[2]

The problem of overcapacities for fighting a war between the superpowers – realizing that far less is enough to deter such a war – was clearly identified in 1973 by Herbert F. York:

It is most important . . . to have clearly in mind what the current technical situation means: the survival of the combined populations of the superpowers depends on the goodwill and the good sense of the separate leaderships of the superpowers. If the Soviet leadership, for whatever reason, or as a result of whatever mistaken information, chose to destroy America as a nation, it is unquestionably capable of doing so in less than half an hour, and there is literally nothing we could now do to prevent it. The only thing we could do is to wreak on them an equally terrible revenge. And, of course, the situation is the same the other way around.[3]

The extent of expected damage is the question of most vital concern to the people living under what they believe is the protection of the terror balance. They must find that the physical, biological, and social consequences of ever *using* what the two sides have in their nuclear arsenals are completely out of line with any reasonable view of what could be the national objectives of the United States or the Soviet Union:

In the event of an exchange of blows by strategic nuclear forces of the U.S. and the U.S.S.R., most of the urban populations of the two countries could be killed, and most of the industry and commerce could be destroyed by the direct and immediate effects of the nuclear explosions. The towns and rural areas of the two countries would at the same time be subjected to varying amounts of radioactive fallout. The details of what would happen to the people living in such areas depend importantly on the weather conditions prevailing at the time and on the details of the attack pattern, but well over one-half of the town and country populations could be killed by the fallout. In addition, the living standards and the life expectancy of the survivors would be substantially reduced by secondary effects, including both the effect of less-than-lethal levels of fallout and the general breakdown of civilized services.[4]

'Most of the urban population' and 'over half of the total population' are current estimates of today. But few visualize the tragic reality that the price, in terms of destruction, is going up all the time, without the concomitant increase in security which the arms escalation was intended to buy. This was irrefutably stated in succinct language as early as 1964, in an article by York and another eminent colleague, Jerome B. Wiesner:

Ever since shortly after World War II the military power of the United States has been steadily increasing. Throughout this same period the national security of the U.S. has been rapidly and inexorably diminishing. In the early 1950s the U.S.S.R., on the basis of its own unilateral decision and determination to accept the inevitable retaliation, could have launched an attack against the U.S. with bombers carrying fission bombs. Some of these bombs would have penetrated our defenses and the American casualties would have numbered in the millions. In the later 1950s, again in its own sole decision and determination to accept the inevitable massive retaliation, the U.S.S.R. could have launched an attack against the U.S. using more and better bombers, this time carrying thermonuclear bombs. Some of these bombers would have penetrated our defenses and the American casualties could have numbered in the tens of millions.

Today the U.S.S.R., again on the basis of its own decision and determination to accept the inevitable retaliation, could launch an attack on the U.S. using intercontinental missiles and bombers carrying thermonuclear weapons. This time the number of American casualties could very well be in the order of 100 million . . .

From the Soviet point of view the picture is similar but much worse. The military power of the U.S.S.R. has been steadily increasing since it became an atomic power in 1949. Soviet national security, however, has been steadily decreasing. Hypothetically the U.S. could unilaterally decide to destroy the U.S.S.R. and the U.S.S.R. would be absolutely powerless to prevent it. That country could only, at best, seek to wreak revenge through whatever retaliatory capacity it might then have left.

Both sides in the arms race are thus confronted by the dilemma of steadily increasing military power and steadily decreasing national security . . . The clearly predictable course of the arms race is a steady open spiral downward into oblivion.[5]

The damage would, however, not be limited to the warfaring nations:

In addition, the lives of many millions of people living in the immediate neighborhood of the superpowers would be imperiled by so-called local fallout, and long-range or world-wide fallout would endanger those living in even remote countries. It is very difficult to make precise estimates, but it seems that a full nuclear exchange between the U.S. and the U.S.S.R. would result in the order of 10,000,000 casualties from cancer and leukemia in countries situated well away from the two main protagonists. In addition, genetic problems that are even more difficult to calculate would affect many, many millions of others – not only in this generation, but for centuries to come. Civilization would survive somewhere, but probably not in the United States or the Soviet Union, and perhaps not elsewhere in North America or Europe.[6]

To add to these already excessive military capabilities without first answering the question of how much is enough to deter a war between them is what the senseless game between the superpowers is about. But it continues. As Henry Kissinger said in one of his unguarded moments:

What in the name of God is strategic superiority? What is the significance of it politically, militarily, operationally at these levels of numbers? What do you do with it?[7]

Gaming over a Passive Europe

The increasingly unthinkable danger to both the contesting superpowers of a head-on war explains their interest in planning for a 'limited' war. Such wars do not imply the use of available strategic nuclear weapons against each other. Rather the homelands of the superpowers become 'sanctuaries', while wars, if and when they would occur, are to be fought in the territories of lesser powers.

For historical reasons 'limited war' primarily has been discussed in regard to Europe.[8] The long history of European wars, ending with World War I and World War II, has stamped the entire postwar discussion with the idea that a war threatening to involve the two superpowers might again originate in Europe. The core idea of the Potsdam Agreement in 1945 was to ensure 'that never more should a war be started from German soil'.

Yet today the consideration of who might ignite a war in Europe has been completely changed. The only possible origin of war would arise from a superpower conflict. The confusion must be shattered: a European war might mean a war fought over Europe and in the European locale but it would not be a war instigated by European states – except, for example, a localized war such as the Greek-Turkish conflict over Cyprus in the unruly Balkan corner. A 'European war' would be categorically different from wars started independently in other parts of the world. In these, superpower interests might be involved, but not involved to the level of confrontation with each other. A few reminders of European history, though abridged to bare essentials, are needed here for an understanding of how the present situation has evolved.

When World War II ended, the larger part of Europe, as well as the Soviet Union, was utterly devastated, suffering all sorts of social and economic disorganization. The Great Alliance from the War was breaking up; soon it would be followed by a gradually intensifying cold war between the United States and the USSR. Though the process ultimately took several years, the East European countries, including the then Soviet zone of East Germany, became satellites of the Soviet Union. There was never any attempt by the United States to suppress similarly the political independence of the West European countries. These were conceived of as democracies, including West Germany emerging at the end of the war from its humiliating defeat and material misery.

There were early moves by some West European countries to join in a defensive military alliance. When in 1948 the Western European Union was formed by Britain, France, and the Benelux countries in response to the Soviet coup in Czechoslovakia the same year, the protective role of the United States was recognized. The United States joined the alliance, the Berlin blockade having provided an additional warning of Soviet attitudes, and NATO was created formally in April 1949. It later included Greece, Turkey, and Portugal. Spain under the Franco dictatorship was never formally accepted as a NATO ally, but through United States bilateral arrangements involving military bases and other priorities it became included in the Western defence system. Finally, West Germany, having undergone transformation from occupation to partnership, was incorporated in NATO in 1955, following a long struggle within Germany and among NATO members over its rearming.

In both Western Europe and the United States, NATO was from the outset conceived as a protective shield for Western Europe; the United States with its then monopoly of nuclear weapons was to provide a nuclear umbrella. When, in September 1949, the Soviet Union exploded its first atomic bomb, this created in many quarters of Western Europe (even if it was seldom expressed publicly) an apprehension that it was becoming engaged in a contest between the superpowers.

The military strategies that evolved became more and more clearly a reflection of the mutual contest between the superpowers, dominated by their shifts in strength. The American military policy was from the outset one of containment, which presumed the active threat of a Soviet military move against the West. As long as the United States had the monopoly of atomic bombs, the threat of counteraction implied security for Western Europe. When the Soviet Union acquired a nuclear arsenal, however, the security of Europe changed into the insecurity of the risk of being dragged into a nuclear confrontation between the superpowers.

Still, the reiterated promises to Western Europe of protection by the United States nuclear umbrella kept the worries from surfacing publicly. Some disquietude was often felt, as when John Foster Dulles in the early 1950s enunciated the doctrines of massive retaliation and roll-back. To the relief of the West Europeans, the latter doctrine was not applied to the uprisings in East Germany in 1953 and

Hungary in 1956. No military countermeasures had been resorted to in Czechoslovakia in 1948 nor were they used later in 1968. The United States by then had apparently accepted the division of Europe as West European governments had done much earlier.

From the beginning the NATO alliance resulted in contributions from the United States other than the promise of an ultimate defence with its nuclear weapons. For many years the United States provided large-scale military aid and seemingly permanent garrisons of American troops to Western Europe. The Western European members of NATO were supposed to have increased their conventional defence; however, in spite of continuous prodding from the United States, to this day it is considered inferior in strength to what the Soviet Union could muster.[9] Some countries even occasionally reduced their forces.

The question of how far the defence of Europe should rely on conventional forces is, in reality, a crucial issue in the NATO strategic debate. While the European allies in NATO were unwilling to make a contribution in conventional forces that would match the Soviet bloc, and the American forces naturally could not be expanded to fill the void, the decision was to rely on nuclear weapons deployed in Europe. That the choice might have been a different one is borne out by the fact that the nonaligned countries of Sweden, Switzerland, and Yugoslavia have proven to be much more willing to build up strong defences with conventional weapons and to rely on their own strength to be independent. They have continued this policy of strong national defence, forsaking not only alliances but nuclear weapons as well.

The real crossroad for the Western European defence strategy, signalled by the deployment of nuclear weapons in Europe, came when the United States, in the face of rising Soviet nuclear capabilities, no longer wanted to be committed to a near-automatic release of its massive nuclear retaliation. During the Eisenhower administration the pos-

strategic – tactical nuclear weapons.

sibility of fighting a more limited war with tactical nuclear weapons was envisioned.

Large numbers of tactical nuclear weapons, intended for use in a local battlefield, began to be shipped to Europe in 1954. Their deployment there was not negotiated, particularly with the major recipient, West Germany, not yet a NATO member. But they were nonetheless accepted, tacitly, as a substitution for stronger local forces, and, more openly, as a reassurance that the United States would not withdraw into isolationism. What was less evident at the time was that these nuclear weapons on European soil inexorably linked the strategies for defending Western Europe with global American strategies for nuclear warfare, which did not necessarily serve Europe's best interests.

These tactical nuclear weapons deployed in Europe remain, like the strategic ones, under United States control. European feelings about this have perhaps been best expressed by Henry A. Kissinger in his earlier period as a professorial writer:

> The very quality of deliberation which makes this strategy militarily desirable for the United States creates a sense of impotence or pressures for autonomy among our Allies. The central command and control system, which is the key feature of the new doctrine, is American. The United States will determine – to the extent that the enemy cooperates – how and with what weapons the war is to be fought and on what terms it will be concluded.[10]

Although this statement refers to the 'flexible-response' doctrine from the Kennedy years, the political, and military, situation has remained basically the same since the 1950s.

With Sputnik in 1957, the Russians demonstrated the possibility of Russian missiles with nuclear warheads reaching the United States and the credibility of the American nuclear umbrella was shaken. The shock of the Soviet testing of a ballistic missile that could cross the Atlantic led the United States in 1957 to negotiate, as a token of increased defence preparedness, installation of intermediate-range missiles (IRBM) in Britain, Italy, and Turkey. However, the IRBMs were never a real threat to the Soviet Union because of its strategic retaliatory force and thus were not effective protection for the Western countries either. They were removed in 1963 in a political bargain, part of the price paid for the withdrawal of Soviet missiles from Cuba. Afterwards, though promises of protection continued to be forthcoming from the United States, whenever new strategic doctrines such as that of 'flexible response' or 'realistic deterrence' were announced from Washington, Europeans experienced growing anxiety. The prospect of the super-powers fighting a limited war in Europe and the idea of their mutually establishing sanctuaries at home produced disaffection, but this was played down in public discussion and papered over in NATO compromises.

The initial premise about Soviet intentions, against which the capabilities had to be built up, became less and less a part of European thinking, though it spread rapidly in the United States. In these early years, because of my assignments in the United Nations and later UNESCO, I had wide contacts in practically all countries of the European continent, as well as in the United States, and can testify to this. In spite of European disapproval of the Soviet postwar annexation of the Baltic states and watchful protest against the Soviet suppression of political self-determination in the Eastern European countries, there was nevertheless a degree of understanding in the Western European countries that, after all the sufferings the Russians had sustained during the War, they could have valid reason to establish a belt of buffer states against Germany, whose onslaught on the European democracies was fresh in memory. In addition, the division of Germany was not felt by its neighbour countries to be entirely unfortunate. Still, overriding such considerations there was in Western Europe the widely shared conviction that the Soviet Union would not attempt to cross the line dividing the two Europes. Active planning by the Soviet Union for a military push westward was not perceived as realistic by most Europeans.

That picture took on a different cast in the minds of Americans. The Marshall Plan aid for reconstruction and development of Western Europe was, from 1947, of a scope and generosity greater than any aid afforded the underdeveloped world, and it continued for many years. The basic American motivation was certainly human solidarity with the distressed European nations from which so many Americans reckoned their ancestry, while their own country had been spared, and this was gratefully acknowledged by Europeans. But, as the cold war between the superpowers gathered momentum, the United States' motivation for providing aid increasingly reflected an anticommunist, anti-Soviet policy.

Western European governments for a time accepted this attitude as being necessary to secure passage of aid bills in the American Congress. Those Western European governments who in the immediate postwar years had included in their cabinets representatives of indigenous communist parties paid the price and excluded them. In addition several Western countries, including some nonaligned, paid the price of cooperating with the United States in a strategic licensing policy aimed at stopping exports to the Soviet sphere of a comprehensive group of commodities. In the United States this policy was widely publicized as being directly aimed at hurting economic development in the communist world. The West European governments' cooperation with the United States in this export embargo policy was kept mostly secret from European peoples.[11]

The West European nations had, in fact, been ready for a detente with the Soviet Union and its allies long before this could be advocated as policy in the United States. Stalin's death in 1953 signalled, from the West European point of view, an important political change. At about the same time Marshall Plan aid was being terminated and United States military aid also was decreased. Almost immediately the West European governments used this greater political independence to quietly liquidate the export embargo policy. What remained of the licensing procedures became more of a bureaucratic nuisance than a serious trade barrier. East-West trade in Europe increased, but the United States continued its discriminatory trade policy.

These historical glimpses, despite omissions, point up the differences of political developments on the European and the American scene. After the War, relations between the two Europes in trade, travel, and cultural contacts have been much closer than those between the United States and the Soviet Union. Europe must be understood to have been reliably cured from any propensity to war. Boundaries between its countries had been increasingly accepted as settled even when peace treaties had not been signed. Finally, there was the acceptance of the division of Germany and the demarcation between East Germany and Poland, the result of Willy Brandt's Ostpolitik at the beginning of the 1970s, which was solemnly countersigned at the European Security Conference in Helsinki on 1 August 1975.

'Limited War' over Europe? The Soviet Point of View

As the available nuclear-weapons strength between the two superpowers grew more equal, at ever higher levels of destructive capabilities, it was inevitable that the idea of using these weapons against each other's homelands lost its appeal. The strategy of preserving the Soviet Union and the United States as sanctuaries is viewed differently by the superpowers than it is by Europe.

So far as one can gather, the official position of the Soviet government is a categorical disbelief in the possibility of a limited superpower war – that is, limited to a local battlefield such as Europe and limited there to the use of tactical nuclear weapons.[12] A. Yé Yefremov, whose book *Europe and Nuclear Weapons* (1972) I have read in a complete Soviet-prepared Swedish translation, is quoted and summarized in *The Role of Nuclear Forces in Current Soviet Strategy*.[13] The use of tactical nuclear weapons in Europe is likely to lead to an escalation. Yefremov asserts that 'military conflict on European territory', given the present network of military alliances, 'would inexorably involve all other states of the world in the orbit of a thermonuclear collision', and that the 'threat to use some of the American tactical atomic weapons to carry out local actions in Europe, figuring that the use of "warning atomic shots" will not lead to escalation and a global thermonuclear war', is obviously 'dictated by propaganda rather than military considerations'.

Some authors are even more outspoken:

> By itself, the idea of introducing 'rules of engagement' and artificial restrictions 'by agreement' is illusory and untenable. It is difficult to visualize that a nuclear war, if it is unleashed, could be kept within the framework of 'rules' and would not develop into an all-out war.[14]

Similar views have been expressed in speeches, articles, and books by high officials, such as Marshal Sokolovski's classic *Military Strategy*, and by the former Soviet Minister of Defence, Marshal Grecko, and by the Marshal of Artillery, Peredelski, and others. In view of some hard facts this position appears reasonable. The most important of these is that Soviet proximity to European countries where United States nuclear weapons are stationed (some with definite capacity to hit targets in the Soviet Union) makes its territory more vulnerable than the territory of the United States. Also, the limited-war concept was part of the United States official strategic doctrine of flexible response, and is endorsed by its allies in Western Europe. As such it makes the Russians suspicious that the United States might pretend to engage in a limited war, and then use the occasion to escalate it.

Reflection on policy statements from Soviet sources raises the question of whether these statements may be merely propaganda threats, a warning to the United States that it will not be allowed to wage war in Europe without risking a nuclear onslaught at home. The Soviet Union must, equally with the United States, fear annihilation of its own country in case of a direct intercontinental confrontation. Thus underlying both strategies is a definite, joint interest in preserving their own territories. A former Secretary of Defense in the United States, David Packard, is quoted as having stated:

> The U.S.S.R. as well as the U.S. are going to use their nuclear potential against each other only when an unavoidable threat appears against their own existence.[15]

It is hazardous to take anything for granted in the gaming between the superpowers. The fundamental difficulty with the sanctuary theory is that the limitation of warfare must rely upon an understanding between the potential main enemies. Such a concordance is highly unlikely. Henry A. Kissinger, when still a professor, insisted that limited war is only possible if the contestants, through diplomatic under-standing, agree to view it as a chance to emerge from the war without too heavy material and human damage and without too much injury to their prestige.[16] No attempt to reach such an agreement or understanding has ever been reported.

In this utterly unclarified situation, it may be surmised that the Soviet Union probably holds all conceivable scen-arios open as alternatives, including that of a limited war in Europe. But in regard to such an eventuality, there seem to be two fundamental differences as to how the two sides view its course. One is that the prevailing view in the USSR has always been that any war should preferably be limited to the use of conventional forces, a hitch being that a smaller or larger part of them may already be concentrated at other frontiers. Upgrading a war to the nuclear level would mean 'unlimiting' it to the bitter end. A second difference is that we can deduce from all that is known about the deployment and composition of Soviet forces that their aim, different from the United States', would be a massive attack or counterattack leading to a quick victory. The USSR could then abstain from a nuclear assault on the United States, lessening the risk of assault on itself. Alternatively, the Soviet Union might use nuclear weapons for an early decisive victory on a European battlefield. The Soviet arsenal of nuclear weapons for war-theatre use is concentrated on systems with higher yields, many in the megatonnage class, and with higher radioactive fall-out than the corresponding United States weapons deployed in Western Europe for tactical warfare purposes. Soviet strategists do not make the same categorical distinction as the United States does between strategic and tactical nuclear weapons and they are evidently ready to use a part of their strategic arsenal on targets in Europe.

Several characteristics of the Soviet military posture point in the direction of a blitzkrieg: the continued resistance to any substantial decrease of its mighty conventional arms build-up; the reluctance, demonstrated by Soviet pronouncements, to draw a clear distinction between strategic and tactical nuclear weapons; and the unwillingness to admit that also for them there is an open choice to resort to limited war – on their terms.

'Limited War' over Europe? The American Point of View

Contrary to Soviet scepticism about the possibility of conducting limited war in Europe with nuclear weapons, it has increasingly become declared policy in the United States to try to keep any war limited. The posture of 'defence for Europe' thus relies more and more on tactical nuclear weapons. (Some 7,000 are now deployed by the United States in Western Europe.) In current doctrines there is an ever clearer preference for, or belief in, limiting a war with strategic offensive weapons to selected targets.

An early reminder that Europe should not rely upon the strategic doctrine of massive retaliation was given by Professor Henry Kissinger in a 1958 interview by Mike Wallace:

Kissinger: Our current military policy is based on the doctrine of massive retaliation – that we threaten an all-out attack on the Soviet Union in case the Soviet Union engages in aggression anywhere. This means that we base our policy on a threat that will involve the destruction of all mankind. This is too risky and I think too expensive.

Wallace: You obviously think it is wrong – dangerous to our security. I wonder if you would expand on that. Just because of what you call the risk and just because of the expense, it is not worthwhile?

Kissinger: What it will mean is that in every crisis an American President will have to make the choice whether a given objective is worth the destruction of American cities. The American President will have to decide whether Beirut or whatever the issue may be is worth thirty million American lives. In practice I am afraid the American President will have to decide that it is not worth it and will therefore encourage the piecemeal taking over of the world by Soviet aggression.[17]

Referring more directly to Europe, Kissinger wrote in 1959:

The defense of Europe cannot be conducted solely from North America, because . . . however firm allied unity may be, a nation *cannot be counted on to commit suicide in defense of a foreign territory.*[18]

In 1965 Kissinger devoted a whole book with the telling title *The Troubled Partnership* to this subject.[19] In spite of considerable inconsistencies, he repeated his warning and continued to see Europe as becoming directly involved in war, although he recognized that war would in essence be a superpower contest. As Secretary of State, Kissinger did not change his view on this particular point, although his pronouncements were adjusted so as not to appear to retract the United States promise to hold a protective nuclear umbrella over Western Europe.

The United States clearly now has a double scenario, one for deterrence and one for war; both are focused on the Soviet Union as the enemy:

(a) deterrence for avoiding a superpower war chiefly through strategic nuclear weapons up to the level of MAD, Mutual Assured Destruction;

(b) if war occurs, it is to be fought as a limited war in Europe, possibly using tactical nuclear weapons as a countermeasure against a conventional attack, but not allowing that war to escalate to intercontinental warfare involving the territories of the superpowers themselves.

For good reasons this scheme is not often presented officially in clear terms. But former Secretary of Defense James R. Schlesinger repeatedly stated the present policy in an authoritative way, for example, in his 1976 budget report to the United States Congress:

We continue to deploy our own theater nuclear forces in both Europe and Asia. In the case of Europe, we have three basic reasons for our deployments. First, the maintenance of theater nuclear capabilities in NATO is essential to deterrence as long as the Warsaw Pact deploys theater nuclear forces of its own. They help to deter the use of nuclear weapons by the Pact and, along with our strategic nuclear and conventional forces, provide a general deterrent across the entire spectrum of possible aggression. Second, should deterrence fail, *our theater nuclear capabilities provide a source of limited and controlled options other than the early use of U.S. and allied strategic forces.* Third, in keeping with NATO's flexible response strategy, we do not rule out the use of nuclear weapons by the United States and its allies if that should prove necessary to contain and repel *a major conventional attack* by the Warsaw Pact.[20]

'Other than the early use of . . . strategic forces' is the crucial point. Even more revealing was a phrase used by Schlesinger in Senate hearings a year earlier when he argued for the strengthening of European conventional defence forces 'so that they could sustain a longer war'.[21] Different from likely Soviet strategy, the United States intention has been that the defensive forces in Europe should be built up, not for a quick victory, but for more enduring operations. Reinforcement from the United States would require time; the logistics have usually been planned for some sixty days before a war would reach its peak. No scenarios have been publicly revealed what would happen then.

The vagueness about what might be the fate of Europe is reflected in the attitudes and opinions of American political leaders, editorial writers, and public opinion. It is fairly certain that neither the United States Congress nor American citizens in general would, even after a hypothetical Soviet attack against Western Europe, be in favour of letting such a war escalate to nuclear attack on the Soviet Union, which would initiate what has aptly been called mutual collective suicide. To judge by the results of some public-opinion polls there are signs that it might even be difficult to bring the nation along in active participation of a limited war. This brings into considerable doubt what is really meant by the loud exclamations that the United States stands firm behind its commitments. The entire doctrine of what is meant by limited war in Europe remains hazy, and ideas of what might trigger such a war are equally hazy if not actually erroneous.

'Limited War' over Europe? The European Point of View

Viewed from the angle of Europe – whether East or West – there are no possibilities for a major war to be launched by a European power on its own initiative. A major war could only originate from the protectors of the two blocs, the gaming superpowers.

If war comes to Europe, it will be because one or the other of the superpowers wishes a contest to be played out there, which probably would be ignited outside Europe, for example, in the Middle East. However, a military test of strength between the superpowers might then be transposed to Europe. Military planning is ready for such a contingency. Thus, the war machines may well begin to roll over Europe as a main battlefield. This kind of transferred incidental war in Europe would not be less gruesome than a deliberate one. No Europeans, East or West, would have their hearts set to win it, only to avoid or delimit it.

The possible origins of a war befalling Europe are not discussed very openly in Europe. Likewise, the nature and consequences of a limited war are not analysed in Europe. This is natural for Eastern Europe, as such a war has never been announced as plausible strategic doctrine by the Soviet Union. There has not been much public discussion in Western Europe of such a war either, in spite of the United States having declared flexible response, with the employment of nuclear weapons, to be NATO strategy. The European allies have duly lined up in support of this doctrine.

Helmut Schmidt was a prominent exception. For a time the leading spokesman on military questions of the Social Democratic Party, he is now the Chancellor of the Federal Republic of Germany. In 1971 Schmidt stated:

We have thus sketched out NATO's dilemma regarding deterrence: effective defence of Europe would only be possible for a short time or in a geographically limited area – and it would lead rapidly to the destruction of Europe.[22]

and he reiterated:

a war which, though regarded as a 'limited war' by the superpowers, would be no less than a war of annihilation for the countries of the battlefield.[23]

Let us separate the problem of a limited war in Europe with the use of tactical nuclear weapons into two aspects.

98

What would be the consequences? What are the political conclusions?

Some experts, mostly German authors, have been quite outspoken about the possible effects. Retired German general H. H. Trettner concludes a systematic review, that a 'tactical nuclear defence of [Western] Europe would lead to its destruction'.[24] Carl Friedrich von Weizsäcker has edited the most intensive study to date, a 700-page collection of detailed expert analyses devoted to appraising the consequences to West Germany's civilian population of a series of war scenarios with differing levels of input of nuclear weapons. Even a brief and locally limited war could mean ten million deaths and cause total destruction of West Germany as an industrial society.[25] Escalation to blind utilization of existing weapons capabilities could mean the extinction of all life in Germany. Von Weizsäcker is reported as having testified elsewhere, in studies for the NATO Nuclear Planning Group, that an input of just 10 per cent of the nuclear weapons now stationed in Europe could practically annihilate both East and West Germany.

Recently a different point of departure has been utilized in a study by Herbert York, but with the same shocking revelations about the consequences of tactical nuclear war in Europe.[26] York finds that the approximately 7,000 tactical nuclear weapons in Western Europe under the aegis of the United States and NATO must be deemed provocative: though they are supposed to serve as deterrents, war plans call for their actual use in case there is any kind of attack, even conventional, on Western Europe. The corresponding Soviet nuclear weapons, designed for tactical use, about half the number but of higher average yield, are said by the Soviets not to be intended for an attack on the West but Soviet officials add that if, for any reason, NATO should use nuclear weapons they will be repaid in kind. York has elaborated in considerable detail what would be the consequences of the use of Soviet weapons.

There is a difference in the targeting pattern of all these

superpower weapons. Several less potent types are meant strictly for use in an ongoing battle and are kept in reserve for an input in Western Europe – that is, to stave off advances over important bridges, etc.

The larger NATO weapons are in the main targeted on Eastern Europe, with a few of longer range targeted or targetable on the Soviet Union. Obviously, if such weapons come to be used locally in Western Europe efforts must be made to limit collateral damage. It is reasonable to assume that those targeted Eastern European countries, which probably have few or no nuclear weapons stationed on their territory, would attempt to avoid massive civilian damage.

Conversely, Western Europe, having tactical nuclear weapons deployed in its midst, cannot avoid itself providing suitable targets for a retaliatory attack by the Soviet Union which, according to its different strategic doctrine, would strike first in a systematic attempt to pre-empt the larger weapons and to destroy command and communication centres which are generally in or near large cities.

York's study elaborates in considerable detail the consequences to Western Europe if the Soviet Union chose to launch just its 600 medium-range ballistic missiles with megaton warheads, specifically designed for bombardment of Europe. The projected result is very similar to von Weizsäcker's, which York presents in pictorial form. In one scenario York describes how 166 one-megaton ground-burst explosions with their wide area of lethal fall-out could cover all of West Germany, killing all persons in the open. In another he describes the possible results of the use of an even smaller number of one-megaton bombs on Western European cities with more than 200,000 population. Fewer than 100 of these bombs against the European NATO countries would destroy these centres and kill at least a third of Western Europe's population.

What are the political and public reactions to these obvious dangers? The peoples of Europe – West, East, and neutral – have not been kept much aware of what is in store for them if the superpower rivalry leads to a military confrontation in Europe. There has been a carefully kept official silence as to the consequences. Only once, in 1955, when a NATO military field exercise, 'Carte Blanche', resulted in 1·7 million Germans 'killed' and 3·3 million 'incapacitated', was a short-lived political furore caused.[27]

It is necessary to remember that Europeans had not asked for tactical nuclear weapons when they were first introduced in Western Europe in 1954. They were also reluctant to approve the United States' strategic doctrines. When finally in 1967 they accepted the flexible-response doctrine, the European NATO members exerted considerable pressure to have greater influence over the use of the nuclear weapons. The only concession they could obtain was the establishment of a Nuclear Planning Group in NATO for joint consultations in regard to, for instance, targeting of possible nuclear weapons operations. West German leaders in particular have wanted a considerably stronger role for the European allies in the control of nuclear weapons in Europe.

Since 1967 there has been little public discussion about any fundamental change in the policies of nuclear defence for Europe, little of the early clairvoyant anxiety of Helmut Schmidt. West European official postures have become frozen in a kind of silent approval of the status quo. In recent years, it has often appeared as if the NATO governments were backing continued deployment of tactical nuclear weapons in their countries even more than the United States. West Germany particularly seems to fear that withdrawal would signify a lessening of the United States commitment to act in the defence of Western Europe.

In 1975 I was conducting a seminar at the Massachusetts Institute of Technology on tactical nuclear weapons in Europe. In order to isolate the determining factors in the justification of deployment of nuclear weapons, we posed the hypothetical question that, if there were now no such weapons, what would be the reasons for introducing them? None of the participants, academics, diplomats, and some military personnel, could give tenable reasons, only numerous counter-reasons for maintaining the status quo. The debate became nonconclusive as most of the participants cut off pursuit of the subject by asserting that any change in the present situation was totally impractical for political reasons – a nuclear-weapon-free Europe being altogether out of the question.

It is refreshing to read the obvious truths so unpolitically presented by Herbert York:

> In summary, today's Western Europeans have chosen to buy current political stability by placing the awful risks described above over their lives and their future. Perhaps their choice was inadvertent; perhaps they did not and even today still do not realize what they have done. In that case, it would seem that they ought to know, and that they ought to reconsider their choice in the light of such knowledge.[28]

Or, even more straightforwardly:

> To say it differently, NATO's plans for the defense of Europe are centered on an awesome bluff . . . In short, the bluff could be called and Europe could be destroyed, not just partially as in 1914–18 and 1939–45, but totally.[29]

The discussion of the potential damage tactical nuclear weapons would inflict now centres around the pending changes in weapons characteristics, the substitution of lower-yield, shorter-range, more accurately targeted missiles for some of those now deployed. This would have the effect of increasing the total number. Plans to introduce a new generation of tactical nuclear weapons into the defence system of Western Europe are being met by criticism in many quarters, though criticism in NATO councils has not been audible outside them.

In the academic debate on strategy, there is open advocacy of using mini-nukes for a rapid first use to fortify the sanctuary of the United States. Some Los Alamos experts openly make a plea for prime consideration of United States national interests by relying on an immediate input of low-yield nuclear weapons for the defence of NATO:

> The strategy proposed in this article . . . calls for immediately engaging an attacker with low-yield nuclear weapons for all but the most trivial incursions. Yet this concept would require no change in NATO's accepted strategy of forward defense, only in its interpretation.[30]

The ulterior motive is to steer war away from United States ✳ territory:

> Discriminating use of nuclear weapons from the outset would enable NATO to conduct a successful defense . . . Dealing with threats of irrational attacks to destroy all or part of NATO is a problem for our European allies to face without counting on U.S. strategic nuclear weapons. It is their survival that such attacks threaten.[31]

As, due to European malaise, there has been little discussion and no public uproar about the plans for a superpower battle over European territory, I find it necessary to speak frankly about the limited-war concept being in reality little more than a plan for sanctuaries. Though there is open discussion of the risk of American *découplement* from Europe, that is not a grave risk at present; what is a risk is the existing *couplement* of superpower conflicts with the potential sacrifice of Europe.

Some other dangers also need attention, although more marginal in this dramatic context. If mini-nukes should become standard equipment, deployed interchangeably with conventional weapons, this would blur the distinction between nuclear and conventional weapons. But the 'fire-break' between them must be absolute. If the present distinction between nuclear and conventional weapons becomes blurred it will be impossible to believe in limited war and to avoid uncontrollable escalation. Further, as communication links to the Supreme Commander in Washington, so far in sole control of the release of nuclear weapons, or with any specifically empowered NATO commanders would be difficult to keep clear, these smaller nuclear weapons would be more exposed to the danger of unauthorized use by overzeal, mistake, a failure of nerve, blackmail, or theft.

Where is the thoroughgoing responsible analysis of all aspects of the deployment of tactical nuclear weapons in Europe? Where is the political debate about the effects of their use in a war and, generally, about their usefulness?

Discussion of the questions raised in expert circles about the wisdom of withdrawing all or certain types of them, the more vulnerable or more offensive, has not reached the peoples of Europe. There is definitely no interest in public discussion of a realistic analysis

(a) of the implications of drawing nuclear fire on to the European countries, or

(b) of the extent to which these countries and peoples would be devastated.

The ostrich attitude became apparent once again when the barter offer in the Vienna negotiations to withdraw a small part of the tactical nuclear weapons from Western Europe became known. In October 1975, Chairman Willy Brandt of the Social Democratic Party in West Germany declared himself in favour of the proposal. The news story was accompanied by some comments:

> But many U.S. allies in Europe, including West Germany, have previously expressed uneasiness over the proposal. They feel that any suggestion that U.S. atomic weapons are being withdrawn from Europe touches off fears that the United States is taking a step toward removing its guarantee of nuclear protection for its allies.[32]

As was already customary in earlier periods, the European partners in NATO have preferred to have little public attention directed towards the possible consequences of their NATO allegiance. Perhaps they feel that they could not handle a twofold argument – continuing to appeal to the

Americans for military commitment while informing the people at home about the insecurity involved. The remarkable thing is that the public has acquiesced. Even in the nonaligned Western countries there has been astonishingly little discussion of these awkward issues or studies examining the consequences of various scenarios, for example, those involving the use of the thousands of tactical nuclear weapons deployed in the midst of Europe. These nonaligned neighbours to NATO countries have demonstrated a kind, but ultimately not very helpful, discretion in questions which concern the destiny of the continent as a whole.

There has as usual been more open discussion in the United States. There it has often been understood that the political consequences of presently relevant scenarios and damage estimates are ominous. As former ambassador to NATO Harlan Cleveland has pointed out:

It is natural for Americans to press for effective, which is to say large-scale, use of nuclear weapons on the battlefield – enough to 'stop the enemy in his tracks.' But this conjures up for Europeans the picture of a Europe devastated while the United States and the Soviet Union remain intact.[33]

In the Brookings Institution study where Cleveland was quoted, the conclusion was put in sharper language:

The idea that tactical nuclear weapons furnish a plausible 'option' for *defending* Western Europe (as distinguished from their escalatory role) has had a lingering half-life. In fact, the use of hundreds of atomic weapons could cause so much collateral damage to the area being 'defended' that the inhabitants might prefer surrender as a lesser evil. This would be less true of certain low-yield or 'clean' weapons; but even if NATO so limited its weaponry, an enemy might not.

The use of these weapons in Europe evokes a potential conflict of perceived interest between elements of the attentive publics in Europe and the United States.[34]

This matter was not brought up at the European Security

Conference, where it ought to have headed an urgent agenda. Nowhere so far are views heard from the citizens of Europe, who will, after all, be the victims if there is a superpower war in Europe.

They should, if they were enlightened participants in a dialogue about the defence of Europe, join with the independent experts and state it clearly: *these tactical nuclear weapons are not needed in Europe, neither for deterrence nor for defence.*

In fact, and that should be the overriding concern, the United States does not need to have these weapons in Europe. If it maintains its strategy of using its nuclear strength to defend Western Europe, it need only detach some of its submarines, equipped with nuclear warheads on ballistic missiles, targeted and ready to fire in case of an attack against Western Europe. That should be sufficient to deter any such attack.

Notes

1. Richard Nixon, address to a joint session of Congress, 1 June 1972, immediately on his return from Russia after SALT I. *Congressional Quarterly Almanac*, 92nd Congress, 2nd Session, 1972, Vol. XXVIII (Washington, 1972), p. 74-A.

2. Jules Moch, *Destin de la paix* (Mercure de France, Paris, 1969), p. 211.

3. Herbert F. York, 'Nuclear Deterrence: How to Reduce the Overkill', in Fred Warner Neal and Mary Kersey Harvey (eds.), *Pacem in Terris III* (Center for the Study of Democratic Institutions, Santa Barbara, Calif., 1974), Vol. 2, p. 25.

4. ibid., pp. 23–4.

5. Jerome B. Wiesner and Herbert F. York, 'National Security and the Nuclear-Test Ban', *Scientific American*, October 1964, p. 35.

6. ibid., p. 24. (N.B. Error in source: 10,000,000 is correct, not 10,000.)

7. Paul H. Nitze, 'The Strategic Balance Between Hope and Skepticism', *Foreign Policy*, No. 17, Winter 1974–75, p. 136.

8. Europe is defined as the whole continent, except the Soviet Union. Eastern Europe refers to those countries allied to the Soviet Union, the membership of WTO being seven; and Western Europe refers to the countries allied to the United States, the membership in NATO being fifteen. In addition there are a few nonaligned countries, from those that remained neutral in the war, like Sweden and Switzerland, to some who joined the nonaligned ranks later, like Yugoslavia after 1948 and Austria after the 1955 State Treaty.

9. There are great difficulties involved in any such comparison, depending on important asymmetries between the superpowers in composition of forces and also in regard to the difference in distances for bringing up reserves.

10. Henry A. Kissinger, *The Troubled Partnership: A Reappraisal of the Atlantic Alliance*, Atlantic Policy Studies, Council on Foreign Relations (McGraw-Hill, New York, 1965), p. 111.

11. Gunnar Adler-Karlsson, *Western Economic Warfare 1947–1967: A Case Study in Foreign Economic Policy*, Acta Universitatis Stockholmiensis, Stockholm Economic Studies, New Series, No. 9 (Almqvist & Wiksell, Stockholm, 1968).

12. To obtain an overview of relevant Russian sources I have found the following useful: Leon Gouré, Foy D. Kohler, and Mose L. Harvey, *The Role of Nuclear Forces in Current Soviet Strategy*, Monographs in International Affairs (University of Miami, Center for Advanced International Studies, Miami, 1974). Manne Wängborg, *Militär doktrin och politik i Sovjetunionen*, Försvar och Säkerhetspolitik (Centralförbundet Folk och Försvar, Stockholm, 1974); Nordal Åkerman, *On the Doctrine of Limited War* (Berglingska Boktryckeriet,

Lund, 1972); Trevor Cliffe, 'Military Technology and the European Balance', *Adelphi Papers*, No. 89 (International Institute for Strategic Studies, London, 1972); R. N. Rosecrance, 'Can We Limit Nuclear War?' *Military Review*, Vol. 38, No. 12, March 1959, pp. 51–9.

13. A. Yé Yefremov, *Yevropa i ladernoe Oruzhiye* (Voenizdat, Moscow, 1972); translated in JPRS, *Europe and Nuclear Weapons*, 14 March 1973, pp. 329, 331; quoted in Gouré *et al.*, *Role of Nuclear Forces*, p. 129.

14. Aratov, *Promlemy Mira i Sotsializma*, No. 2, February 1974, p. 46, quoted in Gouré *et al.*, *Role of Nuclear Forces*, p. 129.

15. David Packard, *Perception of the Military Balance* (prepared for the Europe-America Conference, Amsterdam, March 1973), quoted in Piet Dankert (Chairman of the Foreign Affairs Committee of the Dutch parliament), 'Amerika's veiligheid is de onze niet' (America's security is not ours), *Internationale Spectator*, Vol. 27, No. 12, 22 June 1973, p. 399 (author's translation).

16. Henry A. Kissinger, *Nuclear Weapons and Foreign Policy* (Harper & Brothers, New York, 1957), pp. 174–268.

17. 'Second Edition: Limiting War: A Younger Henry Kissinger Interviewed by Mike Wallace', reprint of a pamphlet originally published by the Fund for the Republic in 1958, *The Center Magazine*, Vol. 4, No. 1, January–February 1971, p. 56.

18. Henry A. Kissinger, 'The Search for Stability', *Foreign Affairs*, July 1959, p. 548. Italics added.

19. Kissinger, *The Troubled Partnership*, passim, e.g. p. 181.

20. U.S. Department of Defense, *Report of Secretary of Defense James R. Schlesinger to the Congress of the FY 1967 and Transition Budgets, FY 1977 Authorization Request and FY 1976–1980 Defense Programs, 5 February 1975* (US Government Printing Office, Washington, 1975), p. III-2. Italics added.

21. *The New York Times*, 24 April 1974.

22. Helmut Schmidt, *The Balance of Power: Germany's Peace*

Policy and the Super Powers, trans. Edward Thomas (William Kimber, London, 1971), p. 196.

23. ibid., p. 76.

24. Heinz Trettner, 'Tactical Nuclear Weapons for Europe', *Military Review*, Vol. 51, No, 7, July 1971, p. 48.

25. Carl Friedrich v. Weizsäker (ed.), *Kriegsfolgen und Kriegsverhütung* (Carl Hanser Verlag, Munich, 1971), p. 10.

26. Herbert F. York, 'The Nuclear "Balance of Terror" in Europe', *Ambio*, Vol. 4, Nos. 5–6, 1975, pp. 203–8.

27. James L. Richardson, *Germany and the Atlantic Alliance: The Interaction of Strategy and Politics* (Harvard University Press, Cambridge, Mass., 1966), p. 40.

28. York, 'The Nuclear "Balance of Terror" in Europe', p. 208.

29. ibid., pp. 203–4.

30. W. S. Bennett, R. R. Sandoval, and R. G. Shreffler, 'A Credible Nuclear-Emphasis Defense for NATO', *Orbis*, Vol. 17, No. 2, summer 1973, p. 465.

31. ibid.

32. *International Herald Tribune*, 7 October 1975.

33. Quoted in Timothy W. Stanley, 'The Military Balance', in John Newhouse (ed.), *U.S. Troops in Europe: Issues, Costs, and Choices* (Brookings Institution, Washington, 1971), p. 45.

34. ibid.

CHAPTER FOUR

Dan Smith
The European Nuclear Theatre

In December 1979 NATO decided it would deploy 572 new American nuclear missiles in West Europe. 108 of them will be Pershing II ballistic missiles, which have a range of about 1,000 miles, and the other 464 will be Tomahawk ground-launched cruise missiles. The NATO plan is for all 108 Pershing IIs plus 112 of the cruise missiles to be based in the Federal Republic of Germany, while Britain takes 160 cruise missiles and Italy 96. Belgium and the Netherlands are marked down to take 48 cruise missiles each, but, because of popular pressure, it looks as if neither of these two countries will take them.

Unlike ballistic missiles, cruise missiles fly all the way to their targets under power – essentially, they are pilotless aircraft. The missile's guidance system works by matching radar readings of the ground over which it is flying with a pre-programmed contour map. Flying at low altitude at just below the speed of sound, it can take as direct or circuitous a route to its target as its programmer wishes. Its low-level flight and small size – around fourteen feet long, depending on the particular version, with a diameter of twenty inches – mean it will be hard to detect on its way to the target, while the guidance system will be able, it is claimed, to provide such accuracy that on average half the missiles launched would fall within a few yards of their targets, having flown distances of 2,000 miles or so from their launching points.

At this stage, however, it is not clear that their technology will actually work reliably. There has been a series of mishaps during US testing of cruise missiles over the past few years. But the US military is so enamoured of them that in March 1980 the US Air Force announced it planned to purchase 3,400 air-launched cruise missiles over the next seven years, at a cost of $4,000 million.[1] These are different cruise missiles from the ones coming to Europe; the air-launched types are to be produced by Boeing, whereas the Tomahawks are a General Dynamics product. Boeing's product will be carried, twenty at a time, on B 52 bombers, while the Tomahawks will be mounted in fours on trucks.

The 160 Tomahawks expected in Britain will be based at Greenham Common near Newbury and at Molesworth near Huntingdon. In times of emergency they will be dispersed around the countryside on their trucks, up to 100 miles away from their bases. Each truck with its four Tomahawks will be a small target, but the area in which they deploy will be one big target. These missiles, in Britain as elsewhere in Europe, will be completely under US control.

At the time the decision was announced, and in all government statements and most press discussion since, the impression has been given that the new missiles represent no more than a response to a new threat from the USSR, and that without them NATO is virtually defenceless. In military policy and in the arguments used to legitimate major decisions, distortions, half-truths and downright lies are common currency. But in the period just before and since NATO's December 1979 decision, new standards have been set.

Europe remains the main site of the military confrontation between the USA and the USSR and their respective allies in NATO and the Warsaw Pact. Detente in Europe removed some of the main bones of regional contention, but military confrontation continued and escalated through the 1970s. European members of NATO now mount armed forces employing 2,779,000 personnel in uniform, in addition to which the USA has 276,700 military personnel in Europe (202,400 in ground forces, the bulk of them in Germany) plus the sailors in its Mediterranean Sixth Fleet, while Canada chips in with 3,000 soldiers. Non-Soviet members of the Warsaw Pact have 1,105,000 people in uniform, in addition to which the USSR has some 618,000 soldiers in the countries of East Europe, plus airmen and ground crew at airfields, together with the sailors of its various fleets in the surrounding seas. This all adds up to well over 5,000,000 people in the regular armed forces of the two alliances in Europe and the seas around it. Further thousands are in the reserves: 3,473,000 in European NATO countries, and 2,148,000 in the Warsaw Pact apart from the USSR.[2]

But the numbers of people serving in the military forces in Europe do not tell the whole story. These forces mount weaponry on an unimaginably destructive scale. Part of the confrontation of these forces consists of around 11,000 nuclear warheads for use in Europe. Of these, about 7,500 are deployed by NATO, while around 3,500 are deployed by the Warsaw Pact. The exact figures on either side are not publicly available, and in recent years estimates for Warsaw Pact nuclear warheads for use in Europe have ranged from 1,750 to 5,000.[3]

These figures may surprise readers who had been led to believe that NATO's tactical or theatre nuclear warheads, (TNW) were vastly outnumbered by the Warsaw Pact's. But the figures are taken from impeccably militaristic Western sources, and, like most such figures, derive by one means or another from US intelligence.

Many of NATO's TNW, however, are mounted on relatively short-range weapon systems, and the complaints about the Warsaw Pact's numerical superiority in TNW have focused on the longer-range systems. Even here we shall find that the picture is rather different from the overwhelming superiority the Warsaw Pact is usually claimed to have. But before looking a little closer at the weapons and the numbers, some further points should be made about these misleading presentations.

Nuclear weapons were first introduced into Europe by

the USA when it stationed strategic nuclear bombers in Britain in 1948. In the mid-1950s NATO took the decisions which built the TNW arsenal up to its present size. Not only did NATO deploy TNW in Europe first, but it has always had a large numerical superiority over the Warsaw Pact in this respect. NATO's emphasis on relatively short-range weapons systems is due to its own preferences and decisions; at any time since the mid-1950s it had the technology and capability to deploy long-range missiles for TNW had it so chosen. It did not. It has now. It has done so, not because there is a qualitatively new threat from the USSR in the form of the SS 20 – the USSR has had long-range nuclear missiles targeted on Western Europe since the early 1960s. Rather, its December 1979 decision was taken because NATO has come to different views about how it wants to prepare for nuclear war in Europe.

In other words, and this brings us to the second point, NATO was not forced into the decision by the Warsaw Pact; it moved into it of its own volition. If NATO spokesmen and government ministers are right that the new missiles represent an important new capability for NATO, then they cannot deny that it is NATO rather than the Warsaw Pact which has given this particular aspect of the arms race its latest new twist. At one time NATO was happy not to have this new capability. Now it wants it. The comparable TNW on the Warsaw Pact side are today much the same as they have been for many years, but rather more modern. But with NATO we are dealing not with more modern versions of the same weapons, but with a totally new capability, and that means NATO's decision bears a particular burden of responsibility for the dangers we now face.

This also means that the term 'modernization' used to describe the decision is thoroughly inappropriate. It is a gentle word which implies nothing more than routine procedure in the arms race, not something which is qualitatively new. In fact, NATO's TNW modernization

programme dates back to 1969, the first year of the first
Nixon administration. It is almost totally a US programme
which the other NATO states have accepted. It has included
the efforts to introduce 'mini-nukes' (referred to by Alva
Myrdal in her contribution to this book) and the neutron
bomb. In both cases, the basic theme was that the greater
precision of the weapons permitted realistic options to be
developed for fighting a nuclear war in Europe. Other
aspects of the programme include the 'hardening' of airfields
and other military facilities so that they remain serviceable
in nuclear war, and the development of communication
systems which would not be blacked out by the effects of
nuclear explosions. The accuracy of the cruise missiles is
the counterpart of the supposed precision of mini-nukes and
the neutron bomb. The theme throughout is the attempt to
make nuclear war in Europe more 'thinkable'.

But, unless the Warsaw Pact decides to join in the rules
of this macabre game, none of it will do anything to reduce
the destructiveness of nuclear war, which was supposed to
be the main problem for NATO in planning to fight one. As
it has done for at least twenty-five years, NATO war
planning amounts to preparing to defend Europe by
blowing it up. The main difference today is that the planning
appears to be more enthusiastic.[4]

The Warsaw Pact's TNW

Nuclear weapons grouped under the heading of TNW vary
widely in the means of delivery to targets, the ranges over
which they can be delivered and their explosive power. The
picture is further confused because both blocs possess 'dual
capable' systems – systems capable of delivering either
nuclear or non-nuclear munitions. What follows is a brief
description of some of the main TNW of each side, separated
into three categories according to their range (over 1,000
miles; between 100 and 1,000 miles; and less than 100

miles), together with some estimates of the numbers. For numbers of TNW carried by 'dual capable' systems I am using estimates from the International Institute for Strategic Studies (IISS) of how many of the total number of systems available would actually be used to carry nuclear weapons.[5]

For longer-range TNW the USSR has land-based missiles and bombers. The SS 4 and SS 5 missiles were first seen publicly in 1961 and 1964 respectively; the SS 4 has a range of about 1,200 miles, while the SS 5's is about 2,300, and both carry single one-megaton warheads. In December 1979 NATO stated that the USSR had 400 of these two missiles.[6] Now replacing these missiles is the SS 20, which has figured so prominently in recent Western news coverage of Soviet armaments. Unlike the older missiles it is mobile on the ground (like Tomahawk cruise missiles) and carries three warheads, each independently targeted, over a range of between 3,000 and 4,000 miles. In December 1979 the US Department of Defense stated that 100 SS 20s had been deployed, 60 of them targeted against Western Europe and the rest against China.[7] We might therefore estimate that another 40 SS 20s may have been produced by October 1980, of which perhaps 25 would be targeted against Western Europe, raising this figure to 85. SS 20 warheads would thus number about 255.

It is now thought in NATO that, since the lead-up to NATO's decision to deploy new American missiles to Europe, the USSR has stopped phasing out the older missiles, in which case SS 20 would be augmenting rather than replacing the SS 4s and SS5s.[8]

The USSR also has about 450 copies of two bombers with ranges around 1,700 miles, the Badger and the Blinder (these are NATO code-names), which were first seen in 1954 and 1961 respectively. Since early 1975 the USSR has also deployed a supersonic bomber, Backfire, with a range above 3,000 miles. At one time the USA was asserting that Backfire was intended for use against it, with the pilots making a one-way trip, but it always seemed more likely that Backfire was meant for use against Western Europe and maritime targets and that if the USSR wanted bombers to attack the USA it would make them specifically for that. Assurances that Backfire is not aimed at the USA were included in a Soviet statement attached to the Strategic Arms Limitation agreement signed with the USA in June 1979, where it is also stated that the production rate will not exceed 30 per year.[9] On the basis of IISS' 1979 estimate of the total number of Backfires, and the proportion of them deployed against Western Europe, it seems likely that by October 1980 the USSR had about 70 Backfires able to carry TNW.

For shorter-range delivery systems, the Warsaw Pact has about 3,600 aircraft, with ranges varying from 275 to 600 miles, capable of delivering nuclear weapons. By no means all of them would be used for that task. The IISS estimates that aircraft from within this total carry about 700 nuclear warheads. These aircraft are based not only in the USSR but also, in varying numbers, in every other Warsaw Pact country. Non-Soviet Warsaw Pact countries also provide sites for Scud nuclear missiles, with a range of 185 miles. Another missile, the SS 12, with a range of about 500 miles, is based in the USSR, as are some Scuds. There are a little over 400 of these two missiles, all carrying single warheads. Finally, the USSR is thought to have about 54 missiles deployed on submarines in the Baltic and North Sea; the range is about 700 miles, and, again, each missile carries a single warhead.

For sending nuclear weapons over ranges less than 100 miles the Warsaw Pact has nuclear artillery and mortars deployed in the USSR (though one assumes they would be moved forward for war), and large numbers of a group of artillery rockets known as FROG. These have a range less than 40 miles, are capable of having nuclear warheads, and are deployed in all the Warsaw Pact countries.

NATO's TNW

NATO currently has no land-based missiles with ranges above 1,000 miles. This is the 'gap' the Tomahawks and Pershing IIs are supposed to fill. But NATO does have long-range submarine-launched missiles, which are usually conveniently forgotten when the time comes round to moan about Warsaw Pact superiority and convince us we need the new missiles. There are 64 British Polaris missiles, with a range of 2,880 miles, and 40 or 45 US Poseidon missiles, carrying a total of 400 warheads over a similar range. In addition, France, which is a member of NATO but whose forces are not under NATO's military command, has 82 submarine-based missiles.

For long-range TNW, NATO has preferred aircraft to missiles. It has a little less than 1,000 bombers with ranges between 1,000 and 3,000 miles. Among several types included here are British Vulcans, now rather aged, and the American F1-11s stationed in Britain. If French long-range bombers are counted, the total of aircraft increases to just on 1,000, and the IISS estimates that about 870 TNW (950 including the French) would be carried by aircraft within this total. Britain is now introducing Tornado multi-role aircraft into its forces, and some will be used to replace Vulcans.

For shorter-range TNW, NATO has 180 Pershing I missiles, with a range of 450 miles, and 490 aircraft (660 including the French) with ranges between 350 and 800 miles. According to the IISS these aircraft would probably carry about 175 warheads (230 including the French).

NATO also has over 780 pieces of nuclear artillery and large numbers of short-range missiles, especially Lance and the French Pluton, with ranges of well under 100 miles. Finally, NATO has TNW in the form of nuclear depth bombs (as does the Warsaw Pact) for anti-submarine warfare; it has some old nuclear-tipped anti-aircraft missiles; and it has atomic demolition munitions, which would be placed in the ground and detonated to put obstructions in the way of Warsaw Pact forces.

Comparing Numbers

The way in which the military strengths of NATO and the Warsaw Pact are compared by most orthodox Western commentators is extremely misleading, very often incompetent and occasionally downright dishonest. At one level the problem starts because these comparisons are usually designed to show that NATO needs more forces. At another level the problem starts because of the habit of comparing numbers, which, even if the quality of weapon systems is taken into account, it is not the whole story: tactics and roles, morale and the quality of command, timing, terrain and several other factors ought by rights to enter into the equation. Having said that, I am now going to join in the numbers game, not in order to arrive at a genuine comparison of the two blocs' military might, but to show how misleading the stock propaganda is (and thus to show that calling it 'propaganda' is an accurate analytical term and not a simple slur).

I have already pointed to NATO's overall numerical superiority in TNW – approximately 7,500 to 3,500. This is not enough for NATO strategists, who have broken the total down (and there is nothing wrong with that in principle) into different categories in order to reveal the Warsaw Pact superiority in land-based missiles with ranges over 1,000 miles, against which Tomahawk and Pershing II are presented as a defensive response. Everything depends on the choice of categories.

If one took all missiles and aircraft able to deliver TNW over ranges above 1,000 miles, and worked from IISS estimates of how many would carry TNW and how many would be serviceable at the right time, the picture is a little different. In that category, NATO has 1,300 warheads,

1,420 if the French are included, against the Warsaw Pact's 1,040. That is, NATO has a numerical superiority, not a large one (the ratio is 1·3 or 1·4 to 1), in precisely that category into which Tomahawk cruise missiles and Pershing IIs will fit. This is a far cry from the crippling NATO inferiority we hear bemoaned so frequently and furiously. However, for aircraft and missiles with ranges between 100 and 1,000 miles, the Warsaw Pact has a larger numerical superiority in warheads: 1,030 to 340 (or 390 if the French are counted). Overall, for TNW which can be delivered over ranges above 100 miles, the Warsaw Pact has the lead: 2,070 to 1,640 (1,810 counting the French). But the ratio of about 1·3 or 1·1 to 1 is not large, and the lower ratio that includes the French on the NATO side, which is how the Soviets must see it, is within the margin of error for estimates of this kind.

I should repeat that this is really an interesting exercise rather than a genuine comparison of military strength. But it may alert readers to a future possibility – the discovery of a new gap in TNW deliverable over ranges between 100 and 1,000 miles. I think I shall not reveal yet the way in which I will play that particular numbers game if and when the time comes.

European Nuclear Disarmament

All this fooling around is interesting and necessary given the way in which government justifications for the new NATO missiles are presented. But it should not distract attention from two critical points. First, these weapons represent an enormous amount of destructive power and the potential for many millions of deaths within the first few hours of a nuclear war in Europe, with many millions more of horrible casualties, a devastated continent in which the basic structures of society apart from the authority of the central state will totally collapse. Second, with the exception of the British and French weapons, they are all under the direct control of the superpowers (and some of the British weapons are only semi-independent).

The appeal for European nuclear disarmament launched in April 1980 is directed against these weapons, against that war, and against that superpower dominance. The idea and the campaign for it are discussed in more detail in other contributions to this book. My business is to consider two likely objections to European nuclear disarmament: first, the objection that if NATO has no TNW, even if the Warsaw Pact has none, NATO will be the worse off because of its inferiority in non-nuclear forces; second, the objection that the implementation of the idea would weaken the unity of NATO at exactly the time when it should be standing more closely together than ever.

Non-nuclear Forces

The point about the first objection is that, when the problem is closely studied, NATO's inferiority in non-nuclear forces is extraordinarily elusive. It has always been the basis of arguments for having large numbers of TNW in Europe and it has long been an obsession in NATO. In fact, in the 1960s and again in the 1970s, the US Department of Defense conducted analyses of both sides' non-nuclear forces which showed that Warsaw Pact superiorities in some categories were more than offset by NATO advantages in other categories it thought were more important. Naturally, these studies never received the kind of coverage from either official spokespeople or the press which is given to the more common reports of Warsaw Pact superiority. It can be added that a comparison of IISS estimates over the years, and these estimates need to be treated with a great deal of care, shows that the Warsaw Pact's military build-up through the 1970s was at least matched by NATO's own military build-up.[10]

I am not going to enter deep into the non-nuclear numbers game here, but just one example may be worthwhile. It is the example of tanks. For years NATO has expressed its anxieties about the much larger number of tanks held by the Warsaw Pact. The Conservatives in the 1980 defence White Paper, like their Labour predecessors in the five previous years, churned out the usual diagram showing NATO tanks outnumbered by 2·8 to 1.[11] This is about the same figure as the IISS gives. But that same diagram somehow forgot to mention NATO's extremely accurate anti-tank weapons. By late 1978, excluding short-range types carried and fired by individual soldiers, NATO had around 193,000 anti-tank guided missiles. This represented an increase of one third over its inventory two years previously. By early 1979 there were over 17,000 ground-based launchers for these missiles, with yet more on helicopters and fixed-wing aircraft. If this rate of deployment has continued, then by October 1980 NATO probably had getting on for 240,000 anti-tank guided missiles; the 1980 White Paper stated that the Warsaw Pact had 18,300 tanks. The age and quality of Warsaw Pact tanks are not usually mentioned either. Non-Soviet countries use Soviet tanks from the 1950s and before. The Soviet tanks produced in the 1960s are almost universally agreed to be of lower quality than the tanks NATO deploys, and these constitute the bulk of Soviet tank forces in Europe. The newer Soviet tanks probably are superior in some respects to NATO's current tanks, but Britain, the USA and West Germany are now in the process of developing and producing new types. It is also not usually mentioned that NATO took a deliberate decision at the start of the 1970s not to match the Warsaw Pact tank for tank – which reveals the dishonesty of comparing tank against tank – and has a policy of going for weapon systems of higher quality – which reveals further dishonesty, since high quality generally means lower numbers.

Of course, the Warsaw Pact may be right from a military perspective to go for quantity rather than quality, and

NATO may be wrong to have decided not to match its adversary tank for tank. The point is that the current situation, usually presented as the result of the USSR's unilateral military build-up, is actually the result also of a series of specific and deliberate decisions by NATO, and that the current situation is always incompletely described by the British government and several others.

If NATO and Warsaw Pact forces are examined in this kind of detail across the board, two main conclusions emerge. First, as far as it can be quantified there is a rough balance of forces in Europe; neither side has an important advantage overall. Second, these forces, even without nuclear weapons, would be immensely destructive of each other and everything around them if war came. Neither conclusion forms the basis for objecting to European nuclear disarmament on the basis of a NATO inferiority in non-nuclear forces.

NATO's Unity

The second objection is that if nuclear weapons are removed from Europe, NATO's unity would suffer. In fact, there is much to be said for this objection; I think it is essentially correct to say that European nuclear disarmament would weaken NATO's unity. In the Warsaw Pact it would have a similar effect, though perhaps weaker in the short term. This objection actually provides an important insight into the role of nuclear weapons in the current constitution of NATO and into the type of unity we are talking about.

The point is, of course, that these are American weapons. They provide the USA with important strategic and thereby political leadership over the West European NATO states. In general terms, American leadership is under challenge from West Europe and Japan and is suffering; but within NATO the currency of American TNW in Europe and of the 'nuclear umbrella' of US strategic forces still buys US hegemony. Indeed, it is precisely when American leadership is sharply challenged in other arenas that one might expect it to try and strengthen its strategic leadership in NATO, and the most obvious way of doing this would probably be to plan to deploy more US nuclear weapons in Europe. Since meetings of the NATO Nuclear Planning Group, which are supposed to involve the rest of NATO in this aspect of strategic planning, are largely taken up by American lectures, it is not too hard to develop momentum behind any American proposal in this field.

Thus unity in this context means acceptance of US leadership. And that brings with it acceptance of US plans for nuclear war in Europe, for fighting a limited nuclear war, limited in the sense that the USA's own territory is not directly involved. Their limited war – our holocaust. Whether the USSR would permit war to remain limited in this sense is very dubious, but beside the point. For the issue which is of overriding importance for West Europeans is that NATO unity means agreeing to be an expendable American asset, a forward line of defence, a battlefield for the two superpowers. For East Europeans, the issue is essentially the same.

The movement for European nuclear disarmament thus gets to the heart of the matter. Precisely because it does challenge NATO's unity it could create the space for developing new and safer ways of ensuring some degree of security in a dangerous world. It is the confrontation between the USA and the USSR which is leading us towards war. European nuclear disarmament offers a possibility for Europe to disengage from that confrontation, to challenge the right of the superpowers to have the power over our fate that they now do, and eventually to eliminate that power. It opens a perspective of new political movement in both East and West Europe, breaking out of the suffocating effects on domestic politics of the superpowers' military confrontation, leading to a greater variety of social and political systems among wholly or partially nonaligned nations. European nuclear disarmament threatens both American and Soviet hegemony. It therefore demands the rethinking of some of the basic and most cherished precepts in both NATO and the Warsaw Pact; for example, it demands seeing a challenge to NATO unity as positive. It thus involves a head-on collision with what NATO would have us believe are the basic 'facts of life' of international politics. Unless we undertake that task, we are all too likely to have those 'facts of life' draw us over the brink into nuclear war.

Notes

1. *The New York Times*, 26 March 1980.

2. These figures are taken from *The Military Balance 1979–1980* (International Institute for Strategic Studies, London, 1979), with the exception of the figure for Soviet troops in Europe, which was not given. I therefore took the figure given in the previous year's edition and subtracted from it the 20,000 troops unilaterally withdrawn from the German Democratic Republic by the USSR since. The figures for NATO include French forces.

3. See, for example, M. Leitenberg, 'Background information on Tactical Nuclear Weapons', in *Tactical Nuclear Weapons: European Perspectives* (Taylor & Francis, London, 1978); *World Armaments and Disarmament: SIPRI Yearbook 1978* (Taylor & Francis, London, 1978), pp. 426–9. The usual figure given for NATO tactical nuclear warheads is about 7,000, but the US Department of Defense has now made it clear that its Poseidon missiles designated for use in Europe are not included in that total, and the higher figure of about 7,500 therefore becomes appropriate: *Department of Defense Annual Report Fiscal year 1981* (US DOD, 1980), p. 92.

4. This issue is discussed in more detail in my *The Defence of the Realm in the 1980s* (Croom Helm, London, 1980), Chapter 4.

5. *The Military Balance 1979–1980*, pp. 114–19. In addition, I have taken information from *Jane's Weapon Systems* and from *SALT and the NATO Allies* (US Senate, Committee on Foreign Relations, Staff Report, October 1979) as well as sources cited below.

6. NATO press statement, 5 December 1979, cited by M. Leitenberg, *NATO and WTO Long Range Theatre Nuclear Forces*, mimeo, April 1980 (available from the Armament and Disarmament Information Unit, University of Sussex); the figure is some 190 missiles lower than the one given by the IISS in *The Military Balance 1979–1980*.

7. US International Communication Agency, 6 December 1979, cited by Leitenberg, *NATO and WTO Long Range Theatre Nuclear Forces*; again the figure is a good deal lower than the one given by the IISS.

8. *Guardian*, 15 October 1979; *International Herald Tribune*, 15 October 1979.

9. Reprinted in *Survival*, September/October 1979.

10. These issues are those in the following paragraph are discussed in detail in Chapter 4 of *The Defence of the Realm in the 1980s*.

11. *Defence in the 1980s*, Cmnd 7826-I (HMSO, London, 1980), p. 18.

PART THREE

The Armourers:
Bureaucracies and Economics

David Holloway
War, Militarism and the Soviet State*

In the military structure of the world the Soviet Union and the United States stand in a class by themselves. They mount the two largest military efforts and between them account for one half of the massive resources which the world devotes to arms and armed forces. There are, it is true, considerable differences between the military forces of the Soviet Union and the United States, but these are insignificant when compared with the differences between them and the forces of other states.

From the armed forces it maintains and the weapons it produces, it is clear that the Soviet military effort is large. It is difficult, however, to say precisely what resources it comsumes. The Soviet government publishes a figure for the defence budget each year, but this is of little help in estimating the military burden because it is not clear what the budget covers. In any event, observers outside the Soviet Union agree that the Soviet armed forces could not be paid for by the official defence budget without the help of very large hidden subsidies. Western attempts to assess Soviet defence spending must be treated with caution too because of the intrinsic difficulties of making such estimates.[1] It is evident, nevertheless, that only a major commitment of resources has enabled the Soviet Union in the last twenty years to attain strategic parity with the United States,

* *Editors' note*: This article was prepared for the Demilitarization Working Group of the World Order Models Project. It appears in a more extended form in *Alternatives: A Journal of World Policy*, Vol. 6, No. 1 (1980), as part of a special issue on demilitarization.

maintain large well-equipped forces in Europe and along the frontier with China, extend the deployment of the Soviet Navy throughout the world, and engage in continuous modernization of arms and equipment.

A military effort of this scale necessarily has a far-reaching impact on the Soviet economy. An extensive network of military research and development establishments is required to develop armaments, while a major sector of industry is needed to produce them in quantity. The Soviet Union has amassed military power roughly comparable to that of the United States, even though its Gross National Product is only about half as large. Consequently a higher rate of extraction of resources has been necessary, with consequences which will be examined below.

The maintenance of standing forces of some four million people (mainly men) has not only economic, but also social and political consequences.[2] Institutional arrangements exist to draft a substantial proportion of each generation of young men into the armed forces. A considerable effort is made to ensure that reserves are available for mobilization if necessary. Voluntary military societies provide moral support for the armed forces and military training for the population at large. Secondary school children are given pre-induction military training from the age of fifteen. In recent years there has been a growing campaign of military-patriotic education which tries to instil in the population the values of patriotism and respect for military virtues. Party leaders seemingly believe that obligatory military service can help to foster social discipline and to bring the different nationalities closer together. They also appear to believe that association of the Party with the armed forces will strengthen Soviet patriotism and the commitment of the people to the existing political order.[3] At the highest political level the close relationship between Party and Army has been underlined by the awarding to General Secretary Brezhnev of various military honours, including the rank of Marshal of the Soviet Union.

All this is a far cry from the vision of socialist society which the founders of Marxism and the makers of the Bolshevik revolution held. Marxist thought has traditionally been marked by a strong antipathy to militarism, seeing war and armies as the product of the world capitalist system. Before 1917 socialists agreed that standing armies were instruments of aggression abroad and repression at home; the proper form of military organization for a socialist state would be the citizen army which would not degenerate into a military caste or create a military realm separate from other areas of social life. Although he had to lead the young Soviet republic against the White armies and foreign intervention, Lenin never succumbed to the worship of things military or tried to enhance his own authority by the paraphernalia of military command.

Why is it then that the country in which the first socialist revolution took place is so highly militarized? Why is Soviet military organization so different from original socialist concepts, with rank and hierarchy distinguished in a very marked way? Why is the defence sector accorded a special place in the economy? Why are the values of military patriotism given so much emphasis? The object of this essay is to examine the obstacles to disarmament and demilitarization in the Soviet Union and to see whether there exists in Soviet society the possibility for initiatives in that direction.

Methodological Issues

Soviet writers claim that there is nothing intrinsic to Soviet society that would generate arms production or armed forces, and that the military effort has been forced on the Soviet Union by the enmity of the capitalist world. This claim is not usually argued at length, and is based on a general statement about the nature of socialism rather than on a specific analysis of the Soviet system. A contrast is drawn with the fundamentally aggressive nature of imperialism and the incentives which the capitalist system offers for arms production. In this view Soviet military policy is purely a response to external stimuli. (Interestingly, the same writers often claim that Soviet society is, for various reasons, peculiarly suited to building up military power; among the reasons given are the disciplined, hierarchical, military-like organization of the Party, and the planned economy which enables the Party to mobilize resources for military purposes.[4])

A rather different view is given by those peace researchers who argue that the East-West arms race is now firmly rooted in the domestic structures of the two military superpowers. The military competition between East and West, it is claimed, did have its origins in international conflict, but has now become institutionalized in powerful military-industrial-scientific complexes. This is why the settlement of major political disputes in Europe in the early 1970s was not accompanied by any significant moves towards demilitarization. This argument points not to specific features of socialism or Russian history, but to characteristics which the Soviet Union shares with the United States.[5]

The Soviet Union has been subjected to this kind of critical analysis primarily since its emergency as a fully-fledged military superpower. The attainment of strategic parity with the United States has made the Soviet Union seem to share full responsibility for the continuing arms race. Soviet arms policies in the 1970s have proved profoundly disappointing to those who hoped that the SALT I agreements would lead to a slackening of the arms race. They, and others, have come more insistently to ask: what drives Soviet arms policies? What are the domestic roots of those policies?

The problem of militarization is, however, wider than that of disarmament. Andreski has pointed out that the term militarism is used in a number of different senses: first, an aggressive foreign policy, based on a readiness to resort to war; second, the preponderance of the military in the state, the extreme case being that of military rule; third, subservience of the whole society to the needs of the army, which may involve a recasting of social life in accordance with the pattern of military organization; fourth, an ideology which propagates military ideals.[6] In this essay I shall use the term militarization to refer to the third of these phenomena, specifying the others when necessary.

In an essay on the militarization of Soviet education William Odom argues that Soviet militarism is to be explained by two major factors.[7] The first of these is the similarity that exists between socialism and the war system. By this he means that both socialism and a state at war 'sacrifice individuals and their private interests for the state's political objectives'. (This is akin to the argument made by Soviet writers who point to the capacity of the Soviet system for creating powerful armed forces.) The second factor is the inheritance by the Soviet state of the military-political tradition of Tsarism. The very process of consolidating Soviet power against external and internal enemies meant that the Bolshevik state 'had to accept as its birthright most of the tensions that had made militarization of the old state seem imperative to the imperial leadership'.[8] The argument here is not that socialism is inevitably militarist, but that the imperial military tradition combined with the Soviet experience to create a form of socialist militarism. In other words, Odom sees the militarization of Soviet society as primarily a product of Russian history and the Soviet system.

There are, of course, many who see the militarization of Soviet society as a consequence of both external and internal factors and explain it in terms of the Cold War rather than of the Russian past. Many socialists and liberals in the West, for example, held the view – particularly in the early years of destalinization – that if the tensions of the Cold War could be relaxed, this would facilitate not only a shift of resources away from military purposes, but also political change in the direction of freedom and democracy. In other words, many of the distortions of Soviet socialism could be explained in terms of the international pressure under which socialist construction had to be carried out in the Soviet Union.

In the mid-1970s E. P. Thompson wrote of the policy of nuclear disarmament and positive neutrality which the New Left advocated in Britain in the late 1950s and the 1960s:

It was a critical part of our advocacy that with each effective movement of detente there would follow a relaxation in military and bureaucratic pressures within the United States and the Soviet Union. Thus the relaxation of Cold War tensions was a precondition for further destalinization, and a precondition for resuming socialist and democratic advances, East or West.

Thompson went on to ask whether Soviet policy in the early 1970s – detente with the West allied with sharper repression of dissidents at home – invalidated this argument. He concluded that it did not, on two grounds: that the detente of the early 1970s amounted only to great power agreement to regulate their interests from above; further, that the repression of dissidents was a sign that even a little detente sharpens internal contradictions in the Soviet Union by threatening to deprive the bureaucracy of its functions and the official ideology of its credibility. Over the long run, he argued, international tension helps to justify repression, while detente will help to weaken that justification and increase the possibilities of movement towards democracy.[9]

It is precisely this kind of argument that has been challenged by those peace researchers who claim that the arms race is so deeply rooted in domestic structures that the lessening of international tension will have no effect on it. Some see the arms race and detente coexisting for a long time; others see detente falling victim to tensions generated by the military-industrial complexes. In either case, the peace research argument is that the resolution of international political disputes may be a necessary condition for disarmament and demilitarization, but that it is by no means a sufficient condition.

This is not a comprehensive, much less an exhaustive, survey of the approaches that have been taken in examining the obstacles to disarmament and demilitarization in the Soviet Union. But it does provide some helpful pointers to the relationships that have to be analysed. The first of these is the interaction of internal and external factors. The particular form which socialist construction has taken in the Soviet Union cannot be understood without reference to the international context in which the Bolsheviks undertook the transformation of Russian society. Consequently the militarization of Soviet society has to be examined in the light of international, as well as of domestic, relationships. Moreover, some attempt must be made to discuss what is specific to militarism in the Soviet Union, and what it shares with militarism elsewhere.

Secondly, it has been seen that different historical perspectives – some rooted in the Russian Empire, some in the Cold War – have been adopted, and this raises interesting questions about the way in which patterns of political relationships are reproduced in a given society. Although it is important to provide a historical perspective, there is the danger that the Russian tradition will be presented as monolithic, and that militarism will be seen as a genetic inheritance, transmitted from one generation (or even one social formation) to the next. This would be disheartening in its suggestion that no change is possible, and also wrong. The Russian political tradition is diverse, embracing not only militarism, but also the anti-militarism of Tolstoy and Kropotkin. The Soviet tradition too contains various strands, and the diversity is very wide if the views of contemporary dissidents are taken into account. Consequently it would be a mistake to begin this analysis by portraying this militarization as either inevitable or all-embracing.

War and the Soviet State

Analysing the militarization of Soviet society involves much more than an effort to identify a military-industrial or military-bureaucratic complex, elimination of which would remove the internal dynamic of Soviet military policy and leave the rest of the social system untouched. The history of the Soviet state is intimately bound up with war and the preparation for war. This is true both in the classical sense that armed force has established the territorial limits of the state and secured internal rule, and in the sense that war and the preparation for it have profoundly affected the internal structure of the state.

It is one of the striking features of the history of Tsarist Russia and the Soviet Union that rivalry with other, economically more advanced, states has provided a major stimulus to economic and political change. This was true of Peter the Great's reforms, and of the reforms which followed the Crimean and Russo-Japanese wars; it was a major factor in Soviet industrialization too. One consequence of this pattern has been the role of the state as the dominant agency of change; it was through the state that social and economic relationships were altered with the aim of mobilizing resources to increase the power of the state.

When the Bolsheviks seized power they faced the problem of consolidating their rule in the face of enemies at home and abroad. The early experience of the young Soviet state – civil war, foreign intervention and internal unrest – had a profound impact on Bolshevik ideas about military organization. The early vision of militia-type forces did not survive the realization that the Bolsheviks faced considerable opposition from inside Soviet society and from foreign powers. The military reform of 1924–5 created a mixed system, with the main emphasis on standing forces; the territorial-militia element was retained for economic reasons rather than on grounds of principle. Trotsky's project of combining labour with military training was not implemented. Of more immediate practical importance was the view advanced by Frunze, Trotsky's successor as Commissar of War, that, in conditions of economic constraints on defence, every civilian activity ought to be examined for the contribution it could make to military preparedness. By the late 1920s the Red Army did have features which distinguished it from the armies of bourgeois states – its social composition and the commissar system, for example – but it was far from embodying the earlier socialist ideas of military organization.[10]

With the failure of revolution in Europe, the Soviet Union was left largely isolated in a hostile world. This helped to stimulate a great debate about the direction of socialist construction, and in the mid-1920s the idea of building 'socialism in one country' began to gain ground in the Bolshevik Party. This idea, as E. H. Carr has noted, marked the marriage of Marxist revolutionary goals and Russian national destiny.[11] The policy of industrialization which was embarked on towards the end of the decade was the practical offspring of this marriage. In 1931 Stalin, now the dominant leader, who had set his own brutal stamp on the industrialization drive, justified the intensity of the policy by referring to the need to overcome Russia's backwardness and thus prevent other powers from beating her.

Do you want our Socialist fatherland to be beaten and to lose its independence? If you do not want this you must put an end to its backwardness in the shortest possible time and develop genuine Bolshevik tempo in building up its Socialist system of economy. There is no other way. That is why Lenin said during the October Revolution: 'Either perish, or overtake and outstrip the advanced capitalist countries.'

We are fifty or a hundred years behind the advanced countries. We must make good this distance in ten years. Either we do it, or they crush us.[12]

Although this justification was not explicitly military, it did

137

prove a clear rationale for the development of the defence industry.

Industrialization was made possible by a massive extraction of resources from the population and their investment in heavy industry. A vast and powerful Party-State bureaucracy ensured that resources were forthcoming, enforced the priorities set by the Party leaders, and managed the new industrial economy. The defence sector was given high priority in the allocation of investment funds, scarce materials, able managers and skilled workers. During the 1930s a powerful defence industry was created which produced large quantities of weapons, some of which were of high quality. The Soviet Union had rejected the idea, which was popular in the West at the time, of building a small, highly mechanized army and sought instead to marry mass and technology – to create a mass army equipped with the best possible armaments. The territorial-militia element of the armed forces was gradually abandoned. Yet for all that had been done, the Winter War of 1939–40 with Finland exposed serious weaknesses in the Red Army, some of which resulted from the great purge which Stalin had inflicted on Soviet society in the late 1930s.

The German invasion of 22 June 1941 took Stalin by surprise, and found the Red Army in a state of unreadiness. The opening months of the war proved disastrous, with the German forces advancing to the outskirts of Moscow. Only by an enormous effort over the next four years was the Soviet Union able to halt the German advance, turn the tide of war and push the German armies back to Berlin. The degree of industrial mobilization was much greater in the Soviet Union than in the other belligerent states, and Soviet losses of people and material goods were immense. The Soviet name for the war with Germany – the Great Patriotic War – symbolizes the appeal which Stalin made to the Soviet people's patriotism. In contrast to the bitter social and political tensions of the 1920s and 1930s, state and people were largely united in the common effort to defeat the Nazi enemy.[13]

Victory brought the Soviet Union gains of territory and influence which had seemed inconceivable in the early months of the war. But victory also brought political conflicts with the war-time allies, and these soon found their expression in intense military rivalry, which centred on the development of nuclear weapons and their means of delivery. By 1947 the Soviet Union had four major military research and development programmes under way: nuclear weapons, rockets, radar and jet-engine technology. After Stalin's death the implications of this 'military-technical revolution' became more pressing. The existence of nuclear weapons in growing stockpiles raised fundamental questions about the relationship of war to policy, and about the appropriate structure for armed forces in the nuclear age – questions which have dominated Soviet military policy ever since.

Khrushchev now put greater stress on peaceful coexistence between East and West, and set in motion major changes in military doctrine and military institutions. In the late 1950s and early 1960s he tried to devise a new military policy, based on nuclear-armed missiles, that would be militarily and diplomatically effective, while freeing resources for civilian purposes. He even floated the idea of restoring the territorial-militia element in the armed forces. But internal opposition, which was strengthened by a succession of international crises (the U2 incident in 1960, the 1961 Berlin crisis and the Cuban missile crisis of 1962) and by the Kennedy administration's build-up of strategic forces, finally defeated Khrushchev's efforts.[14]

If we can speak of a 'Soviet military build-up', then its origins lie in the defeat of Khrushchev's policy. His successors have devoted considerable attention to the all-round strengthening of Soviet military power. A major increase in strategic forces has brought parity with the United States. The Ground Forces have been expanded, in particular along the frontier with China, and have received more modern equipment. The Air Forces too have been modernized. Soviet naval presence has been extended throughout the world. Arms transfers to third world countries have grown substantially in this period. Certainly Soviet policy has been subject to many rash and alarmist interpretations in the West, but the evidence does point to a steady and significant increase in Soviet military power since the early 1960s.[15]

In the first ten years after the end of the Second World War a clear bipolar structure emerged in world politics, with the United States and the Soviet Union as the dominant powers. Since that time new forces have emerged to transform the international system. The creation of the third world as a political force was helped by the existence of the Soviet bloc, which could provide a counterweight to Western power. Fissiparous tendencies, both East and West, have further complicated international politics. By the late 1960s Japan and the EEC had become major centres of economic power, while the rivalry between the Soviet Union and China had assumed military form. From the Soviet point of view the international environment had become more complex, with the ever-present danger that the various centres of power would combine in opposition to it. Indeed, elements of such a combination have been evident in the 1970s, motivated in large part by the desire to offset growing Soviet military power; in its turn, this countervailing power has provided the Soviet leaders with further reasons for military forces.

The Soviet Union now possesses large armed forces, an advanced defence industry and an extensive military R and D network. In no other area has the Soviet Union come so close to achieving the goal of 'catching up and overtaking the advanced capitalist powers'. As a consequence, the law of comparative advantage seems to operate in Soviet external policies, giving a major role to the military instrument. The Soviet Union conducts its central relationship with the NATO powers from a position of military strength but economic weakness. In Eastern Europe the Soviet Union has suffered political setbacks but has used military force, and the threat of military force, to underpin its dominant position. Soviet relations with China have now acquired an important military dimension with the build-up of forces along the Chinese frontier. In the third world the Soviet Union has used arms transfers and military advisers as a major instrument of diplomacy. Thus in spite of the fact that the Soviet concept of the 'correlation of forces', in terms of which international politics is analysed, does not place primary emphasis on military force, military power has become a basic instrument of Soviet external policy.

It is not surprising that the present generation of Soviet leaders should see military power as the main guarantee of Soviet security and of the Soviet position in the world. The men now at the top levels of leadership came to positions of some power in the late 1930s, and Brezhnev and Ustinov are only the most prominent members of this generation to have had a direct part in managing the development and production of arms. Victory in the war with Germany, the attainment of strategic parity with the United States and the long period at peace since 1945 – these are regarded by this generation as among its greatest achievements. When one considers the course of Soviet history from 1917 to 1945, it is no surprise that this should be so.

It should be clear from this brief outline how important war and the preparation for war have been in the formation of the Soviet state. This is not to say that the course of Soviet development has been determined by forces outside the Soviet Union, or that every event in Soviet history is to be explained in terms of external conditions. The rise of Stalin and his system of rule cannot be explained without reference to social, economic and political conditions in the Soviet Union. Moreover, not everything in the Stalinist period can be seen as a response to external threats. The great purge of 1936–8 was justified in this way, but the justification was patently false and the purge greatly weakened the Red Army. But the Stalinist industrialization drive had as its major goal the development of heavy industry as the basis for economic growth and military power, and it was in these terms that it was justified.

This policy involved the extensive mobilization of the resources and energies of Soviet society, and the extraction from society of those resources by the state, which then channelled them towards the ends laid down by the Party leadership. The process was dominated by the Party-State apparatus which forced changes in social and economic relationships, extracted the resources from an often unwilling population, and managed the new economic system. In order to secure the loyalty of the Party-State apparatus special social and economic privileges and distinctions were introduced. (It was at this time that prerevolutionary ranks began to be reintroduced into the Red Army.) The rate of extraction was very high, leaving the mass of the population with minimal living standards and sometimes (as when famine occurred) not even those. Coercion was an intrinsic part of this policy.

Victory in the war seemed to show that, whatever the 'mistakes' of Stalin's policies in the immediate prewar years, the general emphasis on industrialization had been correct. After the war the high rate of extraction continued as industry was reconstructed and military rivalry with the West pursued. But since Stalin's death important changes have taken place which have a bearing on the questions of disarmament and demilitarization. The first is that the rate of economic growth has slowed considerably, provoking intensive debate about economic reform. It has been widely argued inside and outside the Soviet Union that the system of economic planning and administration was suited to the industrialization drive, but has now become a brake on industrial development and in particular on technological innovation. Second, terror has been abandoned as a system of rule and the Party leadership has been searching for new sources of legitimacy for the state. Repression of opposition and dissent still takes place, but greater effort has been made to secure popular support. Among the ways in which this has been done is through the provision of more and better goods and services to the mass of the population, and through appeals to nationalist sentiments. Third, as a result of the greater attention that has been paid to the living standards and welfare of the population, the priorities of resource allocation have become more complex than they were under Stalin.

The Defence Sector and the Soviet Economy

The organization of the defence sector is similar to that of the rest of Soviet industry.[16] The enterprises that produce arms and equipment are controlled by a series of ministries which have responsibility for the different branches of the sector. The work of these ministries is in turn planned by the central planning agencies (in line with the general policy laid down by the Politburo), since the activities of the defence sector must be coordinated with those of the rest of the economy. There are, however, special institutional arrangements in the defence sector which are designed to ensure that military production has priority claim on scarce resources. In this sense the defence sector is distinct from the rest of the economy.

Since the war some important changes have taken place in the defence sector. It has expanded to include new branches of production, in particular nuclear weapons, rockets and electronics. Along with this expansion has come the creation of an extensive network of research and development (R and D) establishments to provide the basis for innovations in weapons technologies. These establishments are controlled by the production ministries in the defence sector. The size of the network is impossible to establish with any precision, but the number of establishments must be in the hundreds, while those engaged in military research and development must number in the hundreds of thousands. Research institutes from outside the defence sector – for example, from the Academy of Sciences – are also drawn into military work.

Military R and D is more effective than civilian R and D in the Soviet Union. The defence sector is well suited to the development and production of follow-on systems (for example, of tanks) where no great shift of mission or technology is required. The Soviet Union has also been able to organize large-scale innovation when the political leaders have deemed it necessary; the R and D system is well suited to the concentration of resources on specific goals such as the development of the atomic bomb or the development of the inter-continental ballistic missile. It is not so well adapted to the lateral or horizontal transfer of technology across departmental boundaries, unless this is organized as a matter of priority from above.[17]

Soviet military-economic policy is supposed to be guided by three main principles:

– to maintain a high level or armaments production;

– to ensure the flexibility of the economy (for example, in shifting from civilian to military production, in raising the rate of arms production or in introducing new weapons);

– to secure the viability of the economy in war-time.[18]

These principles were elaborated in the 1930s and are still taken as the most important indicators of the state's economic potential – that is, of its ability to provide for the material needs of society while producing everything necessary for war.

In spite of the flexibility recommended by these principles the available evidence suggests that there is considerable stability in the defence sector and that this has a major influence on its mode of operation. The research institutes and design bureaux, where new weapons are created, are funded from the budget and their finances do not seem to depend directly on orders for specific systems. Coupled with the institutional continuity of the military R and D network, this provides the basis for a steady effort in the design and development of weapons. Consequently a strong tendency to create 'follow-on' systems can be discerned. Stable production appears also to be a feature of the defence sector, with no major variation in output from year to year.

Besides the stability of its structure and its operations, the defence sector is marked by the continuity of its leading managers. For example, D. F. Ustinov, the present Minister of Defence, became People's Commissar (i.e. Minister) of Armament in 1941 and until his appointment to his present position in 1976 played a major role in weapons development and production. Another example: Ye. P. Slavskii, the Minister of Medium Machine-building (in charge of nuclear weapons development and production) has held that position since 1957 and has been involved in the nuclear weapons programme since 1946.

The managers of the defence industry form a coherent group, with interlocking careers. There is, however, little evidence that they have acted together as a lobby. The one occasion on which they seem to have done so was in the period 1957 to 1965 when they took part, with some success, in resistance to Khrushchev's decentralization of the system of economic planning and management. In 1963, after some recentralization had taken place, Khrushchev indicated his dissatisfaction with Ustinov and the 'metal-eaters' and complained that secrecy made it difficult to criticize the shortcomings of the defence industry.[19]

This is the only occasion on which the performance of the defence sector emerged into the open as an issue in the arguments about economic reform. In the post-Stalin period there have been intensive debates about the need to reform the system of economic planning and administration in order to stimulate technological innovation. In the 1960s it was widely held by Soviet and foreign economists alike that sooner or later the Soviet leaders would have to choose between plan and market, and that any significant reform would involve a move towards some form of 'market socialism'. Such a reform would not be incompatible with a high level of defence expenditure. Even if the Soviet Union now devotes 12 to 15 per cent of its GNP to defence (and this is the upper range of Western estimates) this level could be maintained in an economy where the market played a significant role; after all, some capitalist countries devote a higher proportion of the GNP to defence without instituting a 'war economy'. Thus the present Soviet system of economic planning and management cannot be said to be entailed by the level of defence expenditure. This is not to deny, of course, that the managers who have been used to working the present system might be fearful of changes on the grounds that their high priority position would be jeopardized.

In any event the choice of market socialism has not been made in the Soviet Union. The Czechoslovak crisis of 1968 was a major setback for the Soviet advocates of far-reaching reform, because political developments in Czechoslovakia were widely seen as the consequence of economic reform. The problems of economic growth and technological progress have not vanished in the Soviet Union, however, and piecemeal reform has been under way. Interestingly, the trend of reform in the 1970s has been to take the defence sector as a model for the rest of the economy. At the XXIV Party Congress in 1971 Brezhnev declared that

taking into account the high scientific-technical level of defence industry, the transmission of its experience, inventions and discoveries to all spheres of our economy acquires the highest importance.[20]

In the 1970s certain organizational features and management techniques – especially in the area of technological innovation – have been borrowed from the defence sector and applied in civilian industry.[21] This marks an attempt to use the defence sector as a model or dynamo of technological progress in the economy as a whole.

The priority of military production is a matter not only of central decisions, but also of the structure of industry and the attitudes of workers and managers. This was clearly illustrated by an article in *Literaturnaya Gazeta* in 1972 and the correspondence it provoked. The author of the article pointed out that in numerous ways – in prestige, in the priority given by other ministries (for example, in construction projects), in wages, in cultural and housing facilities, in labour turnover – light industry fared worse than heavy industry.[22] One of the correspondents wrote that

the best conditions are given to the so-called 'leading' branches. Then we have the remaining enterprises in Group A/heavy industry/. Last in line are the Group B enterprises. Naturally the most highly skilled cadres – workers, engineers or technicians – find jobs or try to find them where the pay is highest, so they are concentrated in the 'leading' branches of industry. What is more, these branches receive the best materials, the most advanced technology, the latest equipment etc. etc. . . . Even at the same machine-building enterprise, in the production of 'prestige' output and Group B output, there is no comparison in quality and in the attitude to the categories of output (in terms of technology, design work, management, pay, etc.).[23]

There is little doubt that within heavy industry the defence sector occupies the position of highest prestige, and therefore shows these features to the highest degree.

The Soviet system of economic planning and administration has not been altered fundamentally since it was first established. It remains a relatively effective mechanism for extracting resources from the economy and directing them to the goals set by the political leaders, and one of the most important of these goals has been the creation of military power. The defence sector occupies a key – and in some respects, a privileged – position in this system, not only in terms of central priorities, but also in terms of the organization of industry and the attitudes of workers and managers. The debates about economic reform have resulted in partial and piecemeal changes rather than in a fundamental transformation of the system. There has been a tendency over the last ten years to use the defence sector as a model for the rest of industry. In terms of the militarization of the Soviet economy, this is an ambiguous development. On the one hand, it testifies to a political concern about the performance of civilian industry; on the other, it highlights the special position and performance of the defence sector.

The Armed Forces and the Rationales for Military Power

There is little evidence of opposition inside the Soviet Union to Soviet military policy. Since 1965 there have been few if any indications of disagreement in the Party leadership about the level of military expenditure. This contrasts with the Khrushchev period, when military outlays did provide a focus of political argument. And in the dissident *samizdat* literature, although sharp criticism has been made of many features of Soviet life, few voices have been raised against the military policy of the Soviet state. Almost the only exception is the warnings which Andrei Sakharov has given the West of the growing military power of the Soviet Union; and Sakharov's background in nuclear weapons development makes him in this instance a very special case. Thus the situation is rather different from that in the United States, where militarism and racism formed the chief targets of protest in the 1960s and 1970s. There are many reasons for this difference, but the chief one appears to be that inside the Soviet Union the Soviet military effort is widely seen as legitimate and as pursuing legitimate goals. This is in spite of the fact that the burden of military expenditure is greater than in the NATO countries and that there are many competing claims for the resources which are devoted to defence.

One of the main reasons for the acceptance of Soviet military policy is no doubt that for the last thirty to thirty-five years the Soviet Union has enjoyed a period of peace and internal stability which stands in sharp contrast to the wars and upheavals of the first half of the century. The Soviet armed forces have seen very little combat since 1945 – certainly nothing to compare with the military role of the American, British and French forces. The Soviet claim that Soviet military strength is conducive to peace does not, therefore, fly directly in the face of reality. This is one reason why there has been, in the Soviet view, no contradiction between the processes of political detente and the growth of Soviet military power. Soviet military power is regarded as a crucial element in detente because it makes it impossible for the West to deal with the Soviet Union from a position of strength or to use its armed forces in an unfettered way throughout the world.[24]

Although Soviet forces have been engaged in relatively little combat since 1945, military power is certainly regarded by the Soviet leaders as contributing to their political purposes. The main object of that policy has been to prevent the West from conducting offensive actions – whether military or political – against the Soviet Union and its allies. Soviet military aid to third world countries is to be seen in the same context. Since the 1960s the Soviet Union has come to use its military power – in the form of advisers and arms transfers – more frequently as a way of gaining influence and undermining Western power. (There may now be an economic element in Soviet arms transfers: excess production can be exchanged – in some instances – for hard currency. But the primary rationale is still political.[25])

But military power has also been a major factor in Soviet relations with socialist states. The Soviet Union used military force in Hungary in 1956 and in Czechoslovakia in 1968 in order to maintain its dominant position in Eastern Europe. That position is underpinned by the ever-present threat of military force, even though that threat is not voiced openly. In the 1960s the confrontation with China assumed a military form with the build-up of forces along the Chinese frontier. Thus apart from deterring offensive policies directed against the Soviet Union and helping to destroy Western domination in different parts of the world, Soviet military power has been used as an instrument to create and sustain Soviet domination over other states. Moreover, as Soviet military strength has grown, new roles have been found for it, particularly in the projection of power outside the Soviet frontiers. The intervention in Afghanistan illustrates the Soviet Union's growing ability to use its military power in this way, and – more important – its willingness to do so.

In the late 1960s the Soviet union attained strategic parity with the United States and on that basis entered into negotiations to limit strategic arms.

Of course, it remains extremely difficult to say what constitutes parity or equality (does it mean equality with one particular state, or with all potential enemies combined?), and acceptance of the principle still leaves great scope for disagreement both within and between the negotiating states. Moreover, the principle of parity provides a basis for negotiation between the Soviet Union and the United States only because they have so many more nuclear weapons than other states that even the other nuclear powers can be left largely out of account. But does every state have the right to parity? Obviously not, since the Non-Proliferation Treaty represents a commitment of a kind to stop the spread of nuclear weapons. Negotiations between the superpowers on the basis of parity goes along with the attempt to prevent other states from attaining that status. Precisely because the Soviet Union and the United States are using arms control negotiations in this double-edged way, they are likely to stimulate other states to acquire nuclear weapons of their own. Consequently arms control negotiations on the basis of parity are by no means the foundation for a process of radical demilitarization.

In spite of the acceptance of parity as the basis for negotiations to limit strategic arms, it remains true that there are major differences between Soviet and American strategic thought. American thinking has laid particular emphasis on the ability, under all circumstances, to inflict widespread destruction on the enemy's society. Soviet thinking, on the other hand, has been concerned to limit the damage to Soviet society in the event of nuclear war. Even in a relationship of parity Soviet policy has been directed towards limiting the vulnerability of the Soviet Union to nuclear attack, and ensuring the viability of Soviet society in war-time. Whether this can be achieved seems very doubtful (even though viability is a relative term), but it does appear to be the rationale behind important elements of Soviet military, military-economic and civil defence policies, and it does have important implications for the militarization of Soviet society.

The main bulk of the Soviet forces is made up of the five branches of service: the Strategic Rocket Forces, the National Air Defence Forces, the Air Forces, the Ground Forces and the Navy. There are also special forces which sometimes engage in civilian work. The Construction Troops carry out construction work for the armed forces and on high-priority civilian projects; the Academic City near Novosibiirsk, for example, where the Siberian Division of the Academy of Sciences is based, was built by them. The Railroad and Road Troops play an important part in building and maintaining the Soviet rail and road communications system. These are quite natural offshoots of the Soviet armed forces. But there are three elements of the Soviet military system which are of greater interest from the point of view of the militarization of Soviet society. These are the civil defence organization, DOSAAF (*Dobrovol'noe obshchestvo sodeistviya armii, aviatsii i flotu* – the Voluntary Society for Cooperation with the Army, Aviation and the Navy), and the system of military-patriotic education. All are designed to strengthen the ability of the Soviet Union to defend itself, and all have political functions beyond that goal.

Soviet civil defence has three major objects: to provide

protection for the population against weapons of mass destruction; to ensure stable operation of the economy in war-time; and to eliminate the effects of enemy use of weapons of mass destruction.[26] Civil defence organizations may also take part in disaster relief operations. The effectiveness of the civil defence effort is very difficult to judge because it would depend so much on the way in which nuclear war was initiated. It could not prevent widespread destruction, although it could reduce its scale. It has been estimated that about 100,000 full-time personnel are engaged in civil defence work at all levels of the government and economic structure.[27] There is an extensive programme of education and training which is designed to enable the population to carry out civil defence measures should the need arise.

DOSAAF has as its main aim the strengthening of the Soviet Union's defence capability by training the Soviet people for the defence of the socialist fatherland.[28] DOSAAF is open to all Soviet citizens over the age of fourteen and has about 80 million members. Its main activities are: military-patriotic education; training of young people for service in the armed forces; training in technical skills; dissemination of military-technical knowledge; direction of sports which have military-technical significance. DOSAAF has clubs and sports facilities and is organized at factories, farms, educational institutions and so on. It seems clear that DOSAAF's activities are of substantial help to the armed forces in providing recruits with skills which will be useful during military service, and also in raising the physical and technical level of the Soviet population. For the same reasons its work is useful to Soviet industry. Much of what DOSAAF does is done by non-military organizations in the West. It is nevertheless significant that in the Soviet Union it is the goals of military preparedness and defence capability that provide the justification and the driving force for activities of this kind. Here again the importance of the military factor as a modernizing force in Soviet society is evident.

Both civil defence and DOSAAF contribute to the Soviet Union's ability to defend itself; they also contribute to the more diffuse process of military-patriotic education.

Military-patriotic education is called upon to instil a readiness to perform military duty, responsibility for strengthening the defence capability of the country, respect for the Soviet armed forces, pride in the Motherland and the ambition to preserve and increase the heroic traditions of the Soviet people. Military-patriotic education is carried out in the teaching process in secondary and higher educational establishments, in the system of political education, by means of propaganda in the press, on radio and television, and with the help of various forms of mass-political work and of artistic and literary works. Of great significance for military-patriotic education is the mastery of basic military and military-technical skills which young people acquire in secondary schools, technical schools, higher educational establishments, in studies at the houses of defence and technical creativity, aero, auto motor and radio clubs, at the young technicians' stations, in military-patriotic schools, defence circles, at points of pre-induction training, in civil defence formations. Physical training with an applied military bent presupposes the development of qualities of will, courage, hardiness, strength, speed of reaction, and helps to raise psychological stability, trains the sight, hearing etc.[29]

Military-patriotic education is directed not only towards satisfying the practical needs of the armed forces but also towards increasing support for, and loyalty to, the Party and the Soviet state. It represents a fusion of communist, nationalist and military appeals. The Great Patriotic War occupies a key position in the programme of military-patriotic education as the source of examples and illustrations of the desired qualities. This, as we have noted, was a time when Party and people were most closely united in a common purpose, and military-patriotic education is evidently an effort to recapture and reinforce that bond by tapping a source of strong sentiment in the Soviet people. In this context it can be seen as a response to the problems of legitimation that the Soviet state has faced in the post-Stalin period.

This military-patriotic education does not amount to a glorification of war and should therefore be distinguished from Fascist militarism. Indeed, the Party's peace policy (the effectiveness of which is seen to rest on Soviet military power) is an essential component of the programme of education. Moreover, one might wonder just how effective the programme is in instilling the desired qualities into a population that seems very far from matching the ideal of the 'new Soviet man'. But quite clearly military-patriotic education will help to instil acceptance of the Party's military policy and belief in the importance of military power. In this way it will help to sustain the Soviet military effort and the special position which the defence sector and the armed forces enjoy in Soviet society.

A Military-industrial State?

As a major instrument of Soviet external policy the armed forces naturally enjoy an important position in the Party-State apparatus. The Ministry of Defence and the General Staff are overwhelmingly staffed by professional officers who have spent all their careers in the armed forces. Since 1945 the post of Minister has, more often than not, been held by a professional soldier, although the present Minister, Ustinov, has spent most of his life in the defence industry. The chief functions of the Ministry and the General Staff are those of similar institutions in other countries: to draw up plans, develop strategy and tactics, gather and evaluate intelligence about potential enemies, educate and train the troops, and administer the whole network of military institutions. The Soviet Union, unlike the United States, does not have an extensive network of civilian institutions conducting research into military operations; operational analysis is done very largely within the armed forces.

The existence of a large military establishment within the state might be thought to pose difficult problems of civil-military relations and to threaten the Party's dominant position in Soviet society. It is true that there have been elements of conflict and tension in Party-military relations, but the principle of Party supremacy has never seriously been threatened. Special mechanisms of control exist in the armed forces, the most important being the Main Political Administration, which is both an administration of the Ministry of Defence and a department of the Central Committee. Some Western observers have seen in this organization an institutionalized Party distrust of the military.[30] But in fact this view is mistaken and the Main Political Administration should more properly be seen as a bridge between the Party and the armed forces, symbolizing their unity and the assumptions that they share about the importance of military power for the Soviet state.[31]

The Soviet Union embodies the apparent paradox of a militarized social system in which the military, while an important political force, are not the dominant one. This is not to say, however, that the armed forces – or, more particularly, members of the High Command – have played no role in the political crises of the post-Stalin period. In each case of leadership change – Beria's arrest and execution in 1953, Malenkov's defeat by Khrushchev in 1955, the defeat of the 'anti-Party group' in 1957 and Khrushchev's fall in 1964 – members of the High Command played some role. But military support was one factor among others, and probably not the decisive one. Moreover, Marshal Zhukov's disgrace in 1957, only months after he had helped Khrushchev to defeat the 'anti-Party group' in the Central Committee, shows that engaging in leadership politics can be a risky business for soldiers. The spectre of Bonapartism was conjured up by Khrushchev as a major justification for Zhukov's removal from office. Even though it appears to have been a contrived justification, it underlined the determination of the Party leadership to retain its supremacy over the armed forces. Military involvement has been made possible only by splits in the Party leadership, and on no occasion has it resulted in a conflict in which Party leaders were ranged on one side and the military on the other; the High Command has had its own internal politics and divisions.

The political quiescence of the armed forces is to be explained by reference not so much to the formal mechanisms of Party and secret police control as to the way in which military interests have been given priority in Party policy. To say this is not to minimize Stalin's brutal treatment of the armed forces or to deny that Khrushchev often pursued policies that were to the distaste of the High Command. But by stressing the importance of international conflict and national solidarity the Party has provided an ideological framework which gives a clear meaning to the armed forces' existence. Party policy has also given the officer corps a privileged material position and a high status in Soviet society. Finally, the professional interests of the officer corps have been generally well served, especially in the allocation of resources to defence and in the opportunities for career advancement.

Since Stalin's death in 1953, and more particularly since Khrushchev's fall from power in 1964, officers have been given considerable freedom to discuss questions of military policy and a greater voice in the policy-making process. This has resulted from the general diffusion of power at the centre of the Soviet state, and has parallels in other areas of Soviet life where vigorous debates have been conducted about matters of policy. The Brezhnev Politburo has placed great emphasis on 'scientific' policy-making and on expert and technically competent advice.

The diffusion of power has created what some writers refer to as 'institutional pluralism'.[32] Like all pluralism, however, it is imperfect in the sense that some groups and institutions have more power than others. In this respect the armed forces and the defence industry occupy a special position. The armed forces enjoy wide prestige as the embodiment of national power and integrity – a prestige which is enhanced by the extensive programme of military-patriotic education. The Ministry of Defence and General Staff are institutions of undoubted competence, with a monopoly of expertise in military affairs; there are no civilian institutions able to challenge this expertise. The high priority given to the defence sector remains embedded in the system of economic planning and administration. The defence industry has been in the forefront of Soviet technological progress and is seen by the Party leaders as something to be emulated rather than restricted in the age of the 'scientific-technical revolution'. Finally, key aspects of military policy are shrouded in secrecy, and this limits criticism of the priority given to defence in resource allocation and of the way in which those resources are used.

This is not to suggest that the military policy of the Soviet state has been pursued against the wishes of the Party leadership. The final decisions on military policy rest with the Politburo, and with the Defence Council, which comprises several leading Politburo members under Brezhnev's chairmanship. All the evidence points to a set of shared assumptions among the leaders about military power and military expenditure. There are differences of view, no doubt, but these appear to be marginal, and the overall policy seems to rest on a broad consensus.[33] It is, however, possible that this state of affairs will change in the post-Brezhnev leadership and that the level of military effort will become a contentious issue as it was under Khrushchev. Then the institutional power of the armed forces and the defence industry might be important in determining the outcome of the argument.

Can we speak then of a Soviet 'military-industrial complex'? It is true that there is a large military establishment and a large defence industry. But the term itself often carries theoretical connotations that make it inapplicable to the Soviet Union. Sometimes it suggests a degenerate pluralism in which the balanced interplay of interests has been undermined by links between the armed forces and industry; in this sense it seems not to be appropriate because it implies too great a degree of pluralism – and it implies pluralism as a norm – for the Soviet Union. Sometimes it is implied that the driving force of arms policies is the pursuit of profit by capitalist enterprises; this too would be inappropriate, and for this reason Garaudy has argued that the Soviet Union has a 'bureaucratic-military complex' – that is, a military-industrial complex without the economic driving-force.[34] An objection of a different kind is summarized in the statement that the Soviet Union does not *have* a military-industrial complex, but *is* such a complex. This is too sweeping a statement, but it does make the point that the history of the Soviet Union is so bound up with military power that it seems wrong to speak of a separate military-industrial complex acting within the state.

Whether or not we say the armed forces and the defence industry constitute a military-industrial complex in the Soviet Union matters less than the fact that they exhibit many features that are identified as a characteristic of such a complex. Because of the way in which the Soviet economic system is organized it does exhibit these features in the same way, or to the same degree, as the American defence sector; but it does share them nevertheless. For example, competition is to be found in the weapons development process between offensive and defensive systems, with new technology in one area stimulating innovation in another. This may happen without any direct stimulus from outside. Second, the military R and D system shows considerable inertia in its operations, thus generating strong pressure for follow-on systems. Third, the R and D system does not appear to have a strong innovative dynamic of its own. Intervention by the political leadership is required for major innovations; but because the Party leaders have devoted so much attention to this area, such intervention is often forthcoming. Fourth, the military R and D system is not especially conducive to the cross-fertilization of technologies to produce new weapons, but this may happen as designers search for ways of meeting new requirements. Finally, the steadiness of Soviet arms policies may be accounted for, in part, by the planning to which weapons development and production are subject.

The Soviet military effort, which was created in the course of international rivalry, is now rooted in the structure of the Soviet state. This is not to say, of course, that the external stimuli have vanished. It is clear that foreign actions do impinge on Soviet arms policies and this can be seen both in the histories of specific weapons systems and in the direction of overall policy.[35] The advanced capitalist powers have set the pace in making major weapons innovations, and this has served to stimulate Soviet military technology. Of course it must be borne in mind that military power rests not only on the quality of military technology, but also on its quantity and on the way in which the troops are trained to use it. The arms competition between East and West consists of both qualitative and quantitative elements; although the balance of the two may change, the arms race has never been a question of one of these elements to the exclusion of the other. Western military technology has spurred Soviet weapons development, but has often been justified in terms of superior Soviet numbers.

It would be wrong therefore to deny the effects of foreign actions on Soviet arms policies. But it would be equally mistaken to see Soviet policy as merely a reaction to Western actions. Foreign influences are refracted through the Soviet policy-making process, in which Soviet perceptions, military doctrine, foreign policy objectives and domestic influences and constraints come into play. The effect of foreign actions on Soviet policy is complex and not at all automatic. In many cases the foreign influences combine with domestic factors to speed up the internal dynamic of Soviet arms policies.[36] The very existence of large armed forces, a powerful defence industry and an extensive network of military R and D establishments generates internal pressures for weapons development and production. The interplay of demands and invention gives rise to proposals for new and improved weapons. As a system progresses from conception to development, military and design bureau interests become attached to it, building up pressure for production. If it passes into production – and here a decision by the Party leadership is required for major systems – enterprise managers are likely to favour long production runs.

Dieter Senghaas has pointed to two principles which are important in understanding military-industrial complexes and which can be applied in the Soviet case.[37] The first of these is the principle of 'configurative causality', which states that the overall configuration of the complex can be seen to give rise to pressures for arms production, even though these pressures may vary from case to case and cannot be identified in every specific instance. The second principle is that of 'overdetermination' or 'redundant causation'; to remove one cause or set of causes is not to eliminate the policies themselves, since other causes remain sufficient. This principle lies behind the argument that it is not enough to tackle the international causes of the East-West arms competition; the domestic roots too must be eradicated. These principles are both helpful in understanding Soviet arms policies. Although much of Soviet military policy-making is shrouded in secrecy, enough is known about the structures of the military-industrial-scientific complex to suggest that internal pressures are generated and considerable inertia built up in the military effort. It seems clear too that the removal of external stimuli, while it might alter Soviet arms policies in some important respects (for example, make it less technologically innovative), would not eliminate its driving-force entirely, because much of that force is derived from domestic sources. (Nor could one say that military power would wither away because it had no role: it has been noted already that as Soviet military power has expanded it has acquired new roles.) The question then is: how are these domestic sources to be weakened?

Conclusion

This essay has tried to outline in general terms the domestic sources of the Soviet military effort. It has suggested that these sources are deeply embedded in Russian and Soviet history. Disarmament and demilitarization would involve therefore more than the surgical removal of some element of the Soviet state; it would have far-reaching effects throughout the whole society. Indeed, complete disarmament and demilitarization could come about only with the destruction of the international state system (and would not necessarily happen then). And although the 'withering away of the state' is one of the anticipated consequences of communist construction, the Soviet Union has one of the most powerful and extensive state apparatuses in the world. Yet, although the sources of Soviet militarism are strong, this essay has tried not to present them as absolute, or to suggest that there is no scope for initiatives for demilitarization. There are some developments in the Soviet Union today which suggest that a change of direction is possible. It would be a serious error to overestimate their importance or the degree to which they can be influenced from outside the Soviet Union. But it would be an even greater mistake to suppose that no change is possible or that its direction could not be influenced from afar.

Soviet military policy contains several contradictions which may, with time, become more apparent and exert an influence on Soviet politics. Having attained equality of superpower status with the United States, the Soviet Union is now faced with a new set of questions about military power and the direction of its policy. The Soviet leaders have said that they are not striving for superiority, but they have made it clear that they will not fall behind the United States in military power. The Soviet Union has thus locked itself into a relationship of parity with the United States. At one level the maintenance of parity – along with the arms control negotiations which it underpins – provides the justification for Soviet military policy. At another level, however, the attainment of parity has meant that the Soviet Union has come to share full responsibility for the continuing arms competition. This has had a subtle, yet profound effect on the attitude of many people in the West to Soviet military policy. Many of those sympathetic to Soviet policy deemed it legitimate for the leading socialist state to catch up with the leading capitalist power; but sharing responsibility for the arms race is not regarded so favourably, especially in view of the danger of nuclear war. In a similar way, the continuation of a high level of military effort, even after parity has been attained, may help to breed opposition inside the Soviet Union to the amassing of more military power. It is possible, for example, that Soviet militarism may emerge as a more important focus for dissident criticism, though the strength of nationalist sentiment (including dissident Russian nationalism) and the deep roots of legitimation should not be forgotten.

The Soviet Union shares with the United States the contradiction that growing military power does not bring greater security, even for superpowers. The accumulation of military power may only spur other governments to increase their own forces, thus nullifying the original gain. It is true that military power can further foreign policy, but it cannot ensure complete security in the nuclear age. The 'Soviet military build-up' of the 1960s and 1970s has brought the Soviet Union political gains, but it has also helped to stimulate countervailing actions, and it is highly doubtful whether, in the last analysis, Soviet security is more assured now than it was fifteen years ago. Moreover, the extension of Soviet military power throughout the world increases the risk that the Soviet Union will become embroiled in a military adventure which will arouse opposition at home, just as the American war in Vietnam did, or the Russo-Japanese war of 1904–5. The failure of military power to ensure security should, in principle, provide the opportunity of pressing the importance of pursuing non-military cooperative arrangements for security rather than seeking to provide one's own security at the expense of others'.

These contradictions would be of little importance if there were no possibility of giving them political significance. The last fifteen years have been a period of consolidation and conservative reform in the Soviet Union. But beneath the stable surface changes have been taking place which could result in major shifts of direction in Soviet policy. The rate of economic growth has been declining, thus increasing the prospect that pressure for far-reaching reform will re-emerge. Agricultural performance has improved greatly, but at a very high cost, again raising the prospect of reform. Other pressures exist for changing the priorities of resource allocation – for example, in order to speed up development of Siberia or to raise living standards. The cumulative effect of such pressures might be to weaken the position of the defence sector or to involve it more deeply in non-military functions. But it is not only the economic system that has been the focus of debate; discussion has also been taking place about the Soviet Union's proper relationship to the rest of the world. Some have pressed for as great a degree of autarky and isolation as possible; others have argued for a more outward-looking approach which would recognize that the world faces many problems which can be solved only by common and concerted action.[38] With the impending change of leadership these various factors may combine to create a turning-point in Soviet politics. The present leadership, as has been seen, has given immense importance to military power. It is as yet unclear how the next generation, which will not have been marked so deeply by the war, will view military power.

In pointing to these developments one should not forget the militarizing pressures that were analysed earlier in this paper. Nor should one suppose that a change of course undertaken by a Soviet leadership would amount to radical disarmament or demilitarization. But the possibility for some change does exist and it should be the aim of the peace movement to try to influence that change in the desired direction. There are considerable difficulties in seeking to influence Soviet policy from the outside, for the political system is very impermeable, both in physical and cultural terms: it is hard to gain access to the policy-making process, and foreign attempts to influence policy will automatically be viewed with suspicion.

There are, nevertheless, two courses to be pursued. The first of these is directed at Western governments and should aim at ensuring that they do not foreclose, through their own policies, the possibility of Soviet moves towards disarmament and demilitarization. This course is a natural concomitant of efforts to press Western governments in that direction too. But some attempt is needed to take the Soviet dimension consciously into account, and this means that the causes of Soviet militarism, and the ways in which pressure on Western governments can also serve to influence the Soviet Union, need to be analysed. Such influence need not necessarily be directed solely at disarmament, but could try to draw the Soviet Union into cooperative efforts to solve such problems as the world food supply. This might make it easier subsequently to work out cooperative, non-military security arrangements.

The second course is directed at the Soviet Union and should try to engage people there in a dialogue about the problems of disarmament and demilitarization. Such a dialogue should be as extensive as possible, and should not be confined to officials and representatives of officially approved bodies on the one hand, or to dissidents (whether in the Soviet Union or abroad) on the other. The variety of political views and currents in the Soviet Union is very wide, and dissident and official views overlap and shade into each other; there are, for example, strong nationalist tendencies in both official and dissident thinking, and dissident reformist views find an echo in official circles as well.[39]

The importance of this course is that vigorous debates about Russia's destiny and the proper path of Soviet development are taking place inside the Soviet Union and among Soviet émigrés; in Eastern Europe too there is such argument about the future of state socialism. But the issues of disarmament and demilitarization – which are important for everyone's future – scarcely figure at all in these discussions, even though militarism and the lack of democracy are linked in the Soviet case. If these issues could be injected into the discussions, they would then be subject to a great deal of creative political thinking – and thinking, moreover, that is more attuned to the specific problems and conditions of the Soviet Union. Besides, it has been seen that the military burden in the Soviet Union is very heavy, but that its legitimation is also strong. Debate and discussion about the problems of Soviet militarism might help to weaken that legitimation.

It should not be supposed that everyone will welcome such discussion, and the attempt to generate it may well be regarded as unwarranted interference in the internal affairs of the Soviet Union. But in the nuclear age we are all affected by the military policies of the superpowers, and hence we surely have the right to try to influence them.

Notes

1. The figures available on arms production and force levels give only the roughest indication of Soviet military production. They show no very sharp fluctuations since

1950, but they are too crude to register any but the most massive changes. The late 1950s and early 1960s appear to be the period of lowest effort. Western estimates of Soviet defence spending as a proportion of GNP seem to fit this pattern, with the Khrushchev years as the period when the proportion was lowest. Most estimates, derived by whatever means, fall into the range of 8 to 14 per cent, with the lower estimates for the late 1950s and early 1960s. See, for example, the following: A. S. Becker, *Soviet National Income 1958–64* (Berkeley and Los Angeles, 1969), Chapter 7; F. D. Holzman, *Financial Checks on Soviet Defense Expenditures* (Lexington, Mass., Toronto and London, 1975); H. Block, in Joint Economic Committee, US Congress, *Soviet Economic Prospects for the Seventies* (Washington, DC, 1973), pp. 175–204; W. T. Lee, *The Estimation of Soviet Defense Expenditures 1955–75* (New York, 1977).

2. *The Military Balance* (IISS, London) each year gives a figure for the manpower in the Soviet Armed Forces. In 1979 that figure is 3·6 million (*The Military Balance 1979–1980*, p. 9). This does not include approximately 400,000 KGB and MVD troops. On top of these figures there are the 400,000 troops who engage in construction, railroad, farm and medical work. See M. Feshbach and S. Rapawy, in Joint Economic Committee, US Congress, *Soviet Economy in a New Perspective* (Washington, DC, 1976), pp. 144–52.

3. Defence Minister Ustinov has declared that 'service in the Soviet armed forces is a wonderful school of labour and martial training, of moral purity and courage, of patriotism and comradeship' (*Pravda*, 8 November 1979, p. 2). See T. Rakowska-Harmstone, 'The Soviet Army as the Instrument of National Integration', in John Erickson and E. J. Feuchtwanger (eds.), *Soviet Military Power and Performance* (London, 1979), pp. 129–54.

4. See, for example, *Markizm-Leninizm o voine i armii* (Moscow, 1968), Chapter 5.

5. See, in particular, Dieter Senghaas, *Rüstung und Militarismus* (Frankfurt am Main, 1972).

6. J. Gould, W. L. Kolb (eds.), *A Dictionary of the Social Sciences* (London, 1964), pp. 429–30.

7. William E. Odom, 'The "Militarization" of Soviet Society', *Problems of Communism*, 1976, No. 5, pp. 34–51.

8. Loc. cit., p. 51.

9. E. P. Thompson, 'Detente and Dissent', in Ken Coates (ed.), *Detente and Socialist Democracy* (Nottingham, 1975), pp. 123–5.

10. On these early debates see John Erickson, *The Soviet High Command 1918–1941* (London, 1962), pp. 113–213; I. V. Berkhin, *Voennaya reforma v SSSR (1924–25 gg)* (Moscow, 1958).

11. E. H. Carr, *Socialism in One Country, 1924–1926*, Vol. 2 (Harmondsworth, 1970), p. 59.

12. J. V. Stalin, *Problems of Leninism* (Moscow, 1947), p. 356.

13. This is not to deny that there was opposition to the Soviet state during the war; but the memory of the war is very potent. See, for example, Chapter 12 of Hedrick Smith, *The Russians* (London, 1976).

14. On this period of Khrushchev's rule see especially Michel Tatu, *Power in the Kremlin* (London, 1969).

15. It is also possible to trace the 'Soviet military build-up' to the Central Committee resolution 'On the Defence of the Country' in 1929. But the present phase has its roots in the 'revolution in military affairs' which was the subject of much discussion in the early 1960s.

16. For a discussion of the organization and functioning of the defence sector see my 'Soviet Military R & D: Managing the Research-Production Cycle', in J. Thomas and U. Kruse-Vancienne (eds.), *Soviet Science and Technology*, published by the George Washington University for the National Science Foundation (Washington, DC, 1977), pp. 179–229; for a more detailed discussion see my two chapters in R. Amann and J. Cooper (eds.), *Innovation in Soviet Industry* (forthcoming).

17. See my paper 'The Soviet Style of Military R & D'

in F. A. Long and J. Reppy (eds.), *The Genesis of New Weapons. Decision-Making for Military R & D* (forthcoming).

18. *Markizm-Leninizm o voine i armii* (Moscow, 1968), pp. 258–9.

19. *Pravda*, 26 April 1963; Tatu, op. cit., pp. 343–4.

20. *Materialy XXIV s"yezda KPSS* (Moscow, 1971), p. 46.

21. See especially Julian Cooper, *Innovation for Innovation in Soviet Industry*, Centre for Russian and East European Studies, University of Birmingham, Discussion Paper, Series RCB/11, 1979, pp. 87–92.

22. A. Levikov, ' "A"; "B" ', in *Literaturnaya Gazeta*, 15 November 1972, p. 11.

23. *Literaturnaya Gazeta*, 7 February 1973, p. 10.

24. See, for example, S. Tynshkevich, 'Sootnoshenie sil v mire i faktory predotvrashcheniya voiny', *Kommunist vooruzhennykh sil*, 1974, No. 10, p. 16; N. A. Kosolapov, 'Sotsialno-psikhologicheskie aspekty razryadki', *Voprosy filosofii*, 1974, No. 4, pp. 36–7; V. M. Kulish (ed.), *Voennaya sila i mezhdunarodnye otnosheniya* (Moscow, 1972), Chapter 1.

25. See *World Armaments and Disarmament. SIPRI Yearbook 1979* (London), pp. 172–3; G. Ofer, 'Soviet Military Aid to the Middle East', Joint Economic Committee, US Congress, *Soviet Economy in a New Perspective* (Washington, DC, 1976), pp. 216–39.

26. See the article on civil defence in *Sovetskaya Voennaya Entsiklopedia*, Vol. 3 (Moscow, 1977), pp. 23–5.

27. CIA: *Soviet Civil Defense*, NI 78–10003, Washington, DC, July 1978, p. 2.

28. See Odom, loc. cit., pp. 44–7; *Sovetskaya Voennaya Entsiklopedia*, Vol. 3 (Moscow, 1977), pp. 255–7.

29. *Sovetskaya Voennaya Entsiklopedia*, Vol. 2 (Moscow, 1976), p. 245.

30. This has been a very widespread view, advanced most thoroughly in R. Kolkowicz, *The Soviet Military and the Communist Party* (Princeton, 1967).

31. T. Colton, *Commanders, Commisars and Civilian Authority* (Cambridge, Mass., 1979) argues that the Main Political

Administration in effect identifies with the military. See also R. Fritsch-Bournazel, 'Les Forces Armées et la "société socialiste avancée" ', *Pouvoirs*, 1978, No. 6, pp. 55–64.

32. 'The Soviet System: Petrification or Pluralism', in J. Hough, *The Soviet Union and Social Science Theory* (Cambridge, Mass., 1977), pp. 19–48.

33. For a discussion of marginal shifts of resources see J. Hardt, 'Military-Economic Implications of Soviet Regional Policy', prepared for Colloquium at NATO Economic Directorate, Brussels, April 1979.

34. R. Garaudy, *The Turning-Point of Socialism* (London, 1970), p. 138.

35. A very clear example is Soviet atomic bomb development. See my *Entering the Nuclear Arms Race: The Soviet Decision to Build the Atomic Bomb*, Working Paper No. 9, International Security Studies Program, Wilson Center, Washington, DC, 1979.

36. See my 'Research Note: Soviet Thermonuclear Research', *International Security*, Winter 1979/80.

37. Senghaas, op. cit., pp. 361–4.

38. For a discussion of the different trends see W. Clemens, Jr, *The USSR and Global Interdependence* (Washington, DC, 1978).

39. See, for example, the discussion in R. Medvedev, *On Socialist Democracy* (London, 1975), Chapters 3 and 4.

CHAPTER SIX

Emma Rothschild
The American Arms Boom*

The United States may buy itself two things with its $1 trillion defence budget of 1981 to 1985. The first is an economic decline of the sort that comes about once or twice in a century. The second is a nuclear war.

This country is in the early years – not, despite the new shine of the Carter Doctrine, at the very beginning – of the most expensive military boom in history. In the process, the distinction between the military and the non-military modes of the American economy is being suppressed. So is the distinction between nuclear and non-nuclear war. The continuum of money and destruction is being projected, through investment in military research and development, into the far future.

The expansion in military science and technology is the most ominous component of a defence budget that is dense with the ghosts of past and future wars.[1] The new defence boom has been welcomed – in the US Congress, for example – as a response to recent events in South-West Asia and elsewhere. But its main focus, instead, is on nuclear conflict.

The greatest increase in any major category within the 1981 budget is for 'research, development, test and evaluation', or 'RDTE'. Spending on strategic and other nuclear weapons increases particularly fast, as does futuristic research at the 'leading edge' of military technology. With the money it spends to buy and keep scientists and engineers,

* *Editors' note*: this essay was first published in *The New York Review of Books* under the title 'Boom and Bust'. It is reproduced here by permission of *The New York Review of Books*.

the Defense Department is designing the weapon of ten and twenty years from now. With its research boom, it is defining a revised American doctrine of science-intensive war.

This effort is not new, and it is scheduled to persist for the balance of the five-year defence plan. The proportion of defence spending devoted to research and the procurement of new weapons has increased steadily since 1976. This constitutes, as the Report shows, the first sustained boom in US military investment – investment in South-East Asia aside – since 1960–63.

The RDTE budget for 1981 is \$16·5 billion. The MX missile – the race track of Ozymandias – is its most expensive item. The MX is allocated \$1·5 billion in research money: this is more than the combined RD budgets for the United States Department of Labor, the Department of Education, the Department of Transportation, the Environmental Protection Agency, the Federal Drug Administration, and the Center for Disease Control; over 140 per cent of the RD budget of the National Science Foundation.[2]

This allocation for the MX is only part of a build-up in research on nuclear, anti-nuclear, and post-nuclear weapons systems. The 'science and technology' programme ('advanced research', 'technology opportunities', and so forth) receives special commendation from Defense Secretary Brown, who presided as Director of Defense Research and Engineering in 1961–5 over the first great boom in strategic research, and is now concerned to 'overcome the effects of reduced funding during the 1965–75 period.' It is as though the years of obscurity, of the bargain-basement, low-technology Vietnam war were over; as though military scientists can now step out into the clear light of particle beams, space optics, and blue-green lasers.

The military doctrine that Brown outlines is suited to the epoch of innovative war. He returns again and again to concepts of flexibility, precision, 'selective and measured' attack and calibrated retaliation. Even the hopes and dreams of Russian leaders are measured; to the calibration of retaliation is added a calculus of values, in which the utility of certain 'political control targets' exceeds that of, let us say, the entire city of Gorky, with missile sightings adjusted accordingly. Is there to be a further role for social scientists and moral philosophers in the teams of savants who are nourished by Sea Launched Ballistic Missiles?

The notion of 'flexibility' is a leading piety of American strategic doctrine. Nor is there anything new about the idea of a 'continuum' of nuclear weapons. But it is elevated by Brown into the writing on the wall of future destruction, from bazookas to particle weapons. 'A continuum of deterrence', an 'unbroken continuum' from 'conventional to intercontinental forces': the word occurs five times in a brief discussion of so-called 'theatre' nuclear weapons, for use within one region such as Europe. At one extreme is the American first strike. 'Even supposing a US first strike', Brown muses at one point in the report, the Russians would have many surviving weapons.

This exercise in the use of the conditional is not likely to reassure those, such as the authors of the most recent S I P R I *World Armaments and Disarmament Yearbook*, who see in the M X missile system and in the latest anti-submarine technologies a refinement of the US ability to strike first at its enemies.[3] Next in the continuum come the varieties of intercontinental retaliation dictated by the doctrine of 'countervailing' force. Here again the emphasis is on precision, on choosing frequently among military and political targets, on 'retaining an assured destruction capability' for the weeks of burning cities, social destruction, and ionizing radiation which would follow a limited 'exchange'.[4]

From here to the long-range 'theatre' nuclear weapons – such as the Pershing II and cruise missiles which will be able to strike from Western Europe into the Soviet Union – is a mere nudge along Brown's continuum. Thence to the array of 'battlefield' and other nuclear warheads, of which the United States maintains some 7,000 in Europe alone, and 'many thousands more' elsewhere. 'Conventional' weapons, too, are to be found in the rainbow of modern war, often, indeed, launched from 'dual purpose' nuclear or non-nuclear artillery, missiles, planes and ships. At the end of the continuum, chemical weapons, of which the 'deterrent stockpile' is to be maintained in 1981, which feature ('lethal chemical munitions concepts') in the Army's 1981 research budget, and for which 'a facility that will have the capability to build binary chemical bombs, warheads and projectiles is being designed.'

What is most remarkable about the doctrine of the continuum from non-nuclear to nuclear conflict is the cool and precise rhetoric in which it is described. Brown notes that 'we have no more illusions than our predecessors that a nuclear war could be closely and surgically controlled.' But the Report returns obsessively to the promise of such illusions: to 'increased NATO options for restrained and controlled nuclear responses', to the 'effectiveness and versatility' of nuclear-armed destroyers in the Indian Ocean.

This is the banalization of the nuclear epoch. We no longer find the pious disclaimers, the epithets ('of course, terrible') which earlier Defense Secretaries once appended to the words describing nuclear war. Nor are there frequent references to 'the limited utility of nuclear weapons' (Donald Rumsfeld in the last Republican Defense Budget). The phrase 'total war' is used casually in a discussion of defence spending. The unthinkable is being thought, ignored, presumed upon.

The Report puts forward three sorts of arguments in favour of increased defence spending. The first, and most familiar, suggests that because the Soviet Union is spending much more than the United States on its military effort, the United States must now rearm. The Report is full of speculation on Russian intentions: the fact that their forces in Eastern Europe are 'much too offensively oriented', and that their positions in the Far East are 'apparently designed for offensive operations'; their curious propensity to 'take more seriously than we have done, at least in our public discourse, the possibility that a nuclear war might actually be fought.' But the argument relies in general upon the simple reiteration of relative expenditures.

The shortcomings of such comparisons are well-known, as the Report itself comes close to acknowledging. They are selective, in that they sometimes measure the Soviet Union against the United States and sometimes NATO against the Warsaw Treaty Organization. They pass lightly over the proportion of Russian military efforts which is directed not against NATO but against China. They move even more expeditiously past the sharp qualitative advantages enjoyed by the US, such as the 'rather startling asymmetries' which SIPRI detects in US and Russian strategic sub-marines.[5]

The comparisons of dollar costs are even more misleading. They are measured, the Report explains, 'by what it would cost to buy Soviet programs (including personnel) in the US economy'. Estimates are thus arrived at for such quantities as 'Soviet resources devoted to RDT & E'. One has only to imagine the reverse exercise to see the tenuousness of such calculations. A Russian 'estimate' of American military research would start, to be sure, with the published budget figure of $16·5 billion. To this it would add the $1·3 billion which the Department of Energy will spend on nuclear weapons and other defence research, and a sizeable part of NASA's $5·6 billion RD budget. The Russian economists next need to calculate what portion of RD spending by American business supports the military effort, notably in two industries, aircraft and communications equipment, which are called by the government 'defense product industries'.

At this point, they might decide what it would cost 'to buy' this science and technology in the Soviet Union – to reproduce the utility of Hewlett-Packard's basic research, or of such military contractors as Penn State University.[6] Do they multiply by two? Or three? Or is Penn State unreproducible? All that remains for our diligent academicians is to head, charts in hand, for the Armed Services Committees of Mr Smirnov and Mr Ustinov and the other titans of the Soviet Union's military-industrial complex.[7]

This exercise is not frivolous. Some such sequence may indeed have helped to determine the present arms race. We can assume that the Soviet Union reacted to the American military build-up of the late 1960s – an effort directed in large part at South-East Asia – by investing in military research. The weapons that the Russians are building now are the products of that research. The Americans in turn react by increasing their own research, which will produce the arms race of the early 1990s; such are the dynamics of comparative weaponry.

The second argument in favour of the military boom suggests that the 'growth in international turbulence' in Afghanistan, Africa, the Caribbean, Thailand, and elsewhere makes such an effort essential. One may question whether the times are, indeed, notably turbulent. There are relatively few wars under way, and revolution is distinctly on the retreat. It is even more questionable whether acquiring the capacity to construct particle beam weapons in the 1990s is likely to reduce turbulence in the third world in 1980. One of the major new projects, the CX airlift plane, is recommended for 'contingencies outside of Europe', yet it is some years from being deployed. The strategy of knowledge-intensive war suggests that the United States will look for precision and measured responses in its worldwide military efforts: in other words, the use of tactical nuclear weapons. Is this what the Carter Doctrine requires? Is this what Congress is buying with its bucks?

Brown's report, meanwhile, demonstrates a far more muscular attitude to US military intervention outside Europe than has been seen for some years. 'Our defense establishment could be faced with an almost unprecedented number of demands', Brown writes. We are not far from Henry Kissinger's recent thoughts, when after considering whether US troops would be welcome in Oman he said:

The immediate crisis shouldn't deflect us from other areas of potential danger. The situation in Turkey requires our urgent attention. Thailand could be a dangerous situation. Morocco remains under attack from adversaries armed with Soviet weapons. Central America is in turmoil. We may yet be needed in Southern Africa.[8]

The third argument is the murkiest. It suggests that 'perceptual problems' are critical, that the United States must increase its military spending lest it 'lose, not from war, but from changes in perceptions about the balance of nuclear power'. Even those who accept this argument – I do not – should ask themselves whether the United States is buying the right power and the right perceptions with its new defence dollars. Must it sell the far future with blue-green lasers? Is the Brown Doctrine of science-intensive war the best standard under which to fight the battle of perceptions? It should be added that the Report's calculus of 'perceptual' costs and benefits is bizarre. Thus we learn that 'the aura of great US military power' is 'a legacy of World War II, Korea, the Cuban missile crisis, and even (up to a point) Southeast Asia . . .', that 'the mining of Haiphong Harbor demonstrated the deterrent effect of mines . . .'

The Brown position is based on a view of the American economy and American society as organized around knowledge and science. The Report contrasts the 'manpower-intensive Soviet economy' with the 'more capital-intensive and technologically advanced American economy'. The obvious strategy, thus, is to lead from strength or from comparative advantage; to prepare to fight an automated and innovative war. This choice has the further advantage of appealing to the apparent preferences of the Congress for hardware and for clean wars.[9] Yet even on these terms, the strategy is perilous. The Report is full of allusions to 'problems with materiel readiness, in part because of the advanced equipment coming into the forces'. We learn, in passing, of production problems in constructing nuclear attack submarines, of 'shore processing software, computer loading and array reliability problems' with Navy sensor systems; that the Air Force finds it difficult to maintain 'their increasingly complex equipment', given 'maintenance backlogs' and 'increases in our accident rates'; that the Army's 'telephone switches in Europe are obsolete, require continuous costly maintenance, and often break down', and will be replaced by German digital switches.

We are not far from the more familiar problems of the civilian economy: from subway systems whose sensors break down, and hospitals in which electronic hardware surpasses medical software, from the maintenance problems of DC 10s (the Federal Aviation Administration's budget for civilian RD is less than that allocated to one Navy aircraft). The military has conventionally assumed that because it can afford the most elaborately redundant controls, and because its operations are isolated from the messiness of real-life clinics and sewage tunnels, it is thereby free from such tribulations. Even this may no longer be the case.

There is a related and deeper contradiction in the notion of knowledge-intensive war. The United States is practising a variety of 'la guerre savante', the stylized struggled which has dominated European wars since the sixteenth century. But as Fernand Braudel shows in his Les Temps du Monde, such struggle is only possible when it is practised by both sides at once; the veterans of Flanders campaigns who brought their learned battle formations to Oran in the 1590s and to Brazil in the 1630s found opponents who were playing in a different game.[10] The United States cannot expect that the Soviet Union will continue to join in its high science game, as this game becomes ever more idiosyncratic and ever more indulgent. The American military is choosing those weapons systems which are, in Robert Oppenheimer's phrase, 'technically sweet'. But this sweetness seems increasingly determined by the most introspective of scientific cultures. Are the random dashes and dummy missiles of the MX 'sweet' to Russian probability theorists and computer scientists? The arms race implicit in the new military boom requires the most precise coordination of national scientific emotions, as the United States and the Soviet Union move together toward the MX, to 'invulnerable' missiles for the Russians, pressure on SALT, new missile defences, pressure on the ABM Treaty, laser weapons, even more pressure to abrogate the ABM Treaty, warfare in space.

The epigraph to Brown's Report is a remark made by Abraham Lincoln, in 1861: 'I think the necessity of being *ready* increases – look to it.' That America's leaders should choose, now, to evoke the last war fought in this country is itself awesome. The insignia to the Defense Budget should be not what Lincoln said on the eve of the Civil War, but rather what he said at its end: 'It is sure that I have not controlled events, events have controlled me.'[11]

The last, striking contradiction of the doctrine has to do with its economic costs. These, too, are determined by the technology-intensive character of the projected boom. Yet they have been to an extraordinary extent forgotten in discussions of the Defense Budget. Just as it is assumed that investment in lasers will somehow encourage the loyal Pathans, that the incantation of numbers (4 per cent real growth in defence spending) is itself useful, so too are the economic consequences of the boom ignored.

The Budget was greeted with enthusiasm: 'Defense Stocks Lead Market Up', and a survey of business opinion in the *Wall Street Journal* to the effect that 'we're in a war economy'. There seemed nothing, as in 1950 and 1966, that could so fortify business confidence as a vigorous defence effort. The recession of 1980, it seemed, was 'postponed'. Yet this optimism is founded on a profound misunderstanding of the changes that have taken place in the American economy since 1970, and thus of the likely benefits of the defence boom.

Even the most rosy expectation does not deny that military spending will stimulate inflation. Previous arms booms began in years of moderate price increases (consumer prices increased 1 per cent in 1950 and 2·9 per cent in 1966); United States inflation early in 1980 reached an annual rate of 16 per cent. This tendency is likely to be exacerbated because many engineers, skilled workers, and high-technology components are in short supply; the chairman of General Dynamics (the contractor for the Navy's troublesome attack submarines) looks forward to 'some type of priority system' favouring defence contractors.[12]

It is much less likely that the boom will provide extensive new employment for American workers. In the first place, the character of defence spending is, following Brown's dictum and the exigencies of the times, increasingly capital-intensive. If a billion dollars in the 1960s could procure a sizeable arsenal of General Motors rifles for Vietnam, it will not now pay General Dynamics for a single Trident submarine. Secondly, by cutting into other government programmes, military spending may jeopardize the most precarious of existing jobs.

One mysterious aspect of the economic crisis of the 1970s in the United States is the extent to which employment has continued to increase. This is in part because manufacturing industry there – far more than in France or West Germany – has maintained jobs. But it is also because employment in social and public services, particularly health services, has multiplied. Thus of the 9 million jobs created in the US economy from 1973 to 1978, one half were in services and state and local government (a further quarter were in retail trade). These jobs, often temporary or part-time, are peculiarly at risk in a recession; it is worth recalling that the last great surge in service employment in the United States was in the late 1920s, and was brought to an end by the

Depression.[13] Will the overpaid aeronautical engineers of 1981 spend their disposable income on nursing home services? Or will the Carter administration, cutting government civilian programmes to limit inflation and balance the budget, begin a new crisis of lay-offs in social services?

There is one problem of the US economy which the military boom may be expected to alleviate. This is the decline in rates of growth of labour productivity in the 1970s, with an actual reduction in 1974 and 1979. It seems likely that shifts in the economy away from the production of goods for military consumption and toward the production of social services have reduced growth in productivity. Many industries that are dependent on defence enjoy high levels and high rates of growth of productivity. They buy components, intermediate inputs, from other equally vigorous sectors. The service industries, by contrast, tend to buy paper, construction, other services.[14] Yet even here the stimulus of procurement may be limited. Perhaps modern defence contractors behave, economically speaking, like business services or technology consultants.

US military expenditures started to increase in the mid-1970s. Military contracts for goods and services – what the Defense Department comptroller calls 'procurement', which includes spending for maintenance goods and for foreign military sales – increased from $45·8 billion in 1976 to $55·6 billion in 1977 and $69·0 billion in 1979.[15] Yet this boomlet has done little for productivity growth. The Soviet economy, of course, is a poor example of the economic benefits of militarization. The Defense Department Report is generous with its estimates of Soviet economic growth in the 1980s. How can an elemental enemy be at the same time a pitiful and impoverished giant? Recent figures show, however, that the Soviet economy grew in 1979 at 2 per cent as against a planned 4·3 per cent, and industrial productivity 2·4 per cent against 4·7 per cent, with productivity in agriculture and transport falling.[16]

*

What, in these circumstances, are we to make of the military-induced boom in 'business confidence'? It is perhaps the most ominous of the ghoulish economic indications of the past several weeks, not only for what it reveals about the perversity of capitalist economies. Business optimism, now, is evidence of a keening desire by American industry to return to the old economic and technological patterns of the 1940s, 1950s, and 1960s. The economic changes of the period since 1970 have amounted to a vast, if unintended and perhaps unwanted, transformation of the American economy toward the provision of social security. There has even, within this metamorphosis, been some conversion of scientific and technical efforts toward secular society; some social innovation. Now, every instinct of the American political economy seems to be crying retreat, to be crying war.

If one considers the history of the American economy in the twentieth century, it seems possible that military industries have functioned as a 'leading sector' – in the economist Joseph Schumpeter's sense of a dominant industry – during the long expansion of the 1940s to the 1970s. One does not have to believe in specific explanations of economic cycles such as Kondratieff's to see that modern economic growth is characterized by long periods of expansion, more or less associated with a given 'locus' of innovation. Such periods include, for the world economy, 1848 to 1873 and 1895 to 1920, as well as the post-World War II boom that ended in the early 1970s.[17]

There has been no undisputed leader during the US expansion of the postwar years. Instead, some theorists of economic cycles point to an assortment of leading industries, including electronics, consumer electrical goods, and air travel. What seems possible is that the military industries themselves have constituted such a focus. They do not function as a single or multiple industrial sector, as did the railroads and the automobile and electricity businesses in earlier booms, but rather as a cluster of industries joined by a common objective and a common customer. Their role in the war-time and postwar American expansion would certainly fit Schumpeter's criterion for the longest waves of the economic cycles as 'breaking up old and creating new positions of power, civilizations, valuations, beliefs and policies'; as well as creating new ways of organizing scientific research and innovation.[18]

If this speculation is plausible, what we should have seen in the 1970s was the elaboration and decline of military innovation in the United States. This obsolescence is what Mary Kaldor calls 'baroque technology'.[19] Is it to be glimpsed within the optimism of Harold Brown's knowledge-intensive budget? Will the $200 million to be spent on Very High Speed Integrated Circuits produce some pale imitation of the past triumphs of military electronics and its civilian spin-off? Is the MX the residual monstrosity of the long expansion led by the military, and does it portend the decline not of the auto-industrial but of the military-industrial age, the Edsel and the Vega writ as large as the deserts of Utah?

The defence boom and the business confidence it inspires are from this perspective deeply disturbing. They suggest an instinctive return to the industrial and scientific culture of an obsolete expansion, the power of what Veblen, writing of the British railroad industry in the 1890s, called 'the inertia of use and wont'.[20] Such a reversion can only make the long cyclical decline of military industries more painful and more dangerous.

The United States in 1970 – after the first decline in military spending for Vietnam – consecrated a fifth of its engineers, a fourth of its physicists, a fifth of its mathematicians, almost half of its aeronautical engineers to defence-related employment.[21] Estimates in the Rumsfeld defence budget suggest that the proportion did not fall during the Republican defence recession, and may have increased since.[22] At the trough of the recession in military research, the United States devoted 28 per cent of its national research and development effort to defence, as compared to 7 per cent in West Germany, 19 per cent in France, and 4 per cent in Japan.[23] An economy in the throes of decline cannot afford to lose this portion of its knowledge, of its education system, of its future to old industries, and to destruction.

There is now, as not often in the world since Nagasaki, the intuitive possibility of nuclear war. There is also the possibility of a remilitarized world economy which will make this prospect more imminent, year after year, as the research boom becomes a boom in procurement, in strategic doctrine and in military culture. Very little is more important, as we enter the 1980s, than to act against the one and against the other.

Notes

1. *Department of Defense Annual Report*, Fiscal Year 1981, Harold Brown, Secretary of Defense, Department of Defense, 29 January 1980.
2. *Special Analyses, Budget of the United States Government*, Fiscal Year 1981, pp. 303–33.
3. Stockholm International Peace Research Institute (SIPRI), *World Armaments and Disarmament. SIPRI Yearbook 1979* (Taylor & Francis, London), p. 449.
4. Kevin N. Lewis, 'The Prompt and Delayed Effects of Nuclear War', *Scientific American*, July 1979.
5. *SIPRI Yearbook 1979*, p. 417.
6. 'ARL, Penn State University', is listed as one of the contractors of the Navy's 'Advanced ASW (Antisubmarine Warfare) Torpedo', Department of Defense, *Program Acquisition Costs by Weapon Systems*, Fiscal Year 1981.
7. See Mary Kaldor and Alexander Cockburn, 'The Defense Confidence Game', *The New York Review*, 13 June 1974.
8. Interview with Henry Kissinger, *Wall Street Journal*, 21 January 1980.

9. Deborah Shapley, 'Arms Control as a Regulator of Military Technology', *Daedalus*, Winter 1980.

10. Fernand Braudel, *Les Temps du Monde* (*Civilisation matérielle, économie et capitalisme*, Vol. III) (Armand Collin, Paris, 1979), pp. 44–7.

11. Quoted by Hans Morgenthau in D. Carlton and C. Schaerf (eds.), *Arms Control and Technological Innovation* (Croom Helm, London, 1977), p. 262.

12. *Wall Street Journal*, 1 February 1980.

13. Edward Denison, 'Service Industries – Trends and Prospects', *Survey of Current Business*, January 1945.

14. Wassily Leontief and Marvin Hoffenberg, 'The Economic Effects of Disarmament', *Scientific American*, April 1961; 'The Input-Output Structure of the US Economy, 1972', *Survey of Current Business*, February 1979.

15. 'Procurement' in this sense is different from and larger than 'procurement' of weapons in the budget sense. Procurement for foreign military sales accounted for $5·4 billion of the total in 1979.

16. *Le Monde*, 27–8 January 1980.

17. See Eric Hobsbawm, 'The Development of the World Economy', *Cambridge Journal of Economics*, September 1979.

18. Joseph Schumpeter, *Business Cycles*, Vol. II (McGraw-Hill, 1939), p. 696.

19. Mary Kaldor in *Arms Control and Technological Innovation*, p. 331.

20. Thorstein Veblen, *Imperial Germany and the Industrial Revolution* (paperback edition, University of Michigan, 1966).

21. Estimated in Richard Dempsey and Douglas Schmude, 'Occupational Impact of Defense Expenditures', *Monthly Labor Review*, December 1971.

22. Donald Rumsfeld, *Annual Defense Department Report*, Fiscal Year 1979, p. 102. A recent study of American physicists confirms this tendency. E. L. Woollett, 'Physics and modern warfare: The awkward silence', *Am. J. Phys.* 48 (2), February 1980.

23. Figures for 1975 from Bernard Delapalme *et al.*, *Science and Technology in the New Socio-Economic Context* (OECD, Paris, forthcoming, 1980).

CHAPTER SEVEN

Dan Smith and Ron Smith
British Military Expenditure in the 1980s

During their opposition years in the 1970s the Conservatives always made it quite clear that a major priority when they returned to office was to increase British military expenditure. Indeed, in 1975 the call for higher military expenditure was probably the one policy around which the Conservative Party was united. It was during this period that Margaret Thatcher made the hawkishly vitriolic speeches about foreign policy which led *Pravda*, in a typically miscalculated effort at propaganda, to dub her the 'iron lady' – a tag she was proud to sport. Those speeches not only revealed the centrality in Conservative ideology of perceptions of the Soviet threat and of a strong foreign and defence policy, they also served as a rallying cry for party unity and as a convenient stick with which to batter the Labour government about its head.

The same themes were pursued through the 1970s until the Conservatives were elected in 1979, even if they became rather less prominent as the Conservatives found other policies around which to unite. Increased military budgets, improved military salaries and shopping lists of expensive new weapons projects were the Conservative answer to the Soviet threat, the Conservative solution to the damage allegedly done to British defence policy by the Labour government.

There is, however, something of a paradox here. True to its promises, the Conservative government has increased military spending and has announced plans to go on doing so. The 1980–81 budget shows an increase of 3 per cent in real terms (that is, after accounting for inflation) over the previous year; public expenditure plans for the next two years include the same level of increase per year, while the defence White Paper announced the government's intention to repeat the annual 3 per cent increase through to 1986. Yet this level of 3 per cent is no more than the Labour government had agreed to in 1977 as part of an all-round NATO programme, though implementation was delayed until 1979–80, the last defence budget prepared by Labour, when the actual increase was 4½ per cent. In other words, the Tories are doing no more than Labour was doing by the end of its period in office.

But the paradox has further dimensions. By the late 1970s, wages and salaries had become matters of major grievance in the armed forces; morale was badly affected not only by this but also by often inadequate living conditions, and by the limited availability of supplies and spare parts. The problem was that Labour's budgetary trimming exercises left inadequate resources to sustain the military capabilities it was attempting to mount. The result was a major crisis of morale in the services in 1978, characterized by high rates of early departure, low efficiency, and a deluge of leaks to the press about the inadequacies of British military preparations. The Conservatives have committed themselves to preventing this from happening again. A good proportion of the 3 per cent annual increases will be eaten up by that commitment alone. On top of that, the costs of military equipment, especially the major weapon systems, are climbing at giddy speeds, far outpacing inflation in the civil economy. It is likely that annual increases in real military spending of 3 per cent, even if sustained throughout the 1980s, will not be sufficient to maintain the present range of forces deployed by Britain, especially with the concentration of effort on major and prestigious procurement projects like the replacement of Polaris. In other words, even if real expenditure increases by 3 per cent annually during the 1980s, it is likely that forces will have to be reduced – the very thing the Conservatives' ideology commits them against.

One would therefore expect the Conservatives to seek even larger increases, perhaps up to 6 or 7 per cent annually. But a study of possible British military spending in the 1980s within the context of the likely condition of the national economy shows that there must be serious doubts about the government's ability to sustain annual 3 per cent increases, let alone anything more ambitious.

Economic and Social Constraints

By the end of its period in office the 1974–9 Labour government was firmly committed to increasing military expenditure. It has been succeeded by a Conservative administration distinguished by its enthusiasm for high military spending. Thus over the past few years there has developed, despite the acrimonious debates between Labour and Conservative front benches, a relatively stable consensus in Britain's political leadership in favour of increasing the military budget over the levels of the mid-1970s. But the political and ideological preferences of a government, even if supported by such a consensus, are only one factor, albeit an important one, in setting national military spending levels. Particularly if one is thinking about spending patterns over a fairly long period, such as a decade, it is essential also to consider economic constraints upon the size of the budget and their interplay with other social and political factors. These constraints can be grouped under three headings: resources, allocation and stability.

Resource constraints are possible shortages in the actual physical inputs to military programmes, especially weapons procurement projects: personnel with appropriate skills, industrial capacity, materials. Over a long period this form of constraint may not be binding, since, in principle, appropriate planning could make available the necessary materials, personnel and capacity. In the short run, however, considerable problems can be posed, and are at present being posed for the expansion of US military programmes.[1] Moreover, if there is an expansion in the volume of procurement, or a gradual shift of emphasis towards new military technologies, additional capacity must be created. This is a time-consuming and expensive process, and new capacity is unlikely to function with optimal efficiency at the outset, while, once the first projects have been completed, it is necessary either to continue to employ that capacity, creating permanent upward pressure on the military budget, or to cope with massive adjustment problems in diverting that capacity to different work.[2] The creation of new capacity and, indeed, the provision of personnel and materials do not happen in an economic or social vacuum: there are other calls on these resources.

The effect of these other calls on available resources can be described as the allocative constraint, reflecting socioeconomic choice between various goals. Since resources available to a national economy are finite at any given time, these various goals are mutually competitive and, possibly, they are ultimately mutually exclusive. Thus the allocative choices made express the priority given to military expenditure as against other forms of public expenditure, private consumption, investment or net exports. A government may have a firmly held preference for a particular pattern of resource allocation, but in practice it is never entirely free to implement it. It cannot but respond to economic conditions; it cannot but respond to other politically expressed social priorities. Should it fail to respond adequately, there is in the end the possibility that it will be brought down and replaced by a government which at least claims, at least at the outset, to have a different set of allocative preferences.

In practice, choices about allocation are difficult and uncertain and have been made in inconsistent ways, even by the same government, as a result of which short-term stabilization measures have been required. When choices are made in such a way that planned allocations are greater than can be sustained by the realized output of the national economy, the usual response has been to adjust planned expenditure in the light of a fresh assessment of priorities. The adjustment within defence policy has been to drop roles (largely by military withdrawal from Empire), to cancel projects, to keep military wages down, to run down spares, and so on. Thus, if allocation outreaches feasible levels, as a result, for example, of over-ambitious projections of economic performance or insufficient attention to other social priorities, later correction is a painful business for the armed forces. This process of correction can be thought about in terms of the stabilization constraint. In principle, military planning should aim for long-term stability. If it does not, disruptions will ensue. To achieve long-term stability, planned targets should accord with long-run socio-economic priorities and feasible projections of economic output. Thus, if an attempt is made, through incompetence or, more important, through deliberate political choice about competing allocative demands, to challenge long-run socio-economic priorities in military planning, among the possible outcomes is an extremely disruptive encounter with the effects of the stabilization constraint.

Military Spending and Allocative Choice

The government has declared its support for the NATO aim of annual increases in military spending of 3 per cent in real terms through to 1986. We think it is reasonable to assume that the Ministry of Defence's Long Term Costing, covering a ten-year period, includes a working assumption that this trend will be continued to the end of the decade. In fact, since cuts in forces are a likely prospect even with that level of spending increase, the 3 per cent figure may be viewed in many circles as the lower limit of what is necessary.

The most convenient way of expressing the allocative priority given to military expenditure on the basis of this goal is to take military spending as a share of the Gross Domestic Product (GDP). The rate of growth of this share can be derived from three terms: it is the rate of growth of the volume of military expenditure (3 per cent) plus the relative price effect minus the rate of growth of output. The relative price effect expresses the difference between the rate of inflation for military goods and services and the rate for all domestically produced goods and services; it depends on the relation of import prices to domestic prices, relative productivity growth and the relation of military wages to average wages. The relative price effect was low in the late 1970s because of the squeeze on military wages, which the current government is committed to preventing; our calculations therefore assume a slightly higher effect. The assumed rate of growth of output is 1 per cent annually; this is the rate estimated by the government for the period to 1983–4, and at present there is no basis on which to assume it will be higher through the rest of the 1980s.[3]

Having made these assumptions, the calculation and the conclusion are straighforward. On current government plans and using feasible economic projections, the share of GDP in current prices devoted to military expenditure will rise from 4·6 per cent at present to 5·92 per cent in 1985 and 7·21 per cent in 1990. This will take the GDP share back up to the level at which it stood in the mid-1950s and from which it has since more or less consistently declined.

There is no sense in which this can be taken to represent a feasible programme of military expenditure *given long-run socio-economic priorities*. It will have severe economic repercussions, most notably on civil industrial investment and the balance of payments.[4] It will contribute to a harsher economic crisis and it will retard economic recovery. Ironically, it will thereby undermine the foundations on which stable military programmes might be constructed. The strength of competing economic and social forces is likely, by one means or another, to lead to a change of course unless the current government is able to effect decisive change in social expectations and the balance of social forces.

This, then, is the Conservatives' programme for military spending: nearly 6 per cent of GDP going on the military by the mid-1980s, and just over 7 per cent by the end of the decade. But, as we have argued, the government's preference is but one factor affecting the level of military spending. How can we summarize the possible effects of the other factors?

Some guide to the future can be gained by reference to the past, especially by reference to long-run and relatively stable patterns in the past. While we cannot predict how social judgement of competing priorities will be made in the future, we can assess past patterns and see what would happen in the 1980s if those patterns were to hold.

The volume of British military expenditure over the period 1951–75 is well explained by the relationship between real income, the relative price effect and US and Soviet military expenditures, together with a statistical dynamic adjustment process which captures the fluctuations induced by periodic defence reviews and changes of course.[5] The relationship between US and Soviet military expenditures functions in this equation as a proxy for the international strategic environment, perceptions about which shape military policy and budgets in Britain. Our calculation assumes the same growth in output and the same relative price effect as before; we assume that US military expenditure will increase at 3 per cent annually in real terms, in line with the NATO target, and that Soviet military expenditure will continue to grow by 4 per cent annually (or, to be more precise, will be estimated in the West to grow at that rate).[6] Using the equation which fits the period 1951–75, it is then possible to estimate British military expenditure in the 1980s as a consequence of the relationship of these four variables on the assumption that past long-run patterns will hold.

The conclusion is straightforward. Far from there being an annual 3 per cent increase, the volume of military expenditure would decline over the decade by the equivalent of 1·5 per cent annually. In current price terms, the share of GDP devoted to military spending would decline to 4·5 per cent by 1985 and 4·4 per cent by 1990, continuing its slow move towards the NATO average.

The difference between spending 4·4 per cent of GDP on the military in 1990 and spending 7·2 per cent expresses the difference between the reality of the British state and society for the past thirty years and the state and society the Conservative government wants to construct. To fulfil its military spending ambitions, the government will have to push through profound socio-economic and political changes, yet within the 'new' departures the Conservatives seek there are several very familiar, traditional themes. This can be understood by looking, in turn, at the decision to purchase Trident as the successor to the British Polaris nuclear force, and at the effects on the domestic British scene of its military spending plans.

Military Spending and International Prestige

It is well understood that the government wants to increase British military spending; this, it is supposed, will strengthen Britain's international standing and provide more military power against the USSR. But to say this is not enough. The major decision in British military policy currently is the procurement of a new force to replace Britain's four Polaris submarines. The cost of doing this by purchasing Trident missiles from the USA and constructing five submarines to carry them has been estimated at up to £6,500 million.[7] So far, forward spending plans have not included this massive outlay. If spiralling equipment costs and the commitment to preventing another crisis of morale in the forces are going to put pressure on military budgets even if they increase by 3

193

per cent annually in real terms, then deciding to buy Trident will multiply the problems.

Were the procurement of Trident or any other major nuclear force likely to result in a clear strategic advantage for Britain, or even were it likely to provide an important political instrument, the decision would be understandable within the terms of orthodox strategic debate, though it would not be supportable. But the politico-strategic arguments in favour of Polaris and now Trident are vague, confused and contradictory.[8] The most that emerges is a marginal contribution to NATO nuclear forces that already are thoroughly capable of overkill. And this contribution, even if annual increases of 3 per cent in real terms are sustained, will either require the orderly phasing out of other major military forces or result in extraordinary chaos in military policy and industry around the end of the 1980s. Understanding the emphasis placed on the procurement of Trident is not aided by strategic analysis; we must leave that realm, and enter one of a more elusive political symbolism.

The theme embodied in Polaris and Trident has been extremely durable. Neither changes of government nor failures in the late 1950s and early 1960s, first with the British Blue Streak and then with the US Skybolt, have really dented the theme; the most that happened was the reduction of the Polaris force from five to four submarines by the 1964–70 Labour government, after it had been elected on a manifesto which included a pledge to have nothing to do with the force, and at some severe cost to its credibility with Labour supporters. One may add that this theme has also survived the opposition of one of the largest public movements Britain has ever seen, which was, at the time it erupted on to the political scene in the late 1950s, the first sustained mass movement in Britain since the end of World War II. There is, in short, something very special about this theme.

To these considerations it should be added that for most

of the time Britain has had nuclear weapons in other forms: the V-bomber force, of which only Vulcans now remain; Buccaneer strike aircraft, based both on land and, until recently, at sea; Honest John tactical missiles, now replaced by Lance; nuclear depth-charges and nuclear artillery; Tornado aircraft in the near future. Thus, whatever it is about the Blue Streak-Skybolt-Polaris-Trident theme which gives it its durability, it seems reasonable to suggest it derives not just from the nuclear weapon dimension, but from the fact that they are missile forces, and not just missiles but long-range missiles of the kind the USA or the USSR might have.

Polaris provides not just 'a say in the holocaust',[9] but 'a say' as such. It is a sea-based long-range ballistic missile force. It is the kind of thing the USA and the USSR – the superpowers – possess. It provides the British state with a tinge of great power standing, in times when it has had precious few other such tinges. This tinge seems appropriate to a state with Britain's history, itself a former superpower, with the greatest ever formal empire, which could still play a major role in the alliances of World Wars I and II; which became a permanent member of the UN Security Council and, at the formation of NATO, was clearly number two in the alliance, meaning number one in West Europe, and received appointments within the NATO command structure to match; and which long cherished, and still tries to revive from time to time, a 'special relationship' with the USA.

In other words, perceptions that Britain requires a long-range nuclear missile force derive in the last instance not from strategic calculations (although strategic calculations can be adjusted to match) nor even from political calculations (though these can also be adjusted for the sake of compatibility). Rather, they derive from a basic belief that Britain, being *Britain*, with all that means, with all that history, ought naturally to be in on this, the most devastating military instrument. They derive, in other words, from deeply assimilated but thoroughly anachronistic beliefs and pretensions about what Britain is. For these beliefs to be effective, to result in a series of policy decisions over time which lead to Polaris and beyond, there is no need for them to be shared by other states. Arguments which demonstrate the weakness of claims that possessing a force like Polaris provides particular status thus miss the point. What other states believe about Britain is here secondary, almost irrelevent. What matters is what the British state believes about itself. Thus it is equally irrelevant to comment that the way Britain procured Polaris would hardly provide much status in the eyes of others. What matters is that Britain has Polaris, and thus, in its own eyes, it has the requisite tinge of greatness.

Polaris and Trident are therefore concrete indications of the difficulty the British state has found in modernizing itself in the past thirty years, in accustoming itself to a permanently reduced international position. It is a semi-autistic response to international political realities. This difficulty is seen elsewhere in British defence policy, particularly in the continual process of seeking greater military capabilities than the resources can be provided to sustain. Of course, some adjustments have been made; the military withdrawal from Empire is one such, the abandonment of major aircraft-carriers is another, yet this decision itself has been partially negated by the procurement of the Invincible class of anti-submarine warfare cruisers – mini-aircraft-carriers. Some adjustments have been made; some have been made and then qualified; others have not been made. The difficulty of making the adjustments has been great, and the consequence of the inability to scale desired capabilities down to available resources has been a pattern of constant chops and changes.

The difficulty in modernizing, in coming to terms with the second half of the twentieth century, is felt elsewhere in British state policy; its sources lie in the history and structure of the state and in Britain's economic and social relations.

This anachronistic inertia is inherent in the British state as it is now constituted. In some ways, and in some instances, the British state has been able to modernize, but rarely with any ease. And it is perhaps not surprising that it is in the field of defence policy, so closely related to imperial military traditions, that the difficulty has been the greatest. For all the apparent modernity of British armed forces, for all the Ministry of Defence's ability to function in sophisticated, modern (usually Americanesque) levels of discourse, major aspects of British defence policy are totally anachronistic. Polaris and Trident are their highest embodiment.

Neither Polaris nor Trident is really about 'defence' at all. The submarines and missiles are there to sustain the self-image of the British state and ruling circles, an attempt to maintain the appearance of being a major world power long after the fact has ended. The emphasis placed upon the procurement of a replacement for Polaris, despite the damage this will do to the rest of British military preparations, is a very good indicator of the hollowness and self-defeating nature of the Conservative government's international aspirations.

Indeed, it is all too reminiscent of the nineteenth-century British view of the world. Britannia (tries to) rule the waves, when it no longer can. The archaism of this view of Britain's role in the world is interestingly paralleled by the Conservatives' economic policies. We are thinking first and foremost of the ideology of 'laissez-faire' and the rhetoric of reducing the role of the state, but also of the increased emphasis on internationalizing British capital, together with the expansion in the City's business as a result of the strength of the pound sterling in international markets. The removal of controls on currency exchange and the opposition by both the City and the government to controls on the Eurodollar market are a further part of the pattern.

The rule of Britannia and 'laissez-faire', however, make up only a part of the picture of nineteenth-century Britain.

A third aspect can be simply summarized as coercion, writ large.

Social and Political Costs

We have argued that if past social and political patterns hold, the Conservatives will be unable to sustain annual increases in military spending of 3 per cent in real terms. In fact, evidence from analysing those past patterns suggests that military spending will actually decline in the 1980s. Clearly then, despite the traditionalism which lies at the heart of much Conservative thinking on international and economic issues, compared to the past thirty years a genuine and profoundly new departure is required if Conservative military plans are to be implemented.

What this means is that the British people would have to pay costs for sustaining the imperial self-image on a scale which we have not been willing to pay for three decades. We would have to accept the closures of more hospitals, the further run-down of the National Health Service, so that good health becomes a privilege once again, not a right. We would have to accept the closure of schools and the enlargement of classes, the continuation of outdated and inadequate educational facilities. We would have to accept the steady elimination of many of the services and amenities in local communities we have taken for granted, together with the further decay of inner-city areas. And we would have to accept these and other costs, not as a temporary break, but for many, many years. For the resources which military expenditure and military industry utilize are also those which could be utilized for civil investment. In other words, we would also have to agree to put off economic recovery, to throw revenues from North Sea oil down the military drain, to watch the civil economy stagnate yet further while the military economy booms.

There are two main reasons why the British people might,

if only for a period, agree to pay these costs. We might agree out of conviction, or out of fear. The war psychology which we see being created today, which is necessary to legitimate the replacement of Polaris and the devotion of enormous resources to the military, is one side of the coin. The other side is the increased authoritarianism of the state in dealing with 'dissident' groups, the transfer of military techniques learned in Northern Ireland to the British mainland, the growth of the Special Branch and the political role of the police. The British state had already increased, in the 1970s, under a Labour government, the attention it pays to domestic propaganda and techniques of political repression; the process would have to continue and reach into yet more areas of our social and political life.

Thus, the Conservatives' rhetoric around international questions is in direct conflict with their rhetoric of reducing the role of the state, because to sustain their international aspirations and to impose the consequent social and political penalties on the British people would require a major expansion of the role of the state in particular areas. The ideology of economic 'laissez-faire' is at odds with the means which would have to be employed to implement Conservative ambitions in the international arena. Since the ideology of 'laissez-faire' is already at odds with the reality of economic policies, it seems to us more likely that the ideology would, over time, be jettisoned or downplayed, rather than that propaganda and coercion would be jettisoned for the sake of the ideology.

The Conservatives' Forthcoming Failure

This nightmarish prospect has been mapped out in deliberately stark terms. It is predicated on the government being successful in increasing military expenditure and reconstructing British politics and society. There are three main reasons why it could fail: the first leads to a failure worse than success; the second leads to a failure about as bad as success; the third is rather more agreeable.

Firstly, failure might result from over-success. The government performs in the international as well as the domestic arena. In the domestic arena it exploits the genuine dangers in the international situation, but by so doing it also contributes to an exacerbation of those dangers. Building up a war psychology in Britain contributes to greater tensions and greater dangers of war. And the government is not immune from the effects of its own propaganda. Thus the Conservative government is currently contributing to the possibility of a major war, of a nuclear holocaust. We presume that even the government would accept that, were such a war to occur, it would be some evidence that its policies had failed.

Secondly, as we have already argued, annual increases in real military spending of 3 per cent through the 1980s will undermine the economic basis on which stable military programmes might be built. Accelerating economic decline would hit the mass of the British people hard, but might finally drive home the impossibility of current military plans and force a change of course.

But this is more likely to happen, and to happen sooner rather than later, if, thirdly, a powerful and conscious popular mobilization seeks a change of course. This implies a resistance both to propaganda and coercion and the capacity to go beyond resistance into the development of a new and saner course for British policy. To return to the terms we used earlier in this essay, this means a forceful assertion of allocative choices which are different from those of the current government. The strength of this assertion would then result in a stabilization, in the closure of the Conservatives' new yet traditional departure.

We have argued that Conservative plans for military expenditure in the 1980s conflict with the social, economic and political realities of late-twentieth-century Britain. But these realities are not mechanical forces which automatically assert themselves. They will be asserted by people and movements struggling against coercion, the removal of social services and the threat of war, seeking a secure future and a reasonable standard of living. Within the context of a general economic crisis, this requires a very different allocation of resources from the Conservatives' preference and a different set of policies. We believe that different social and economic priorities will be asserted, because we believe that social and political forces exist which are capable of doing that. But the point is that these 'forces' are made up of people and of many kinds of groups and organizations who must first decide that they will actively oppose the Conservatives' policies. The first task in mobilizing those forces is to convince the people.

Notes

1. *Business Week*, 18 February 1980, carries a major article on this theme.

2. This is not to argue that such an adjustment is impossible. Work done on the possibility of converting military industry to non-military uses shows the adjustment is possible, but it has also shown that a successful transition depends on a series of political preconditions, to which the Conservatives would be thoroughly opposed. See, for example, M. Kaldor, D. Smith and S. Vines (eds.), *Democratic Socialism and the Cost of Defence* (Croom Helm, London, 1980).

3. Sources used were *National Income and Expenditure 1979* (HMSO, London, 1979) and *Economic Trends*, April 1980 (HMSO). For the years 1974–9, the average relative price effect was 1·36 per cent as against 2·23 per cent for 1968–79; for reasons stated in the text we have assumed a figure for the 1980s of 2 per cent. The *National Income and Expenditure* figures for current expenditure on goods and services for military defence were used, since long runs of data are available in current and constant prices for this definition.

It is a slightly lower figure for the GDP share (4·6 per cent in 1979) than the official figure (4·9 per cent). Although these data provide the longest consistent series for the relative price effect, it is difficult to match these estimates with those implied by Table 5.12 of the public expenditure White Paper, *The Government's Expenditure Plans 1980–81 to 1983–84*, Cmnd 7841 (HMSO, London, 1980).

4. For detailed argumentation see R. P. Smith, 'Military Expenditure and Capitalism' and 'Military Expenditure and Capitalism: A Reply', *Cambridge Journal of Economics*, March 1977 and September 1978.

5. The estimated long-run relationship can be summarized as

$$M = 0·224g - 1·09\,RP - 0·26A + 0·306R$$

where M is the rate of growth of real military expenditure, g is the rate of growth of output, RP is the relative price effect, A is the rate of growth of real US military expenditure, and R is the rate of growth of real Soviet military expenditure: see R. P. Smith, 'The Demand for Military Expenditure', *Economic Journal*, forthcoming.

6. *Defence in the 1980s*, Cmnd 7826–I (HMSO, London, 1980), para. 104.

7. See D. Greenwood, 'The Polaris Successor System: At What Cost?', in *The Future of the British Nuclear Deterrent*, Bailrigg Paper No. 1 (University of Lancaster, 1980).

8. See D. Smith, 'After Polaris', in *Politics and Power 2* (Routledge & Kegan Paul, London, 1980).

9. A. J. R. Groom, 'The British Deterrent', in J. Bayliss (ed.), *British Defence Policy in a Changing World* (Croom Helm, London, 1977), p. 153.

CHAPTER EIGHT

Mary Kaldor
Disarmament: The Armament Process in Reverse

Stopping cruise missiles is not just a matter of convincing the politicians. Time and time again, the statesmen of the world have met together in international fora and expressed lofty and commendable ambitions for peace and disarmament. Yet hardly anything of practical value has ever been achieved. New and more deadly kinds of weapons continue to be acquired; war and militarism continue to characterize international relations. It appears as though disarmament, which is viewed as an international act of will, is quite unrelated to armament, which is a national process involving people, money and institutions deeply embedded in the fabric of our society.

If the campaign for European nuclear disarmament is to succeed, we need to see it, not just as a campaign to change the political will of Europeans – important as that is – but, more profoundly, as the first step in a process which reverses the process of armament. The aim would be to undermine the ideas and institutions which foster the arms race, to rechannel the energies which are currently devoted to militarization into other new directions and create, so to speak, a vested interest in socially productive as opposed to destructive ends. The act of will that is currently thought of as disarmament would present the final blow to a crumbling military-industrial edifice, the last and perhaps least act in a series of events which totally transforms the current political, social and economic environment of armaments.

Every armament process has its time and place. The culture which invented the stirrup was quite different from the one which developed the gun. The capitalist armament process and what is more or less its mirror image in the centrally planned economies has its own unique properties. This essay is an attempt to sketch out these properties and to see what they imply for disarmament.

The Armament Process

Modern armed forces both East and West are dominated by armaments: what one might call the fixed capital of warfare. In countries like the United States, Britain or France which are major arms producers, the procurement of arms accounts for about half the military budget and the same is probably true of the Soviet Union. Moreover, the procurement budget is dominated by a few major weapon systems, i.e. warships, aircraft or armoured fighting vehicles, that combine a weapons platform, a weapon (gun, missile, torpedo) and the means of command and communication. In the US, for example, the Trident submarine, the new nuclear-powered aircraft-carrier, and a handful of guided missile destroyers and frigates, account for about two thirds of the naval procurement budget. The MX missile, together with the latest air force fighters F 15 and F 16, is equally important for the Air Force, while the new XM 1 battle tank accounts for a major share of the Army budget. The same is true in Britain and France. In Britain, the Multi-Role Combat Aircraft (MRCA) Tornado accounts for around 40 per cent of the Royal Air Force (RAF) budget; the three anti-submarine warfare cruisers, which are actually small aicraft-carriers with their associated escort and support ships, probably account for a fifth to a quarter of the British naval procurement budget.

The concept of the weapon system can be said to have originated in the first prolonged period of high peace-time military spending, namely the Anglo-German naval arms race before World War I. Socially, the rise of the concept may be likened to the replacement of tools by machines. Whereas formerly the weapon was the instrument of man, now it appears that man is the instrument of the weapon system. A weapon system demands a rigid technical division of labour that admits little variation in the social organization of the men who operate it. Equally, the weapon system, like the machine, guarantees the existence of certain types of industry for its manufacture.

Although in almost all industrialized countries, armed forces have been pruned and centralized since the war, they remain functionally organized around the weapon system. Hence, navies are organized by ship, with groups of ships organized hierarchically into task forces. At the apex of the American surface Navy is the aircraft carrier, requiring destroyers and a submarine or two for protection, aircraft to fly from its deck, and supply ships of various kinds for replenishment. The bomber and the battle tank have a similar role in the Air Force and Army. The Air Force is divided into bomber, fighter and transport commands. The Army is made up of armour, artillery, parachute or infantry units, but the armoured units are the core of the combined arms team. The functional autonomy of individual services or military units is achieved through independent strategies associated with particular weapon systems. This would explain why strategic bombing is so central to the US Air Force or why the British Navy remains committed to an ocean-going role associated with carriers long after the abandonment of overseas commitments. In the Soviet Union, for example, land-based medium- and long-range ballistic missiles constitute the basis for a separate service, the Strategic Rocket Forces.

The strategic doctrine of any particular military unit can thus be expressed in the military specifications for a particular weapon system; that is to say, in a set of specified performance characteristics. These, in turn, are the product of the manufacturing capabilities of a particular enterprise. Hence, the weapon system is the link between the enterprise and military unit, the embodiment of a persistent military-industrial alliance.

Western Countries

In the West, the design, development and production of weapon systems is, by and large, undertaken by a few large companies known as prime contractors. In general, the prime contractors are the manufacturers of weapon platforms-aircraft, shipbuilding, automobile or engineering companies; they assemble the complete weapon system, subcontracting subsystems, like the weapons, the engine and the electronics, and components in such a way as to create an interdependent network of big and small companies. The prime contractors tend to specialize in particular types of weapon systems: Boeing and Rockwell are bomber enterprises; Dassault in France and British Aerospace make combat aircraft, Westland Aircraft makes helicopters; Electric Boat (now part of General Dynamics) and Vickers Barrow (now part of British Shipbuilders) make submarines.

The prime contractors are among the world's largest companies. Since World War II, between forty and fifty US companies have regularly appeared on *Fortune*'s list of the top 100 companies and on the Pentagon's list of the 100 companies receiving the highest prime contract awards. Their stability, in both America and Europe, has been widely noted. Firms have been amalgamated or nationalized, especially in Europe, but basically there has been very little rationalization. The plants which receive prime contracts for major weapon systems have remained much the same, under different names, for thirty years. There has been more specialization and an increased amount of subcontract work both among the prime contractors and the outside firms, especially in the electronics industry. Also, the composition of subcontractors has varied enormously along with changes in technology and the business cycle – thousands of subcontractors regularly go bankrupt during recession. But among the prime contractors, there have been few, if any, actual closures in the postwar period. Equally, there have been no new entries into the major weapons markets. The consequence is that a specific mix of skills and physical equipment, and a specific set of relationships with customers (the military units) and suppliers (the subcontractors), has been preserved – in effect, a specific manufacturing experience which corresponds to a specific military experience.

Although several of the big arms manufacturers in Europe have been nationalized, the prime contractors operate according to the principles of private enterprise. They need to maintain their independent viability and this, in practice, means the constant search to find new markets, and to maintain or increase profit margins. Frequently, US defence contractors testify to the intensity of competition – 'a continuous life and death struggle to obtain defense contracts'.[1] The fact that this competition takes a technological rather than price form has to do with the peculiarity of the arms market – the government as sole customer. Firms put more emphasis on the ability to offer improvements to the product than on the ability to reduce the cost of production – in the end, the government pays.

In essence, then, the Western armament process is characterized by a contradictory combination of stability and competition. The armament sector could be described as a semi-planned sector. On the supply side, it is monopolistic, i.e. has one customer, and on the demand side, it is oligopolistic, i.e. has a few competitive suppliers. On the demand side can be found all the complex mathematical techniques that are typical of a centrally planned system and, on the supply side, can be found the preoccupation with profit margins, contracts, markets, etc. that are the hallmark of private enterprise. Inevitably, these two aspects are reflected in the final product, the weapon system.

In a planned system, unless there is some overriding objective like victory in war, a plan tends to reflect the objectives of the institutions that participate in the plan, to express the various interests of the plan's constituencies. In other words, consumer sovereignty in a planned system is rare because the people who draw up the plan are strongly influenced by the people who carry it out. In peace-time, without external stimulus of war, decisions about what is 'needed' for defence tend to be taken by the 'experts', generally those who have gained their formative experience in the armament sector. Such decisions tend to be 'autistic' – the outcome of the institutional interests of users and producers. Because the Soviet Union has always lagged behind the United States, technologically, the need for any particular weapon system has been assessed against an idea of what the Soviet Union might possess when the weapon system eventually, five or ten years later, enters operational service. This idea owes more to the subjective imagination of the designers than to any hard knowledge about what is happening in the Soviet Union.

The designers are the products of their military-industrial environment. The *competition* between prime contractors propels technology forward as each corporation attempts to offer something better than its competitor and something the military, at least in the US, can justify to Congress. And yet this technological dynamism is confined within certain limits – limits that are defined by the *stability* of military and industrial institutions, a stability which is guaranteed by the planning system. The result is an entirely introverted form of technological change, something which has been described as 'trend' or 'routinized innovation'.[2]

Trend innovation has found its characteristic form in the follow-on imperative.[3] The form and function of the weapon system have not changed much since 1945. Technical change has largely consisted of improvements to a given set of performance characteristics. Submarines are faster, quieter, bigger and have longer ranges. Aircraft have greater speed, more powerful thrust and bigger payloads. All weapon systems have more destructive weapons, particularly missiles, and greatly improved capabilities for communication, navigation, detection, identification and weapon guidance. Each contractor has designed, developed and produced one weapon system after another, each representing an incremental improvement on the last. For Boeing, the Minuteman Inter-Continental Ballistic Missile followed the B 52 strategic bomber, which followed the B 47. Between 1952 and 1979, Newport News's yards have produced no fewer than nine aircraft-carriers, each bigger and better than the last, bow to stern in the best follow-on tradition. And in Europe, Dassault has produced the famous series of Mirage fighters; Westland has manufactured one helicopter after another; and the submarine which the British propose to construct in order to launch the American Trident missile is likely to continue a tradition at Vickers Barrow that goes back, with interruptions, as far as the 1890s.

The idea that each weapon system must have a follow-on has become self-perpetuating. Each corporation has a planning group whose sole function is to choose suitable successors for weapons currently being produced and which maintain close contact with consorts in the military. The planning procedure is supposed to be an exercise in prediction. In actual fact, because of the intimate relationship with the armed services it becomes a self-fulfilling prophecy. Even so the system has not worked smoothly, and it has taken periodic industrial crises to initiate the full range of new projects. Such was the crisis which followed the winding down of the Vietnam War in the early 1970s. The pressure on the defence budget which we are now witnessing is partly the result of projects initiated during that period.

Each follow-on is bigger and 'better' than its predecessor. As weapon systems approach the limits of technology, they become increasingly complex and costly. It becomes harder and harder to achieve incremental improvements to a given set of performance characteristics. Although the basic technology of the weapon platform may not have changed much, such improvements have often entailed the incorporation of very advanced technology, e.g. radical electronic innovations such as microprocessors, or nuclear power for submarines, and this has greatly increased the complexity of the weapon system as a whole. And as the weapon system becomes more complex, more labour and materials are required for development and production, greatly increasing the total cost.

The weapon systems of the 1970s represent what one might describe as a quantum leap in expense and grotesque elaboration. The monstrous MX missile with its ludicrous race-track system will cost somewhere from $33 billion (the official figure) to over $100 billion (an estimate made in April 1980).[4] It will involve the biggest construction programme in the history of the United States. The obese Trident submarine, which is too big to get out of the channel where it was built, will cost much the same. The real cost of producing the British-German-Italian Multi-Role Combat Aircraft will be slightly greater than the *entire* production costs of the Spitfire before and during World War II. A recent US General Accounting Office report concluded:

> The cost problem facing the US military is growing worse and no relief is in sight. The so-called 'bow wave' of future procurement costs is growing beyond the point of reasonableness. Current procurement programs are estimated to total about $725 billion. If these costs are spread over the next ten years (a conservative projection) the annual average of $72·5 billion will be more than twice the current funding levels.[5]

Yet many people, and not just those who question the whole basis of modern strategy, are beginning to wonder whether the extra money will buy any real increase in military utility. A number of strategic writers have come to criticize the criteria for technical improvements to weapon systems.[6] Many of the indicators of military effectiveness are thought to be no longer relevant to modern warfare. For example, the development of naval aircraft and submarines has meant that speed is no longer important for surface ships. Likewise, aircraft speed is only of advantage in fighter roles. The cost, complexity and size of modern weapon systems consequent upon the so-called improvements in performance characteristics may turn out to be a positive liability. In the hostile environment of the modern battlefield, where the accuracy and lethality of all munitions have greatly increased, size and vulnerability go hand in hand. Complexity greatly increases unreliability, reduces manoeuvrability and flexibility, and creates enormous logistic problems. The US Air Force's First Tactical Air Wing, whose motto is 'Readiness is our Profession', recently failed a test given by the Air Force's Tactical Command to see if it was ready to mobilize for a war in the Middle East. Only 23 of the 66 F 15 aircraft were 'mission capable' because of engine and parts failures, lack of spares, shortages of skilled technicians, etc. – and these problems are not untypical of Western weapon systems in general. Likewise, cost is a disadvantage because of the high attrition rates of modern warfare and because budgetary limitations lead to savings on such essentials as ammunition, fuel, spares, military pay, training, etc. The huge support systems and the overburdened centralized command systems associated with the modern weapon system are very vulnerable and could be easily disrupted in a war. Indeed, the experience of war in Vietnam and the Middle East – the problems of vulnerability, logistics, communications, etc. – has called into question the whole future of the weapon system. Destructiveness and effectiveness are no longer synonymous – if they ever were.

The degeneracy of the weapon system is not without its effects on Western economy and society as a whole. As an object of use, the weapon system is the basis of military organization both within individual nations and within the alliance as a whole. It is, at once, a symbol of legitimacy and

Western unity. The dominance of American weapon systems reflects the dominance of American strategic thinking and the American defence industry. The proposals for ground-launched cruise missiles could be interpreted as an attempt to reassert that dominance. As the military rationale for such systems becomes more and more remote and rarified, so their usefulness in holding together, as it were, the Western alliance becomes more open to question.

As an object of production, the weapon system is part of modern industry and its development has to be understood as consequence and cause of broader industrial tendencies. In a capitalist system, the market mechanism ensures rapid technical change. As production processes are adapted to meet changing demands, the whole economic structure undergoes radical alterations. Companies, industries, sectors and regions rise and fall according to the dictates of the market. As the product of a semi-planned sector, armaments can interrupt this process. In so far as they guarantee the stability of military-industrial institutions, of the major corporations, armaments can help to alleviate crises. But capitalist crises produce change. That same stability has the effect of freezing industrial structure and postponing change. In so far as armaments are themselves subject to the capitalist dynamic they can also drag the economy along their own technological cul de sac, passing on the degeneracy of overgrown trend innovation. In effect they can preserve and even extend industries that would otherwise have declined and at the same time fetter the emergence of new dynamic industries. This is one reason for the persistence of mechanical engineering and shipbuilding in Britain or the automobile and aircraft industries in the United States. The absorption of resources by these declining sectors, the distorting effects of armament-induced ways of thinking about technology on new as well as older industries, are among the factors which help to explain the backwardness of arms-intensive economies like Britain and the United States compared with, say, West Germany and Japan.

The Soviet Union

There is a remarkable parallel to be drawn with what happens in the Soviet Union. The armament sector in the Soviet Union could be described as the inverse of the Western armament sector. On the supply side, arms are produced by the same kinds of enterprises that characterize the centrally planned economy as a whole. Unlike those in the West, research institutes, design bureaux and production plants are organized as separate entities under the control of nine different defence ministries. The stability of these institutions, together with their suppliers, is guaranteed by the system of planning and budgeting. Unlike in the West, where competition, the pressure for technical advance, the winning or losing of contracts may lead to the amalgamation of design teams and prime contractors and to massive shifts in the composition of subcontractors, the various industrial organizations are assured of a steady flow of work. If the stability of the prime contractors slows down the process of industrial change in the West, then this same tendency for conservatism and continuity is typical of the Soviet economy as a whole.[7]

On the demand side, however, armaments are characterized by competitiveness (with the West). Armaments in the Soviet Union are privileged products; it is often said that the armament sector is the only sector in the Soviet system which enjoys consumer sovereignty, and this is evident in the priority system. The armament sector receives the best machinery and parts; it can commandeer scarce materials; defence employees earn higher incomes and obtain better non-monetary benefits; requests and orders from the administration tend to be dealt with more quickly. Many commentators have remarked on the unusual degree to which the consumer can ensure that specifications are met and can overcome resistance to demand-induced changes. From time to time, the leadership has imposed new solutions for forcing technology in order to initiate such programmes as nuclear weapons, jet engines, missiles, etc. In general, these programmes were a response to developments in the West, which was always one technological step ahead of the Soviet Union.

Hence, because of the degree of consumer sovereignty, the armament sector can represent a mechanism for change in the Soviet system. This was certainly the case in the 1930s, when military competition with Germany could be said to have been the overriding objective of the Soviet planning system. It can be argued that it was through the armament sector that the economy was mobilized.[8] The armament sector continues to transmit new technology into the Soviet system; however, precisely because of the nature of Western armaments, technologically induced change of this kind may prove distorting and not progressive.

Disarmament

The weapon system is the basis of modern military organization. It holds together the two great military alliances and divides East from West. And yet, paradoxically, the sector which produces the weapon system is also the conceptual *link* between the two societies. For it introduces an element of planning into the capitalist system; it thus helps to stave off crisis but, at the same time, slows down change. And it introduces an element of competition into the Soviet Union, inserting a mechanism for change.

In the past, the armament sector may have worked quite well in blunting some of the contradictions of each society. This is no longer true. The declining military effectiveness and growing cost of armament are gradually undermining the political weight of the superpowers and sapping their economic strength. The crisis of the armament sector has thrown up new forms of conflict and protest. New political and economic rivalries in the West, and consumer dissatisfaction, dissidence, and increased repression in the Soviet

Union are all elements of a wider breakdown in the postwar international system of which the armament sector is a central part. The crisis has drawn a response from within the armament sector, as well as elsewhere, from soldiers ill-prepared for new forms of conflict (as in Vietnam) and from workers in the defence industry, concerned about employment. The new situation represents an opportunity for change. It entails the risk of war and of rearmament. But it could alternatively initiate a process of disarmament by channelling the new protests into positive directions.

Most disarmament efforts are aimed at the role of armaments as objects of use. To reverse effectively the armament process, we also need to undermine their role as objects of production. We need to campaign against cruise missiles. But we also need to change the military-industrial culture which created them.

Industrial conversion is one way of achieving this. In a sense, any form of economic development represents a continual process of conversion – of finding new products and phasing out old ones. The conversion from arms to peaceful production would be merely one aspect of this process. Different societies have different mechanisms for conversion. The capitalist economy depends on the market as a method of allocating resources. It involves anarchy, dislocation, structural unemployment and periodic crises. The alternative is the central planning mechanism of the socialist countries which leads to rigidity because biases in government reflect vested bureaucratic interests. It thus avoids crises but, at the same time, is much more resistant to change than is the capitalist system.

The conversion from war to peace needs to be seen *not* as the *technical* process of converting swords to ploughshares, but as a *social* process of finding a new mechanism for the allocation of resources. Mere technical conversion from war to peace could never be sufficient. In a sense, we have already experienced this in the non-military products of the arms companies – the US and Soviet space programme,

Concorde and the TU 144, nuclear energy, various American rapid urban transit systems and environmental products. These have become what one might call quasi-weapon systems – similarly elaborate and expensive, with, in the end, similar economic consequences. Further, these products could never provide perfect substitutes for armaments since they do not command the same urgency. It would be difficult to justify increased expenditure on space or artificial hearts in times of economic recession.

Conversion needs to be seen as a way of creating a new economic system which would minimize those problems that create opportunities for conflict and the pressure for armaments. Such a system would combine the positive elements of planning with positive elements of free enterprise, instead of, as in the armament sector, the negative elements of both. The Western armament system, as we have seen, is characterized by planning on the demand side and competition on the supply side. The Western form of military technical change, the outcome of this system, is transferred to the Soviet Union through the consumer sovereignty that is the unique characteristic of the armament sector in the Soviet Union. What is needed is a system of consumer sovereignty in which the consumer is not a military establishment engaged in a competitive arms race but an ordinary person – in other words, planning, under democratic control. How is this to be achieved in practice?

A sturdy democracy originates in popular movement, even though such movements must eventually find an institutional expression. Already, trades unions in the defence industry in Britain, West Germany, the United States, Italy and Sweden have begun to express interest in the idea of conversion. This interest has proceeded farthest in Britain, where the workers of Lucas Aerospace and Vickers have earned a world-wide reputation for their proposals and campaigns to achieve socially useful production.

The principle that underlies the Lucas Aerospace Corporate Plan,[9] the Vickers pamphlets,[10] and various proposals from workers in other companies, including Rolls-Royce ('Buns Before the Gutter'), BAC, and Parsons, is the simple but revolutionary idea that in a society where there are substantial unfilled needs it makes no sense to put people, who could be making products to fill those needs, on the dole or into arms manufacture. Neither the market mechanism nor central planning has proved very efficient at marrying social need to available resources. The alternative is to propose products which emanate from direct contacts between producers and consumers. This is the basis of the various worker plans.

In developing their ideas, the unions found it necessary to develop links with unions in supplier industries and with consumer organizations. Partly, this was in order to establish technical and social feasibility. For example, proposals by Rolls-Royce workers for gas turbine propulsion for merchant ships turned out to be an oversophisticated, marginally useful suggestion. More importantly, it provides a more effective method of putting political pressure on management and the government. Many of the ideas clash with priorities currently established by the government, which tend to reflect existing vested interests. Hence the shop stewards proposed energy conservation equipment and alternative forms of energy based on wind or waves; yet official energy priorities stress North Sea oil, coal, and nuclear energy. They also proposed new kinds of rail vehicles or ways of revitalizing Britain's canal system; yet transport policy places the emphasis on roads rather than railways or canals. The workers have consequently joined forces with organizations like the anti-nuclear energy movement or Transport 2000, which lobbies against the unplanned growth of the automobile infrastructure. On more mundane levels, unions in British Leyland pressed their management to purchase a scrap metal baler, one of the ideas put forward by the Vickers Shop Stewards. Lucas Aerospace Shop Stewards at Burnley worked closely with the local council with the idea of meeting local needs. These informal alliances between producers and consumers could provide the basis for future planning agencies which would reflect a different set of social priorities from those that currently hold sway.

Ideally, these links should be international, for there is always the risk that social criteria for resource allocation could turn out to be national, and hence divisive on a global scale. At both Vickers and Lucas Aerospace, some international links have been forged. Vickers workers have visited India (where they helped to establish a tank factory) and Iran (where they were shocked to hear of the way Chieftain tanks had been used). They have proposed various kinds of equipment for irrigation and for water purification. Lucas Aerospace workers have discussed the possibility of adapting a road/rail vehicle they have invented for use in Tanzania and Zambia with the governments of those countries.

The Lucas Aerospace workers have actually achieved some success in pressing their management to undertake the manufacture of socially useful products. For the first time, workers are inserting their own criteria, as both producers and consumers, into the choice of products. They are, in a sense, developing a new mechanism for conversion, which, if it spreads, could change the composition of power in existing institutions—local councils, regional development councils, the Industrial Manpower Commission, the Atomic Energy Commission, for example – and which could eventually be embodied in a new set of planning institutions which set priorities according to the social needs of consumers and which guarantee stable, although mobile, employment.

Any campaign for disarmament must join forces with workers in the defence industry in demanding conversion. Conversion – along with other more traditional disarmament issues – could build upon the growing fissures within the armament system and direct current frustrations towards disarmament rather than war. It could help to initiate a process of conversion which would *precede* disarmament. Conversion would thus be seen as a way of achieving disarmament rather than a thorny problem to be solved after the politicians had finally willed the reduction of armaments. Conversion would not just be a matter of turning swords into ploughshares. It would be a matter of creating a new mechanism for the wider process of economic conversion, matching the desperate needs of the modern world with resources that are either misused or not used at all. It could thus undermine the political and economic basis for armaments in advanced industrial countries and it would help to overcome the structural problems, weaknesses and divisions of different economic systems. Hence it could help to remove the causes of war.

Notes

1. National Security Industrial Association, quoted in J. E. Fox, *Arming America: How the US buys Weapons* (Harvard University, 1974), p. 101.
2. See Morris Janowitz, *The Professional Soldier* (Free Press, New York, 1960).
3. See James Kurth, 'Why we Buy the Weapons We Do', *Foreign Policy*, No. 11, New York, 1973.
4. Science Supplement, *The New York Times*, 15 April 1980.
5. *Impediments to Reducing the Costs of Weapons Systems*. Report to the Congress of the United States by the Comptroller General, PSAD-80-6, November 1979, p. 3
6. See, for example, Stephen Canby, 'The Alliance and Europe, Part IV, Military Doctrine and Technology', *Adelphi Papers*, No. 109 (International Institute for Strategic Studies, London, Winter 1974–5).
7. See Alec Nove, *The Soviet Economic System* (Allen & Unwin, London, 1977).
8. See Julian Cooper, 'Defence Production and the Soviet

Economy, 1929–41', CREES Discussion Paper, Soviet Industrialization Project Series SIPS No. 3, 1976.

9. Lucas Aerospace Combine Committee, *Corporate Plan*, 1976.

10. Vickers National Combine Committee of Shop Stewards, *Building a Chieftain Tank and the Alternative Use of Resources* and *The ASW Cruiser: Alternative Work for Naval Shipbuilding Workers* (1978).

PART FOUR

Europe:
Theatre of Peace

CHAPTER NINE

Appeal for European Nuclear Disarmament
launched on 28 April 1980

We are entering the most dangerous decade in human history. A third world war is not merely possible, but increasingly likely. Economic and social difficulties in advanced industrial countries, crisis, militarism and war in the third world compound the political tensions that fuel a demented arms race. In Europe, the main geographical stage for the East-West confrontation, new generations of ever more deadly nuclear weapons are appearing.

For at least twenty-five years, the forces of both the North Atlantic and the Warsaw alliance have each had sufficient nuclear weapons to annihilate their opponents, and at the same time to endanger the very basis of civilized life. But with each passing year, competition in nuclear armaments has multiplied their numbers, increasing the probability of some devastating accident or miscalculation.

As each side tries to prove its readiness to use nuclear weapons, in order to prevent their use by the other side, new, more 'usable' nuclear weapons are designed and the idea of 'limited' nuclear war is made to sound more and more plausible. So much so that this paradoxical process can logically only lead to the actual use of nuclear weapons.

Neither of the major powers is now in any moral position to influence smaller countries to forgo the acquisition of nuclear armament. The increasing spread of nuclear reactors and the growth of the industry that installs them, reinforce the likelihood of world-wide proliferation of nuclear weapons, thereby multiplying the risks of nuclear exchanges.

Over the years, public opinion has pressed for nuclear

disarmament and detente between the contending military blocs. This pressure has failed. An increasing proportion of world resources is expended on weapons, even though mutual extermination is already amply guaranteed. This economic burden, in both East and West, contributes to growing social and political strain, setting in motion a vicious circle in which the arms race feeds upon the instability of the world economy and vice versa: a deathly dialectic.

We are now in great danger. Generations have been born beneath the shadow of nuclear war, and have become habituated to the threat. Concern has given way to apathy. Meanwhile, in a world living always under menace, fear extends through both halves of the European continent. The powers of the military and of internal security forces are enlarged, limitations are placed upon free exchanges of ideas and between persons, and civil rights of independent-minded individuals are threatened, in the West as well as the East.

We do not wish to apportion guilt between the political and military leaders of East and West. Guilt lies squarely upon both parties. Both parties have adopted menacing postures and committed aggressive actions in different parts of the world.

The remedy lies in our own hands. We must act together to free the entire territory of Europe, from Poland to Portugal, from nuclear weapons, air and submarine bases, and from all institutions engaged in research into or manufacture of nuclear weapons. We ask the two super-powers to withdraw all nuclear weapons from European territory. In particular, we ask the Soviet Union to halt production of SS 20 medium-range missile and we ask the United States not to implement the decision to develop cruise missiles and Pershing II missiles for deployment in Western Europe. We also urge the ratification of the SALT II agreement, as a necessary step towards the renewal of effective negotiations on general and complete disarmament.

At the same time, we must defend and extend the right of all citizens, East or West, to take part in this common movement and to engage in every kind of exchange.

We appeal to our friends in Europe, of every faith and persuasion, to consider urgently the ways in which we can work together for these common objectives. We envisage a European-wide campaign, in which every kind of exchange takes place; in which representatives of different nations and opinions confer and co-ordinate their activities; and in which less formal exchanges, between universities, churches, women's organizations, trade unions, youth organizations, professional groups and individuals, take place with the object of promoting a common object: to free all of Europe from nuclear weapons.

We must commence to act as if a united, neutral and pacific Europe already exists. We must learn to be loyal, not to 'East' or 'West', but to each other, and we must disregard the prohibitions and limitations imposed by any national state.

It will be the responsibility of the people of each nation to agitate for the expulsion of nuclear weapons and bases from European soil and territorial waters, and to decide upon its own means and strategy, concerning its own territory. These will differ from one country to another, and we do not suggest that any single strategy should be imposed. But this must be part of a trans-continental movement in which every kind of exchange takes place.

We must resist any attempt by the statesmen of East or West to manipulate this movement to their own advantage. We offer no advantage to either NATO or the Warsaw alliance. Our objectives must be to free Europe from confrontation, to enforce detente between the United States and the Soviet Union, and, ultimately, to dissolve both great power alliances.

In appealing to fellow-Europeans, we are not turning our backs on the world. In working for the peace of Europe we are working for the peace of the world. Twice in this century

Europe has disgraced its claims to civilization by engendering world war. This time we must repay our debts to the world by engendering peace.

This appeal will achieve nothing if it is not supported by determined and inventive action, to win more people to support it. We need to mount an irresistible pressure for a Europe free of nuclear weapons.

We do not wish to impose any uniformity on the movement nor to pre-empt the consultations and decisions of those many organizations already exercising their influence for disarmament and peace. But the situation is urgent. The dangers steadily advance. We invite your support for this common objective, and we shall welcome both your help and advice.

CHAPTER TEN

Ken Coates
For a Nuclear-free Europe

One day after Mr Francis Pym, the British Secretary of State for Defence, revealed his plans for the placement of 160 cruise missiles in Britain, Russian sources leaked a 'captured' file from American commando headquarters in Europe. This had been stolen almost two decades earlier by a Soviet spy, US Army Sergeant R. L. Johnson. Johnson had later been apprehended by the FBI, and sentenced to twenty-five years in prison. His son subsequently shot him dead during a prison visit. Reporting this rather bizarre story, the *Sunday Times* (22 June 1980) gave a revealing glimpse, but no more, of what Major-General B. E. Spivy, director of J-3 division, had been organizing for the 'defence' of his European allies. Unsurprisingly, perhaps, his schedules included a budget for 'pre-emptive strikes at hundreds of cities in the Soviet Union'. But they also included numerous similar nuclear assaults on 'places in neutral or friendly countries, to deny their resources to Soviet troops'. The lists included named cities: '69 in Yugoslavia, 36 in Austria, 13 in West Germany, 21 in Finland and five in Iran'. A more detailed report was later furnished in the *New Statesman* (27 June 1980). The documents, it explained, appear

to contain over 2,800 targets – possibly double that number – throughout Europe and parts of the Middle East. The targets are not strategic and do not include missile silos, but consist for the most part of lists of airfields and other facilities . . . railway and highway bridges, railway marshalling yards and sidings, military headquarters and camps, troop concentrations, waterways, port areas, motorway junctions and major and minor airports . . .

The weapons designated for this work ranged from 2·5 kilotons to 1·4 megatons.

All this had been worked out back in 1962. At that time the US Air Force was ready to drop '18 to 20 thousand megatons of nuclear weapons in Europe and the USSR within a 24-hour period'. Curious observers will note, so prolific was the armoury by the time of the early sixties, that it was thought prudent to assign it to such hitherto unanticipated targets as bridges and motorway junctions.

Up to the mid-1960s the United States had enjoyed a preponderating lead over the USSR in the numbers and refinement of its nuclear weapons. For this reason, during this time, Western military doctrine was based upon 'massive retaliation'. This much was always public knowledge. What was not public was the information that much of this 'retaliation' was designed to forestall any regrettable tendency among allies or neutrals to be over-run. 'Assured destruction' was openly defined by US Defense Secretary Robert MacNamara as the capacity to eliminate up to one quarter of the population of the Soviet Union, and up to half its industry. But the proportion of the allied populations scheduled for similar elimination was not public knowledge during the years of those calculations.

Today, we have no way of knowing what secrets are locked in the military planning compounds in either the United States or the USSR. But from what is publicly known it is clear that Europe is in a far worse position at the beginning of the eighties than was even secretly thinkable twenty years ago.

It was as early as the mid-1950s that so-called 'tactical' nuclear weapons were brought into widespread deployment in Europe. By 1960 the USSR had an answering arsenal, all capable of targeting on European cities. A decade later, NATO had several thousand 'theatre' or 'tactical' nuclear weapons, while the USSR was thought in the West to deploy 600 medium-range missiles and 1,000 'tactical' weapons in Eastern Europe. Overall, by 1978, the equipment of the world's armies was costing substantially over a billion dollars a day, and the 'overkill' capacity involved had become quite staggering. But the sinister leapfrog between Eastern and Western weapons developments was producing an even more sinister jump in the established theory of mutual deterrence. In the late seventies, that large part of the world production of atomic explosives which was sited in Europe included, in Central Europe alone, 7,000 American and probably 3,500 Russian 'tactical' warheads, with a destructive potential at least fifty times that of all the weapons used in the Second World War, the Korean War and the war in Vietnam combined.

The conventional notion of deterrence had always been wrapped in swathes of assurances by its proponents that the actual use of nuclear weapons was unthinkable. This had been apparently borne out during the Cuba crisis, when, as one American commentator put it, 'we were eyeball to eyeball with the Russians, and they blinked'. But in today's world, nuclear forces in the superpowers are at near parity, so that nowadays *Time* magazine offers up the pious hope that, next time, both parties might blink at once.[1] Meantime, so vast are the investments tied into the manufacture of nuclear warheads and their delivery systems that, in any real war, it is not their use but their non-use which has become 'unthinkable'. Since we must still presume that neither major power really wishes to destroy the world, we may begin to understand why more and more weight has therefore been placed on the notion of 'theatre' weapons, which, it is canvassed, might be actually employed without annihilating the whole of civilization.

This is the unlooked-for transformation which has come over the logic of deterrence. It followed the development of highly accurate, adaptable and lethal weapons delivery systems. Now this threatens the very survival of European civilization. In his last speech, to the Stockholm International Peace Research Institute, the Earl Mountbatten seized the heart of the question:

It was not long, however, before smaller nuclear weapons of various designs were produced and deployed for use in what was assumed to be a tactical or theatre war. The belief was that were hostilities ever to break out in Western Europe, such weapons could be used in field warfare without triggering an all-out nuclear exchange leading to the final holocaust.

I have never found this idea credible [my italics]. I have never been able to accept the reasons for the belief that any class of nuclear weapons can be categorized in terms of their tactical or strategic purposes.[2]

Lord Zuckerman has also declared that he sees no military reality in what is now referred to as tactical or theatre warfare.[3] 'I do not believe,' he told a Pugwash symposium in Canada,

that nuclear weapons could be used in what is now fashionably called a 'theatre war'. I do not believe that any scenario exists which suggests that nuclear weapons could be used in field warfare between two nuclear states without escalation resulting. I know of several such exercises. They all lead to the opposite conclusion. There is no Marquess of Queensberry who would be holding the ring in a nuclear conflict. I cannot see teams of physicists attached to military staffs who would run to the scene of a nuclear explosion and then back to tell their local commanders that the radiation intensity of a nuclear strike by the other side was such and such, and that therefore the riposte should be only a weapon of equivalent yield. If the zone of lethal or wounding neutron radiation of a so-called neutron bomb would have, say, a radius of half a kilometre, the reply might well be a 'dirty' bomb with the same zone of radiation, but with a much wider area of devastation due to blast and fire.[4]

It is often claimed that 'It is not where nuclear weapons come from that matters, it is where they land.' To that we must add that it does not matter, when they land, whether some occult philosopher of war has originally styled them 'tactical' or 'strategic', 'theatre' or otherwise. Once we have seen the trend involved in reasoning about theatre war we cannot fail to draw some very unpleasant conclusions about it.

First, if Mountbatten and Zuckerman are right, any 'theatre' in which such weapons of whatever provenance are used will be eliminated. Second, the corollary is that if there is any meaning in the restriction implied in the concept of 'theatre' weapons, it is not that they will be selective within a particular zone, but that they might possibly be unleashed in one comparatively narrow area rather than another wider one. That is to say, and this is the whole point, they might be exchanged in Europe prior to 'escalation', which in this case would mean extending their exchange to the USA and the USSR. This carnivorous prospect is not at all identical with the simple supposition with which supporters of nuclear disarmament are often (wrongly) credited, that 'one day deterrence will not work'. It rather implies that there has been a mutation in the concept of deterrence itself, with grisly consequences for us. In fact, deterrence is now so very costly that 'conventional' responses are becoming impossible, to the point where even superpowers find themselves stalemated unless they are willing to discover means of 'conventionalizing' and then actually employing parts of their nuclear arsenals. If the powers want to have a bit of a nuclear war, they will want to have it away from home.

If we do not wish to be their hosts for such a match, then, regardless of whether they are right or wrong in supposing that they can confine it to our 'theatre', we must discover a new initiative which can move us towards disarmament. New technologies will not do this, and nor will introspection and conscience suddenly seize command in both superpowers at once.

We are looking for a *political* step which can open up new

forms of public pressure, and bring into the field of force new moral resources. Partly this is a matter of ending superpower domination of the most important negotiations.

But another part of the response must involve a multinational mobilization of public opinion. In Europe, this will not begin until people appreciate the exceptional vulnerability of their continent. One prominent statesman who has understood, and drawn attention to, this extreme exposure, is Olof Palme. During an important speech at a Helsinki conference of the Socialist International, he issued a strong warning:

Europe is no special zone where peace can be taken for granted. In actual fact, it is at the centre of the arms race. Granted, the general assumption seems to be that any potential military conflict between the superpowers is going to start someplace other than in Europe. But even if that were to be the case, we would have to count on one or the other party – in an effort to gain supremacy – trying to open a front on our continent, as well. As Alva Myrdal has recently pointed out, a war can simply be transported here, even though actual causes for war do not exist. Here there is a ready theatre of war. Here there have been great military forces for a long time. Here there are programmed weapons all ready for action . . .[5]

Basing himself on this recognition, Mr Palme recalled various earlier attempts to create, in North and Central Europe, nuclear-free zones, from which, by agreement, all warheads were to be excluded. (We shall look at the history of these proposals below.) He then drew a conclusion of historic significance, which provides the most real, and most hopeful, possibility of generating a truly continental opposition to this continuing arms race:

Today more than ever there is, in my opinion, every reason to go on working for a nuclear-free zone. *The ultimate objective of these efforts should be a nuclear-free Europe* [my italics]. The geographical area closest at hand would naturally be Northern and Central Europe.

If these areas could be freed from the nuclear weapons stationed there today, the risk of total annihilation in case of a military conflict would be reduced.

Olof Palme's initiative was launched exactly a month before the 1978 United Nations Special Session on Disarmament, which gave rise to a Final Document that is a strong, if tacit, indictment of the frenetic arms race which has actually accelerated sharply since it was agreed. A World Disarmament Campaign was launched in 1980 by Lord Noel Baker and Lord Brockway, and a comprehensive cross-section of voluntary peace organizations: it had the precise intention of securing the implementation of this Document. But although the goal of the UN Special Session was 'general and complete disarmament', as it should have been, it is commonly not understood that this goal was deliberately coupled with a whole series of intermediate objectives, including Palme's own proposals. Article 33 of the statements reads:

The establishment of nuclear-weapon-free zones on the basis of agreements or arrangements freely arrived at among the States of the zone concerned, and the full compliance with those agreements or arrangements, thus ensuring that the zones are genuinely free from nuclear weapons, and respect for such zones by nuclear-weapon States, constitute an important disarmament measure.[6]

Later, the declaration goes on to spell out this commitment in considerable detail.

The process of establishing such zones in different parts of the world should be encouraged with the ultimate objective of achieving a world entirely free of nuclear weapons. In the process of establishing such zones, the characteristics of each region should be taken into account. The States participating in such zones should undertake to comply fully with all the objectives, purposes and principles of the agreements or arrangements establishing the zones, thus ensuring that they are genuinely free from nuclear weapons.

With respect to such zones, the nuclear-weapon States in turn are called upon to give undertakings, the modalities of which are to be negotiated with the competent authority of each zone, in particular:

(a) to respect strictly the status of the nuclear-weapon-free zone;

(b) to refrain from the use or threat of use of nuclear weapons against the States of the zone . . .

States of the region should solemnly declare that they will refrain on a reciprocal basis from producing, acquiring, or in any other way possessing nuclear weapons and nuclear explosive devices, and from permitting the stationing of nuclear weapons on their territory by any third party and agree to place all their nuclear activities under International Atomic Energy Agency safeguards.

Article 63 of this final document schedules several areas for consideration as nuclear-free zones. They include Africa, where the Organization of African Unity has resolved upon 'the denuclearization of the region', but also the Middle East and South Asia, which are listed alongside South and Central America, whose pioneering treaty offers a possible model for others to follow. This is the only populous area to have been covered by an existing agreement, which was concluded in the Treaty of Tlatelolco (a suburb of Mexico City), opened for signature from February 1967.

There are other zones which are covered by more or less similar agreements. Conservationists will be pleased that they include Antarctica, the moon, outer space, and the seabed. Two snags exist in this respect. One is that the effectiveness of the agreed arrangements is often questioned. The other is that if civilization is destroyed, the survivors may not be equipped to establish themselves comfortably in safe havens among penguins or deep-sea plants and fish, leave alone upon the moon.

That is why a Martian might be surprised by the omission of Europe from the queue of continents (Africa, Near Asia, the Far East all in course of pressing; and Latin America, with the exception of Cuba, already having agreed) to negotiate coverage within nuclear-free zones. If Europe is the most vulnerable region, the prime risk, with a dense concentration of population, the most developed and destructible material heritage to lose, and yet no obvious immediate reasons to go to war, why is there any hesitation at all about making Olof Palme's 'ultimate objective' into an immediate and urgent demand?

If we are agreed that 'it does not matter where the bombs come from', there is another question which is more pertinent. This is: where will they be sent to? Clearly, high-priority targets are all locations from which response might otherwise come. There is therefore a very strong advantage for all Europe if 'East' and 'West', in terms of the deployment of nuclear arsenals, can literally and rigorously become coterminous with 'USA' and 'USSR'. This would not in one step liquidate the alliances, or end all the tension. But it would constitute a significant pressure on the superpowers, since each would thenceforward have a priority need to target on the silos of the other, and the present logic of 'theatre' thinking would all be reversed. None of this would lift the threat of apocalypse, but it would be a first step in that direction. As things are, we are in the theatre, and they are hoping to be able to watch us on their videos.

Nuclear-free Zones in Europe

If Europe as a whole has not hitherto raised the issue of its possible denuclearization, there have been a number of efforts to sanitize smaller regions within the continent.

The idea that groups of nations in particular areas might agree to forgo the manufacture or deployment of nuclear weapons, and to eschew research into their production, was first seriously mooted in the second half of the 1950s. In 1956, the USSR attempted to open discussions on the possible restriction of armaments, under inspection, and the prohibition of nuclear weapons within both German states and some adjacent countries. The proposal was discussed in the Disarmament Sub-Committee of the United Nations, but it got no further. But afterwards the Foreign Secretary of Poland, Adam Rapacki, took to the Twelfth Session of the UN General Assembly a plan to outlaw both the manufacture and the harbouring of nuclear arsenals in all the territories of Poland, Czechoslovakia, the German Democratic Republic and the Federal German Republic. The Czechoslovaks and East Germans quickly endorsed this suggestion.

Rapacki's proposals would have come into force by four separate unilateral decisions of each relevant government. Enforcement would have been supervised by a commission drawn from NATO countries, Warsaw Pact adherents, and nonaligned states. Inspection posts, with a system of ground and air controls, were to be established to enable the commission to function. Subject to this supervision, neither nuclear weapons, nor installations capable of harbouring or servicing them, nor missile sites, would have been permitted in the entire designated area. Nuclear powers were thereupon expected to agree not to use nuclear weapons against the denuclearized zone, and not to deploy their own atomic warheads with any of their conventional forces stationed within it.

The plan was rejected by the NATO powers, on the grounds, first, that it did nothing to secure German reunification and, second, that it failed to cover the deployment of conventional armaments. In 1958, therefore, Rapacki returned with modified proposals. Now he suggested a phased approach. In the beginning, nuclear stockpiles would be frozen at their existing levels within the zone. Later, the removal of these weapon stocks would be accompanied by controlled and mutually agreed reductions in conventional forces. This initiative, too, was rejected.

Meantime, in 1957, Romania proposed a similar project to denuclearize the Balkans. This plan was reiterated in 1968, and again in 1972.

In 1959, the Irish government outlined a plan for the creation of nuclear-free zones throughout the entire planet, which were to be developed region by region. In the same year the Chinese People's Republic suggested that the Pacific Ocean and all Asia be constituted a nuclear-free zone, and in 1960 various African states elaborated similar proposals for an All-African agreement. (These were re-tabled again in 1965, and yet again in 1974.)

In 1962 the Polish government offered yet another variation on the Rapacki Plan, which would have maintained its later notion of phasing, but which would now have permitted other European nations to join in if they wished to extend the original designated area. In the first stage, existing levels of nuclear weaponry and rocketry would be frozen, prohibiting the creation of new bases. Then, as in the earlier version, nuclear and conventional armaments would be progressively reduced according to a negotiated timetable. The rejection of this 1962 version was the end of the Rapacki proposals, but they were followed in 1964 by the so-called 'Gomulka' plan, which was designed to affect the same area, but which offered more restricted goals.

Although the main NATO powers displayed no real interest in all these efforts, they did arouse some real concern and sympathy in Scandinavia. As early as October 1961, the Swedish government tabled what became known as the Undén Plan (named after Sweden's Foreign Minister) at the First Committee of the UN General Assembly. This supported the idea of nuclear-free zones and a 'non-atomic club', and advocated their general acceptance. Certain of its proposals, concerning non-proliferation and testing, were adopted by the General Assembly. But the Undén Plan was never realized, because the USA and others maintained at the time that nuclear-free zones were an inappropriate approach to disarmament, which could only be agreed in a comprehensive 'general and complete' decision. Over and again this most desirable end has been invoked to block any less total approach to discovering any practicable means by which it might be achieved.

In 1963, President Kekkonen of Finland called for the reopening of talks on the Undén Plan. Finland and Sweden were both neutral already, he said, while Denmark and Norway, notwithstanding their membership of NATO, had no nuclear weapons of their own, and deployed none of those belonging to their Alliance. But although this constituted a de-facto commitment, it would, he held, be notably reinforced by a deliberate collective decision to confirm it as an enduring joint policy.

The Norwegian premier responded to this *démarche* by calling for the inclusion of sections of the USSR in the suggested area. As long ago as 1959, Nikita Khrushchev had suggested a Nordic nuclear-free zone, but no approach was apparently made to him during 1963 to discover whether the USSR would be willing to underpin such a project with any concession to the Norwegian viewpoint. However, while this argument was unfolding again in 1963, Khrushchev launched yet another similar proposal, for a nuclear-free Mediterranean.

The fall of Khrushchev took much of the steam out of such diplomatic forays, even though new proposals continued to emerge at intervals. In May 1974, the Indian government detonated what it described as a 'peaceful' nuclear explosion. This provoked renewed proposals for a nuclear-free zone in the Near East, from both Iran and the United Arab Republic, and it revived African concern with the problem. Probably the reverberations of the Indian bang were heard in New Zealand, because that nation offered up a suggestion for a South Pacific free zone later in the same year.

Yet, while the European disarmament lobbies were stalemated, the Latin American Treaty, which is briefly discussed above, had already been concluded in 1967, and within a decade it had secured the adherence of twenty-five states. The last of the main nuclear powers to endorse it was the USSR, which confirmed its general support in 1978. (Cuba withholds endorsement because it reserves its rights pending the evacuation of the Guantanamo base by the United States.) African pressures for a similar agreement are notably influenced by the threat of a South African nuclear military capacity, which is an obvious menace to neighbouring Mozambique, Zimbabwe, and Angola, and a standing threat to the Organization of African Unity. In the Middle East, Israel plays a similar catalysing role, and fear of an Israeli bomb is widespread throughout the region.

Why, then, this lag between Europe and the other continents? If the pressure for denuclearized zones began in Europe, and if the need for them, as we have seen, remains direst there, why have the peoples of the third world been, up to now, so much more effectively vocal on this issue than those of the European continent? Part of the answer surely lies in the prevalence of the nonaligned movement among the countries of the third world. Apart from a thin scatter of neutrals, Europe is the seed-bed of alignments, and the interests of the blocs as apparently disembodied entities are commonly prayed as absolute within it. In reality, of course, the blocs are not 'disembodied'. Within them, in military terms, superpowers rule. They control the disposition and development of the two major 'deterrents'. They keep the keys and determine if and when to fire. They displace the constituent patriotisms of the member states with a kind of bloc loyalty, which solidly implies that in each bloc there is a leading state, not only in terms of military supply, but also in terms of the determination of policy. To be sure, each bloc is riven with mounting internal tension. Economic competition divides the West, which enters the latest round of the arms race in a prolonged and, for some, mortifying slump. In the East, divergent interests are not so easily expressed, but they certainly exist, and from time to time become manifest. For all this, subordinate states on either side find it very difficult to stand off from their protectors.

But stand off we all must. The logic of preparation for a

war in our 'theatre' is remorseless, and the profound worsening of tension between the superpowers at a time of world-wide economic and social crisis all serves to speed up the Gadarene race.

The European Appeal

It was in this context that, at the beginning of 1980, the Russell Foundation joined forces with a variety of peace organizations in Britain (CND, Pax Christi, the International Confederation for Disarmament and Peace, among others), to launch an appeal to do precisely this.

An early draft of the appeal was written by E. P. Thompson. This was then circulated very widely in Europe, as a result of which a completely new draft was prepared incorporating the ideas of correspondents in many different countries, in Northern, Western, Southern and Eastern Europe. The appeal then took on its final form after a meeting in London in April 1980 at which French, British, West German and Italian supporters were present.

The appeal was announced at the end of that month and signatures were still being canvassed both in Great Britain and the rest of Europe up to Hiroshima Day, 6 August 1980. It calls upon the two great powers to 'withdraw all nuclear weapons from European territory' and urges the USSR to halt the production of its SS 20 missiles at the same time that it calls on the USA not to implement its decision to develop and install Pershing II and cruise missiles in the European 'theatre'. The aim is the removal of all nuclear air and submarine bases, nuclear weapons research, development and manufacturing institutions, and nuclear warheads themselves, from the whole continent, 'from Poland to Portugal'. This convenient slogan does not imply an unwillingness to negotiate the denuclearization of European Russia, up to the Urals: it merely registers the existing real division between superpowers, East and West, on the one side, and the states of Europe, which are caught up in the effects of the arms race between those powers, like corks bobbing in the flood, on the other.

The initial response to what has already become known as the European Nuclear Disarmament movement was quite extraordinary. Thousands of people signed the launching appeal within a few weeks. It quickly became very evident that European hesitations about nuclear armament were in no way less developed than the reservations of Africans, Latin Americans, or Asians.

The British appeal soon gathered a galaxy of well-known names: more than sixty MPs, a number of representatives of Christian churches and peace movements, several peers, trade union leaders and a remarkable cross-section of men and women from the liberal professions. The composer Peter Maxwell Davies joined the painter Josef Herman with Moss Evans, the trade unionist. Melvyn Bragg, John Arlott, Glenda Jackson, Susannah York, and Juliet Mills of a newer generation joined with earlier anti-nuclear campaigners like J. B. Priestley, Lord Brockway and Peggy Duff. But the growing swell of support included hundreds upon hundreds of other names which were not household words, but which reflected a real movement of opinion. Dockers, coalminers, students, housewives, busmen and computer programmers sent in the printed appeal forms, often affixed to home-made petitions listing dozens of adherents.

The approach to Europe was different. It was not possible and not desirable for British activists to attempt to prescribe what courses of action were most relevant in all the different nations of the continent. Not only were the individual states within the two blocs quite different, one from another, but each of the important neutral states was caught in its own distinct patterns of affinities, from Yugoslavia, the inspirer of nonalignment, to Spain, recently emancipated from Franco, and poised before a variety of choices about possible future alliances. Facing up to this complexity, the Russell Foundation agreed to circulate the British appeal with a separate European call for a conference to elaborate whatever distinct approaches to continental disarmament might be practicable and necessary.

Already, as the British supporters were agreeing on their first moves, mass movements had grown up in Holland, Belgium and Norway. The Dutch and Belgians were able, in the swell of protest, to postpone the implementation of the NATO agreement to install cruise missiles in their countries. An important resistance was developing in Denmark. Very soon after the agreement of the text of the END appeal, contact between these movements took place. Key activists from each of these countries joined with eminent political leaders in supporting the proposed European Convention. In France, the END initiative was announced by Claude Bourdet, the editor of *Témoignage Chrétienne*, at a national press conference in Paris. Similar announcements were made in Oslo and Berlin at the same time, and a variety of organizations and individuals gave their support. From Spain, the well-known eurocommunist spokesman Manuel Azcarate was joined by Dr Javier Solana Madariaga of the Socialist Party and by the distinguished Catholic writer Joaquin Ruiz-Gimenez Cortes, together with Joan Miró, the artist. An international meeting was organized by the Spaniards to ventilate the argument in the days before the recalled Helsinki Conference on European Security, scheduled to meet in Madrid in November 1980. Italian support was enthusiastic. An early signatory was Professor Giovanni Favilli, the scientist who had, from the beginning, been actively involved in the Pugwash movement. He happened to be a councillor in the city of Bologna, and in association with the town's mayor he convened meetings in all of the quartieri (or communal councils) of the region to consider the appeal, which was widely published in the civic journal and elsewhere. A Greek committee began to take shape, with the support of Andreas Papandreou, the opposition leader, amongst others. In Berlin, Professor Ulrich Albrecht, the peace researcher, gave extensive publicity to the appeal and gathered important support for it. At the same time, Rudolf Bahro, the East German author who had been imprisoned for publishing a book in the West and was subsequently deported after an amnesty, brought the adherence of the Green Party (with which he is currently working). Portuguese supporters included Ernesto Melo Antunes, the former Foreign Minister, and Francisco Marcelo Curto, Minister of Labour in the Soares government, alongside other members of parliament. By mid-July there were supporters in Finland and Turkey, Hungary and Czechoslovakia, Ireland and Sweden. The roll-call reached from Roy Medvedev in Moscow to Noel Browne, the former Health Minister, in Dublin, and from Gunnar Myrdal in Stockholm to ex-premier Hegedus in Budapest.

This extensive response was reinforced by the encouragement of lateral appeals, in which groups in one country made direct appeals to similar groups in another. Several members of the British TUC General Council wrote to their opposite numbers in France, and a British trade union group soon received approaches from Oslo. Members of British universities appealed to colleagues overseas. As the campaign gathers weight, this kind of initiative will gain importance, because it does not depend upon centralized networks of communications, and is a practical, as well as a symbolic, assertion of a growing all-European consciousness. Already efforts are being made to 'twin' Cambridge and Siena, which share the burden of proximity to planned bases for cruise missiles. Such arrangements are possible at a multiplicity of different levels, between women's groups, churches, civic and industrial bodies, students, or a wide variety of sporting and cultural associations.

The problem of East-West contact may be especially susceptible to this kind of treatment. The appeal is quite specific about the need for such meetings:

we must defend and extend the right of all citizens, East or West, to take part in this common movement and to engage in every kind of exchange.

At the same time, the appeal insists that

> We must resist any attempt by the statesmen of East or West to manipulate this movement to their own advantage. We offer no advantage to either NATO or the Warsaw alliance. Our objectives must be to free Europe from confrontation, to enforce detente between the United States and the Soviet Union, and, ultimately, to dissolve both great power alliances.

No one should seek to minimize the difficulties involved in this task, but neither should they be magnified. On both sides of the European divide, and in the middle of it, there is a very considerable, and rapidly growing, awareness of the great folly of the arms race, which in the appeal is justly styled 'demented'. Whilst there are big differences in the scope for public campaigning in countries which support the two blocs, it is not possible for governments in either camp to ignore the pressure of informed and active public opinion in the other, still less when vast movements are developing a deliberate policy of lateral appeals to one another, and to the peoples of those nations as yet uninvolved in the campaign.

The movement for European nuclear disarmament, then, is a movement to transform the meaning of these blocs, and to reverse their engines away from war. If all previous efforts to denuclearize parts of Europe have foundered, this is in large measure because they have all been partial, and thus incapable of mobilizing counter-pressures to dual bloc dominance on a wide enough scale. The paradox is that if President Ceausescu still wants a nuclear-free Balkan Zone, or if President Kekkonen still aspires to a denuclearized Baltic, then both are more likely to succeed within the framework of an all-European campaign than they would be in separate localized inter-state agreements. This is not at all to argue that denuclearization might not come about piecemeal: of course this is quite possible, even probable. But it will only come about when vast pressures of public opinion have come into being; and these pressures must and will develop, albeit unevenly, over the continent as a whole. Europe is not Antarctica, but Europeans have at least as much right to live as do Penguins.

For this reason, people must begin to organize, in what will become a gigantic transnational campaign. If this task is difficult, postponement will not make it easier. A pan-European Convention will only be the beginning, although the organizational problems involved in this first step are large enough in all conscience. There must be meetings of many kinds, demonstrations, cross-frontier marches, concerts and festivals. We must melt the ice which binds our continent. Since, unlike governments, we possess no elaborate lasers or thermonuclear devices, we shall have to rely on more democratic powers: the light of our reason, the generosity of our hopes and the warmth of our love for one another. Europe is full of clever, resourceful and kindly people. When they reach out to each other, this daunting labour will shrink to human size, and solving it may then become simplicity itself.

Notes

1. *Time*, 23 June 1980.
2. *Apocalypse Now?* (Spokesman Books, Nottingham, 1980), p. 10.
3. ibid., p. 21.
4. F. Griffiths and J. C. Polanyi, *The Dangers of Nuclear War* (University of Toronto Press, 1980), p. 164.
5. The text of this speech is reproduced in the Bertrand Russell Peace Foundation's *European Nuclear Disarmament – Bulletin of Work in Progress*, No. 1, 1980.
6. This document is reproduced in *Apocalypse Now?*, pp. 41–60.

CHAPTER ELEVEN

Bruce Kent
Notes from the Concrete Grass Roots

Since the beginning of 1980 I have wandered from one end of the country to another taking part in disarmament meetings of various sorts. In schools and colleges, village halls and municipal libraries, in cathedrals and in Quaker meeting houses, I have been involved in meetings innumerable and meetings usually also encouraging and stimulating.

This experience is my only qualification for contributing a small section to this book. If I do not claim expertise in much else I think I have some knowledge of how those who bother to come to such meetings are reacting to the new move of militarism which is so obvious in so many aspects of the life of this country. Such people are, of course, hardly a random sample. They bother, or they would not come. For the most part they are sympathetic, anxious and interested. Quite probably they are not representative of the country as a whole, whose citizenry still believes, for the most part without question, whatever the opinion-formers want them to believe, and who still think that the more weapons we have then the safer we must all surely be. It is therefore well that from time to time I also visit semi-hostile groups who manifestly look on an evening with a middle-aged peacenik with the honest joy of those on their way to a bull-fight. The more upsetting for them often enough because the bull is not meant to know more about the contest than the matadors. Yet such is usually the case. In short, as I have travelled from Dundee to Barnstaple, from Sevenoaks to Carlisle, from York to Cardiff, and have seen King's Cross Station in the dismal early hours more times than I care to count in these last few months, there ought to be some reflections worth sharing.

The first is a very obvious one. The issue of disarmament, low key for so long, has now come well up front in the public mind. People are very interested and concerned. They want to learn and they want to discuss their fears. They want to know if we are going to have another war and what such a war might mean for them and their families. They are ashamed of the waste of the arms race and they are deceived no longer by the dogma, acceptable in pre-1939 days, that more weapons means more security.

No one can know exactly what has set this new wave of interest going. A mixture of factors, no doubt. That our government has over-reached itself on the civil defence issue is clear enough. There is too much in HMG's ill-fated *Protect and Survive* that is simply too ludicrous for it to be credible. Therefore the fears that the recent wave of civil defence propaganda, and it has been nothing less, have aroused may be expressing themselves in growing interest in the disarmament issue itself.

I have been asked many times about these extraordinary civil defence recommendations, and it has not been too difficult to make clear that it is just because we *are* a nuclear weapon state that we are at risk as targets in a nuclear war. 'What about Switzerland?' says the lady at the back of the hall. As soon as she realizes that civil defence in a nuclear weapon state, especially if seriously undertaken, is actually a new twist in the spiral of the arms race, then she too starts to think in disarmament terms.

The recent spate of nuclear weapon computer errors in the USA has certainly also brought many into the disarmament lobbies. People are not stupid and they know perfectly well that the more complicated a mechanical and electrical system is, the more likely it is that one day things will go wrong. Our world now has its stockpile of 60,000 nuclear weapons. People do not have to have a Ph.D. to know the risks that deterrence involves with first-strike potential on the way. Nor are they much reassured by Mr Francis Pym, who, at the celebrated Cambridge debate with Lord Soper, said more than once that we have not had a serious accident yet with nuclear weapons, 'touch wood'. The time for touching wood is running out, and the country knows it.

Finally, I cannot help feeling, because it is so often mentioned, that people have now a far better idea of the cost of the arms race than ever they had before. At a time of national affluence, real or imagined, it may not seem to matter much what slice of the weekly wage is on its way to the 'defence' budget. When all seems to be going downhill, when productivity is more important than people, when hardly an aspect of the social services has not had its cuts, then there has to be very powerful justification for a weekly national average expenditure of almost £3.80 per person on the military. It seems to me to be dawning that the threats of 'the enemy' are not as credible as the government would like them to be and that it has occurred to many that preparing to blow up a great deal of the civilized world may not in fact be the best way of protecting anyone against anything.

The shrill voice of the cold war has been heard incessantly on our media, and the result in some sections of the population has not been acquiescence or a war-fighting mentality, but horror and indignation. I do not know how otherwise to explain not only many meetings, but meetings packed out time and time again. New peace groups continue to multiply in the country beyond counting. In East Anglia, no fewer than thirty groups and committees sprang up in the first six months of 1980.

Alongside the new interest there are a number of other general public attitudes and preoccupations. Those of us working in a realistic way for a more international, less violent, less paranoid world, directed not to the peace of status quo but peace of social justice, ought to take note of them. Everyone concerned with the problems of social change, and the move away from militarism in just such a change, ought to read Saul Alinsky's *Rules for Radicals*. Alinsky was a very practical organizer. One of his basic commonsense rules was that in any process of change you have to start from where people are rather than from where you would like them to be. We in the peace movement have not always remembered that.

In practical terms my experience tells me that people are 'at' a number of basic positions. Impotence hangs heavy over many. Despite the interest, hardly a meeting goes by without someone saying frustratedly that there is 'nothing we can do'. Secondly, the belief that military violence is ultimately the only way of dealing with international conflict is very deeply rooted. 'What would you have done in 1939?' is a very regular question and it usually springs from two connected national dogmas. One is that in 1939, owing to the misguided efforts of pacifists and peacemongers, we in this country were militarily defenceless. The other is that there was no other way of dealing with Hitler. That the results of World War II appear to have little enough to do with its original aims seems hardly to have been noticed. Our treaty obligations to Poland somewhere got lost down the labyrinthine ways of six years of what turned out on both sides to be total war.

Finally, there is a third major conviction. The idea that military 'balance' actually means something in the era of nuclear overkill still goes very deep. Not surprisingly, since it is regularly presented as the justification for spending more and more and more. As Mary Kaldor once well said, 'If the Russians decided to buy elephants for military purposes no doubt we would think it necessary to follow them.' Beyond 'balance' lies the belief that the Russians are not only aggressive and expansionist but also the possessors of a much greater military arsenal than our own. No serious international survey would support such a position and I believe that our 'free' media bear a very heavy responsibility for its uncritical acceptance of NATO propaganda on this issue. Nowhere has this been more true than in the run up to the cruise missile controversy. The SS 20, evil monster of the European war theatre, has been made the centre of a giant numbers fraud. However, most people do not find it difficult to believe that, should the horrific day of a nuclear war come, it will not much matter to the Soviets where a missile came from if it lands on their territory. More than that, it takes only a little unravelling of propaganda to demonstrate that if all 'theatre' systems are actually counted, submarine- and carrier-based as well as land-launched, then there is something like parity in theatre warheads between NATO and the Warsaw Pact.

It is, of course, perfectly easy to understand that to be able to kill only four times, rather than five times, is not actually much of a disadvantage. People know too that something funny must be going on if the cruise missiles, so desperately necessary for our well-being, are not due to arrive for another three years, and yet still those horrible Russians don't attack.

In short, there are three major popular positions – the sense of helplessness, the acceptance of war as a normal conflict-solving system and the fears of vast Soviet superiority. In crude ways, no doubt, and without any suggestion that all the answers are in my hands, at least I have tried to grasp these problems. I hope Alinsky would approve.

It is a mystery to me, one, I suspect, that is becoming a mystery to many more people, that the military solution should be thought of as the normal method of conflict resolution at international level. At village, town or city level, or within all the interstate organizations from cricket clubs to trade unions, to threaten to kill someone, let alone to actually kill them, is not only abnormal, however lively the dispute, but actually criminal. Somehow, at nation-state level and upwards there is a blockage in the pipe.

All those concerned with the extension of the rule of law into international society must be about the business of exploring alternative defence systems. Part of the process has to be the sorting out of real from exaggerated or even invented threats. But part of it also must be the exploration of other kinds of defence, both violent and non-violent. This is not the pious pipe dream of the comfortable liberal. If the present system is more of a risk than a protection, and the UN Special Session on Disarmament in 1978 said no less, then to get away from that system just makes sense.

In the hour or so of question time at most disarmament sessions there is not much chance to do more than shake a few cherished dogmas. Not so cherished any longer, perhaps. One does not have to serve on a Parliamentary Select Committee to know that the largest and best equipped military force in the area did nothing to protect the Shah of Iran. It vanished like the morning mist in front of popular indignation and religious feeling. It is not necessary to be an international financier to know that the war in what was Rhodesia was prolonged for years by companies which flouted trading sanctions with British government connivance. It is not necessary to be a Free Presbyterian to note that in 1974 the British Army was roundly defeated in Northern Ireland by nearly a million people who refused to do anything – a refusal which frustrated the will of the Westminster parliament to which they all claimed to be loyal. It is not necessary to be an admirer, though I am, of President Nyerere of Tanzania to be obliged to admit that his military action against Amin was only a last resort which would have been quite unnecessary had the petrol flow to Uganda been terminated and had this country ceased to supply his army with its monthly ration of luxuries flown out from Stanstead airport almost until the time of the collapse. One could go on, and I often do. The Swiss, the Swedes, the Costa Ricans, the Yugoslavs and the Vietnamese have all in their different ways things to tell us about alternative defence. So have a long list of authors from Dr Gene Sharp to Sir Stephen King-Hall. My experience in recent months is that lots of people are now thinking about defence in more intelligent terms than those of the cash register and the biggest bang. The East-West campaign for a European nuclear-free zone is part of that process.

Nevertheless, there is an even bigger problem lurking in the woodshed. It is the problem of the horrible Russians, ruthless, expansionist, over-armed, untrustworthy . . . you have heard it all. We are free, just, peace-loving and defensive – they are monsters. We judge ourselves by our stated intentions, but they are to be judged by their capabilities. I once heard a most distinguished bishop who looked at a CND crowd one Easter. His pronouncement was very brief: 'Better dead than red!' The churches have played a very sad part in stimulating the demonic content of the arms race. How, then, to meet the honest inquirer who is frightened and who has seen some very nasty bits of Russian military activity in recent years? Hungary, Czechoslovakia and Afghanistan will not easily be forgotten.

I only ask for two things. If there is to be any progress, then we have both to try and understand the fears of the 'enemy' and to judge his behaviour by standards which we apply equally rigorously to ourselves and to those with whom we ally ourselves. There is a very long list of countries with whom we have economic and military alliances and to whom we supply weapons who also have a dreadful record of violating human rights. If Afghanistan is a shocker, then so was the inhuman war in Vietnam, and so is the present Indonesian invasion of East Timor, the South African military occupation of Namibia, the Turkish invasion of Cyprus and the collapse of constitutional government in Chile. To understand that the Soviets also have fears is a great step forward. Once we realize that the West has effectively made a military alliance with the Chinese, who regularly talk about war with the Russians, we can understand that the Russians might well have reason for a certain amount of additional anxiety.

On the issue of who has got what in terms of weapons, I never try to do more than say that it is very unwise to rely on sources connected with 'our' side – or 'theirs'. The military have an obligation to present a worst-case analysis, and even in our free country the amount of Ministry of Defence, Foreign Office and NATO money which washes through to 'independent' centres of information and the media is not inconsiderable. There are, of course, Eastern bloc sources of information equally and often more obviously subject to the same process. The argument about balance is often not over fact, but over which facts are to be selected in presenting a general picture. Happily, the Stockholm International Peace Research Institute produces an annual digest that is quite within the capacity of anyone who can work out how to fill in a passport application or an income tax declaration, and it is provided with nice little graphs as well. With an initial shove, anybody can get through it perfectly happily.

Finally, the 'what can I do?' question badly needs an answer. Perhaps the first response should be that the signs of history being made are all around us. Social change happens, and its direction depends often enough on the energy, sacrifice and determination of quite small groups of people. The iniquities of nineteenth-century industrialism did not come to an end (in so far as they have in this country) by chance. That women have a great deal more in the way of equal opportunity now than they had at the turn of the century is no accident. The overseas aid movement, a fragile post-World War II creation, partly radical, partly remedial, had to be built. The awareness created by Amnesty that torture and imprisonment without trial are as much features of the nonaligned countries and the West as of the East, and that there are ways of working to end such abuses wherever they occur, is a very recent initiative indeed.

The impotence syndrome is not really true to history, past or recent. The first challenge is, of course, the challenge of getting involved. Someone once said that s/he loved humanity but could not bear people. To get involved in practical disarmament activity must mean joining some movement and getting down to hard, often boring work. Disarmament is too important for ego trips. The National Peace Council, 29 Great James Street, London, WC1, can supply a long list of the active organizations now at work, and the annual Peace Diary produced by the admirable Housman's Bookshop, 5 Caledonian Road, London, N1, lists not only national but international peace groups. They range far and wide, from the United Nations Association to the Campaign for Nuclear Disarmament, from the Peace Pledge Union to the Campaign against the Arms Trade, from Pax Christi to the Fellowship of Reconciliation, from the World Disarmament Campaign to the Women's International League for Peace and Freedom. Some are pacifist, some are not. Some have a religious base and others a humanist one. Some work within the nation-state framework, some reject it. Some are affiliates of political parties whilst some are outside any party framework.

All are actively engaged in the business of public education about the risks and the costs of the arms race. It does not require some special or unusual skills to collect petition signatures against the arms race and British participation in it from your friends and neighbours. It is not so hard to arrange a fund-raising jumble sale or some other cash-producing event. The peace movements have at least all got poverty in common. It is not difficult to hire a film like *The War Game*, still banned from TV showing by the BBC which commissioned it. Out of date now in some technical respects, *The War Game* is still the most powerful piece of motivation in the business. But it would be quite impossible to list the actions and endeavours open to ordinary people from different walks of life aimed at increasing knowledge of the facts and the perils of the arms race. Letters to local papers, street theatre, phone-in radio programmes, outdoor vigils, for instance on Hiroshima or Nagasaki Day (6 and 9 August), leafleting at railway stations or shopping centres, wearing peace badges or displaying car stickers – all these and many more are ideas which local groups are already putting into practice.

Few of us are without involvement in organized groups of one sort or another. Few people have no connection of any sort with the educational system, either as parents, teachers, pupils or administrators. Schools can do so much. They can pass on myth and prejudice, violence and national militarism, or they can more constructively transmit a message of internationalism, alternative defence and the heroism of the pioneers of constructive social change. No secondary school should be without a specific course on international institutions and the history and consequences of the arms race.

Schools are not the only such community focus. Hundreds of thousands of generous people are today involved one way and another in the work of the development agencies – Oxfam, Christian Aid, War on Want and so many others. All responsible development agencies know that the education of the public here about the causes of third world poverty is an essential part of their work. Yet the unmistakable fact that the arms race, now running at about $550,000,000,000 a year, is the greatest single cause of world poverty has yet to become a serious part of development agency programmes. To accelerate that process is a vital task.

I could, of course, fill a book with groups where the anti-arms race message should be heard and acted upon. Trade unions, political parties, medical associations, legal groups (what price Nuremberg?), the ecology and energy lobbies – the list is as long as one cares to make it. From a personal point of view I think with a heavy heart especially of the churches. The Society of Friends apart, how little they have so far done and how tied they are to national prejudices, how wedded to a moral theology of war that makes counting angels on the tips of needles sound by comparison a most constructive pastime. Yet the potential is so great. So often, at so many meetings, the frustrated laity of the mainstream churches are there but their clergy not. How can church leaders be so concerned about inter-communion and charismatic experience while we balance our world society at scandalous cost on a knife-edge of murderous intention? I do not know, and I rejoice in any signs of change. The splendid, careful British Council of Churches resolution of November 1979 opposing the renewal of Polaris is a model of its kind. In short, if you have any church connection there is a job to be done.

This, however, is only a ragbag of ideas, not an exhaustive manual of 'what I can do' prepared for every situation. The short answer is to take a few first steps. Once that threshold is passed, there is no doubt whatever that your road will open ahead of you. It may mean that you will be thought odd, indeed a little cracked, perhaps. It is more than possible, however, that you are actually a symbol of sanity in an international society of manipulated sleepwalkers and that the future of the world is in your hands.

Further Reading
Compiled by Harry Dean

There is a large and varied body of literature concerning armament and disarmament. The following list of journals, books and official publications is not a comprehensive bibliography, but simply a guide to some of the more interesting and useful material available.

Journals and Periodicals

1. *ADIU Report*. Bi-monthly newsletter of the Armament and Disarmament Information Unit, University of Sussex. Contains analyses, news and a bibliographical section. Available from ADIU, University of Sussex, Falmer, Brighton, Sussex.

2. *Arms Control*. A new journal intended to 'probe and understand the nature of arms control', published three times a year. From Frank Cass & Co., Gainsborough House, Gainsborough Road, London E11. £18 p.a. for individuals.

3. *Bulletin of Peace Proposals*. Quarterly publication containing original articles, current documentation and an abstract of relevant materials. $20 p.a. from Universitetsforlaget, Journals Department, PO Box 2959, Tøyen, Oslo 6, Norway.

4. *Bulletin of the Atomic Scientists*. Monthly. Carries articles, discussions and reviews on armaments and disarmament. $23.50 p.a. for individuals in Europe. 1020–1024 E 58th Street, Chicago, Illinois 60637, USA.

5. *The Defense Monitor*. Published monthly by the Center

for Defense Information, which 'supports a strong defense but opposes excessive expenditure or forces'. Each issue concentrates on one topical issue. $1 per issue. 122 Maryland Avenue NE, Washington, DC 20002, USA.

6. *Disarmament Campaigns*. Reports on disarmament activities throughout Europe. Published quarterly by Nonviolent Alternatives, Kerkstraat 150, B-2000 Antwerp, Belgium. $6 p.a.

7. *Peace News*. For nonviolent revolution. Fortnightly: 20p per issue or £7·80 p.a. 8 Elm Avenue, Nottingham.

8. *Proceedings of the Medical Association for the Prevention of War*. 50p; free to members. Membership Secretary: H. L. Brown, 57b Somerton Rd., London NW2.

9. *Sanity*. Bi-monthly magazine of the Campaign for Nuclear Disarmament. Reports, analysis and news of the movement. £1·50 p.a. (free to members), from 29 Great James Street, London WC1.

10. *State Research Bulletin*. Bi-monthly. State Research is 'an independent group of investigators collecting and publishing information from public sources on developments in state policy', including internal security and the military. £4 p.a. for individuals from 9 Poland Street, London WC1.

Books

Nuclear Weapons and Nuclear War

Bolsover, P., *Civil Defence – The Cruellest Confidence Trick* (Campaign for Nuclear Disarmament, 1980), 23 pp., 40p.

Cox, J., *Overkill* (Penguin Books, Harmondsworth, 1977), 80p.

Glasstone, S., and P. J. Dolan, *The Effects of Nuclear Weapons* (3rd edition, US Department of Defense and Department of Energy, 1977), 653 pp.

Griffiths, F., and J. C. Polanyi, *The Dangers of Nuclear War* (University of Toronto Press, 1980), 216 pp., $5·95.

How to Survive the Nuclear Age (The Ecology Party, 1980), 22 pp., 80p.

Laurie, P., *Beneath the City Streets* (civil defence preparations in Britain) (Panther, London, 1979), 313 pp., £1·95.

Earl Mountbatten, Lord Noel-Baker and Lord Zuckerman, *Apocalypse Now?* (Spokesman Books, Nottingham, 1980), 64 pp., £1·50.

Theatre Nuclear Weapons: European Perspectives (Stockholm International Peace Research Institute (SIPRI), Taylor & Francis, London, 1978), 371 pp., £10·50.

Van Cleave, W. R., and S. T. Cohen, *Theatre Nuclear Weapons: An Examination of the Issues* (MacDonald & Jane's, London, 1979), 119 pp., £8·50.

Soviet Union

Alexander, A. J., 'Decision Making in Soviet Weapons Procurement', *Adelphi Papers*, No. 147–8 (International Institute for Strategic Studies (IISS), London, 1978).

Bonds, R. (ed.), *The Soviet War Machine* (Hamlyn, London, 1976), 247 pp., £4·95.

Holzman, F. D., *Financial Checks on Soviet Defense Expenditure* (Lexington Books, Mass., 1975), 103 pp.

Scott, H. F. and W. F., *The Armed Forces of the USSR* (Westview, Colorado, 1979), 139 pp., £16·25.

Sonnenfeldt, H., and W. G. Hyland, 'Soviet Perspectives on Security', *Adelphi Papers*, No. 150 (International Institute for Strategic Studies, London, 1979).

USA

Blechman, B. L., *et al.*, *Force Without War: US Armed Forces as a Political Instrument* (Brookings Institution, Washington, DC, 1978), 584 pp.

Bonds, R. (ed.), *The US War Machine* (Hamlyn, London, 1978), 271 pp., £8·95.

The Boston Study Group, *The Price of Defense: A New*

Strategy for Military Spending (Times Books, New York, 1979), 397 pp.

Gervasi, T., *Arsenal of Democracy: American Weapons Available for Export* (Grove Press, New York, 1977), 240 pp., $7·95.

Mellman, S., *The Permanent War Economy* (Simon & Schuster, New York, 1975), 384 pp., $10·95.

Britain – General

Bayliss, J. (ed.), *British Defence Policy in a Changing World* (Croom Helm, London, 1977), 295 pp., £9·95.

Cook, R., and D. Smith, 'What Future in NATO?', *Fabian Research Series 337*, (Fabian Society, London, 1978).

Greenwood, D., *Budgeting for Defence* (Royal United Services Institute, London, 1972), 99 pp., £1·25.

Kaldor, M., D. Smith and S. Vines (eds.), *Democratic Socialism and the Cost of Defence*, Report of the Labour Party Defence Study Group (Crook Helm, London, 1980), 576 pp., £17·95.

Smith, D., *The Defence of the Realm in the 1980s* (Croom Helm, London, 1980), 276 pp., £6·95.

Britain and Nuclear Weapons

Nailor, P., and J. Alford, 'The Future of Britain's Nuclear Deterrent Force', *Adelphi Papers*, No. 156 (International Institute for Strategic Studies, London, 1980), 37 pp., £1·50.

Smart, I. *The Future of the British Nuclear Deterrent: Technical, Economic and Strategic Issues* (Royal Institute for International Affairs, London, 1977), 82 pp., £4.

The Future of the British Nuclear Deterrent, Bailrigg Paper No. 1 (Centre for the Study of Arms Control and International Security, University of Lancaster, 1980), 157 pp.

'The Future of the British Nuclear Deterrent', *A Report to the British Council of Churches by the Council on Christian Approaches to Defence and Disarmament* (The Division of International Affairs of the British Council of Churches, 1979), 19 pp., £1.

Greenwood, D., 'The Polaris Successor System: At What Cost?', *Aberdeen Studies in Defence Economics No. 16* (Centre for Defence Studies, Aberdeen University, 1980), 42 pp., £2.

Britain – Official Documents

Defence in the 1980s, Statement on the Defence Estimates (HMSO, London, 1980), Vol. 1, Cmnd 7826-I, £4·50; Vol. 2, Defence Statistics, Cmnd 7826-II, £4.

Protect and Survive (HMSO, London, 1980), 30 pp., 50p.

'The Future of the UK Nuclear Weapons Policy', *Sixth Report from the Expenditure Committee*, Session 1978–79, HC 348 (HMSO, London, 1979), 270 pp., £4.

'The Future United Kingdom Strategic Nuclear Deterrent Force', Defence Open Government Document 80/23 (Ministry of Defence, July 1980), 27 pp.

War and Militarism

Eide, A., and M. Thee, *The Problems of Contemporary Militarism* (Crook Helm, London, 1980), 416 pp., £14·95.

Galbraith, J. K., *How to Control the Military* (Doubleday, New York, 1969).

Kaldor, M., and A. Eide (eds.), *The World Military Order: The Impact of Military Technology on the Third World* (Macmillan, London, 1979), 306 pp., £15.

Luttwak, E., *A Dictionary of Modern War* (Penguin Books, Harmondsworth, 1971), £3·75.

Messelson, M., and Julian Perry Robinson, 'Chemical warfare and chemical disarmament', *Scientific American*, April 1980.

Wright Mills, C., *The Causes of World War Three* (Simon & Schuster, New York, 1958), 172 pp.

Roberts, A., *Nations in Arms: The Theory and Practice of Territorial Defence* (Praeger, New York, 1976), 288 pp.

Sigmund, E., *Rage Against The Dying* (Pluto Press, London, 1980), 128 pp., £1·95.

Arms Control and Disarmament

Arms Control: A Survey and Appraisal of Multilateral Agreements (Stockholm International Peace Research Institute, Taylor & Francis, London, 1978), 238 pp.

Bertram, C. (ed.), *New Conventional Weapons and East-West Security* (International Institute for Strategic Studies, Macmillan, London, 1978), 97 pp.

Burns, R. D., *SALT, Nuclear Proliferation and Nuclear-Weapons-Free Zones* (Center for the Study of Armament and Disarmament, California State University, 1979), 62 pp.

Coffey, J. I., *Arms Control and European Security: A Guide to East-West Negotiations* (Chatto & Windus, London, 1977), 271 pp., £10.

Epstein, W., and T. Toyoda (eds.), *A New Design for Nuclear Disarmament* (Spokesman Books, Nottingham, 1977), 338 pp., £5.

Jolly, R. (ed.), *Disarmament and World Development* (Pergamon, London, 1979), 185 pp.

Kincade, W. H., and J. D. Porro (eds.), *Negotiating Security: An Arms Control Reader* (Carnegie Endowment for International Peace, Washington, DC, 1979), 321 pp.

Myrdal, A., *The Game of Disarmament: How the US and Russia Run the Arms Race* (Pantheon, New York, 1976; Manchester University Press, 1977), 397 pp., £9·95.

Postures for Non-Proliferation: Arms Limitation and Security Policies to Minimise Nuclear Proliferation (Stockholm International Peace Research Institute, Taylor & Francis, London, 1979), 168 pp., £6·50.

Russett, B. M., and B. G. Blair, 'Progress in Arms Control?', *Readings from Scientific American* (W. H. Freeman, San Francisco, 1979), 238 pp.

Sims, N. A., *Approaches to Disarmament* (Quaker Peace and Service, London, 1979), 180 pp., £1·50.

The United Nations and Disarmament, 1945–1970, Chapter 15, 'On Nuclear Weapons Free Zones' (Department of Political and Security Council Affairs, United Nations, 1971), 515 pp.

The United Nations and Disarmament, 1970–1975, Chapter 5, 'On Nuclear Weapons Free Zones' (Department of Political and Security Council Affairs, United Nations, 1976), 267 pp.

Annual Publications

1. *International Institute for Strategic Studies* (IISS), 23 Tavistock Street, London, WC2E 7NO. IISS publishes *The Military Balance* and *Strategic Survey* each year, *Survival* (six times a year), and the *Adelphi Papers* series.

2. *Stockholm International Peace Research Institute* (SIPRI), Sveavägen 166, S-113 46 Stockholm, Sweden. In addition to a number of books on many aspects of armaments and disarmament, SIPRI publishes annually the *SIPRI Yearbook of World Armaments and Disarmament*. This series began with the 1968/69 edition and a cumulative index covering 1968–79 is also now available; *World Armaments and Disarmament, SIPRI Yearbooks 1968–1979* (SIPRI, Taylor & Francis, London, 1980), 90 pp., £5.

3. *United Nations* (UN). Since 1976 the UN has published a *Disarmament Yearbook*. It also publishes *Disarmament*, a periodic review ($3·50 per issue); both are available from the Sales Section, United Nations, New York 10017, USA.

4. *World Military and Social Expenditures* (WMSE). WMSE is an annual digest listing and comparing national military and social expenditures. It is available for £2 from WMSE Publications, c/o CAAT, 5 Caledonian Road, London N1 9DX.

Acknowledgements and Notes on Contributors

Ken Coates is a director of the Bertrand Russell Peace Foundation, and co-author with Tony Topham of *Trade Unions in Britain* (1980).

Harry Dean is Information Officer of the Armament and Disarmament Information Unit, University of Sussex.

David Holloway lectures in politics at the University of Edinburgh and is author of a number of essays on Soviet military questions. He and the editors are grateful for permission to publish here an abridged version of a study originally prepared for the World Order Models Project and first published in *Alternatives* (1980). His thanks also to Silviu Brucan, Judith Reppy and William Sweet for comments on an earlier draft.

Mary Kaldor is Research Fellow at the Science Policy Research Unit, University of Sussex, and author of *The Arms Trade with the Third World* (1971), *The Disintegrating West* (1978) and *The Baroque Arsenal* (to be published by Deutsch in spring 1981).

Bruce Kent is the General Secretary of CND and a former chairman of War on Want.

Alva Myrdal is a former Swedish cabinet minister and leader of the Swedish delegation at disarmament negotiations in Geneva and New York, and has been the Swedish Ambassador to India. She is the author of *The Game of Disarmament* (1977) and the first winner of the Einstein Peace Prize in 1980. The editors are grateful to Manchester University Press for permission to publish here parts of *The Game of Disarmament*, Chapter II.

Henry T. Nash is Professor of Political Science at Hollins College, Virginia, and a former analyst with the US Department of Defense. He is the author of *Nuclear Weapons and International Behavior* (1975) and *American Foreign Policy: Changing Perspectives on National Security* (1978). The editors are grateful to *The Bulletin of Atomic Scientists* for permission to publish here 'The Bureaucratization of Homicide'.

Emma Rothschild is Associate Professor in the Science, Technology and Society programme at the Massachusetts Institute of Technology and author of *Paradise Lost: The Decline of the Auto-Industrial Age* (1973). The editors are grateful to *The New York Review of Books* for permission to publish here 'Boom and Bust' under a different title.

Dan Smith is Research Officer in the Department of Economics, Birkbeck College, and author of *The Defence of the Realm in the 1980s* (1980).

Ron Smith is Reader in Applied Economics, Birkbeck College, and author of 'Military Expenditure and Capitalism', *Cambridge Journal of Economics* (1977), and of several other articles on the economics of military spending.

E. P. Thompson, historian and writer, is the author of *The Making of the English Working Class* (1963) and *Writing by Candlelight* (1980). He wishes to thank Norman Minaur, Dan Smith and Dorothy Thompson for help with an earlier draft and all connected with the Bertrand Russell Peace Foundation, which, together with CND, published the first version of *Protest and Survive* as a pamphlet.

The editors warmly thank Neil Middleton and his colleagues at Penguin Books for the speed and care with which this work has been produced.

More About Penguins And Pelicans

For further information about books available from Penguins please write to Dept EP, Penguin Books Ltd, Harmondsworth, Middlesex UB7 0DA.

In the U.S.A.: For a complete list of books available from Penguins in the United States write to Dept CS, Penguin Books, 625 Madison Avenue, New York, New York 10022.

In Canada: For a complete list of books available from Penguins in Canada write to Penguin Books Canada Ltd, 2801 John Street, Markham, Ontario L3R 1B4.

In Australia: For a complete list of books available from Penguins in Australia write to Marketing Department, Penguin Books Australia Ltd, P.O. Box 257, Ringwood, Victoria 3134.

NUCLEAR POWER

Second Edition

Walter C. Patterson

Can nuclear power stations be operated safely? Can their radioactive wastes be managed without posing a threat to future generations? Can there be adequate safeguards to prevent misuse of dangerous nuclear materials? Just how necessary is the nuclear option, anyway? In one forum after another, expert contradicts expert, and the man in the street looks on in nervous uncertainty.

To those who feel that nuclear matters should not be left to the battling experts, NUCLEAR POWER offers essential support. In lively everyday language it describes nuclear technology and how it works – and sometimes fails to work. The author surveys the development of nuclear power worldwide, and delineates the issues, not only technical but also economic, social and political, which now preoccupy the policymakers. An extensive annotated bibliography provides guideposts to further investigation by the concerned reader.

A Pelican Original

THE ENERGY QUESTION

Second Edition

Gerald Foley with Charlotte Nassim

This book surveys the world's energy resources and their potential for development. Living standards and social development possible for any society depend on the input of energy; even the world's food supplies depend on the ability of modern farming to turn fossil fuels into food.

It is now clear that if some of our plans for the future are fulfilled then others must be abandoned. This book explains the facts on which such choices must be based. It is neither optimistic nor pessimistic – but it enables the reader to form his own judgements.

'Its arguments are always precise and supported by as much data as are necessary but no more. Technical terms are used, but explained carefully, so that the information they convey is available to the non-expert . . . compelling reading'.
THE ECOLOGIST

'. . . a useful reference book on almost every aspect of energy production and use'.   TRIBUNE

'A remarkable book'.   NEW STATESMAN

A Pelican Original

DISASTERS

The anatomy of environmental hazards

John Whittow

A disaster is categorized as such only when there is loss of human life or property. A volcanic eruption, a massive earthquake or a landslide in barren terrain is not a disaster. Yet over the last four or five years rarely a month has gone by without a major disaster being reported from somewhere in the world – the Bangladesh cyclone; the Huascaran avalanche in Peru; the Nicaraguan earthquake; the Turkish earthquake; the Honduras floods spawned by Hurricane Fifi; the Sahel drought of North Africa. Hundreds of thousands of lives have been lost. The disastrous year of 1976 appeared to be the final cataclysm, when earthquake shocks, volcanic eruptions, tidal waves, hurricanes, floods, blizzards and drought combined to give the impression that the earth was in turmoil, the day of reckoning was at hand.

What is going on? Is it possible to predict such events or to alleviate their effects? John Whittow not only summarizes the disasters which have caused such widespread death and destruction but also explains, as far as possible, why they occur and whether man is partly to blame.

A Pelican Original

INFLATION

A guide to the crisis in economics

Second Edition

J. A. Trevithick

Inflation, accompanied by economic disarray and popular despair, continues to offer a major challenge to the credibility of economic science.

As the flow of explanations bids fair to match the growth in the money supply, Dr Trevithick gives – in this Pelican Original – an introductory guide to the problems, the jargon and the panaceas. The characters in his drama include Milton Friedman, Keynes, Hayek and the 'New School' at Cambridge, while the plot encompasses the Phillips Curve, trade union power, helicopter money, rational expectations, floating currencies, incomes policy, import controls and indexation.

In this new edition the author brings us up-to-date with such things as Friedman's Nobel Lecture in 1977, and Lord Kaldor's injection of a new convincingness to the cost-push theory, as well as analysing the latest manifestations of current monetarist orthodoxy in both Britain and North America. He also tells us his view of what will have to be done.

INTERNATIONAL PEACEKEEPING

United Nations forces in a troubled world

Anthony Verrier

Irish squaddies are shot in a squalid encounter in the Middle East and the newspapers are pious for a week until the next bit of international 'news' displaces them. Unlovely acronyms, ONUC, UNFICYP and UNIFIL are trotted out for a bemused and bored public, but they conceal a real and urgent, a terrifying and crucial, a randomly violent half-war.

These are the visible bits of an astonishing and largely hidden military crusade. It is the struggle for peace waged, sometimes uncertainly but unceasingly, by the United Nations Peacekeeping Forces. The funny armies made up of amazing mixtures of people speaking lots of different languages under, for most of them, an alien command, keep warring factions apart.

This book describes the ways these unsung heroes work, shot at by all but unable, for the most part, to shoot back. Verrier recounts their history, their defeats and their victories. He shows how the strategies work or are improvised and, above all, how vital is their role in international politics.

A Pelican Original